MW01005046

LEARN MY LESSON

KATEE ROBERT

TRINKETS AND TALES LLC

To Jenny and Sarah -
Hades wouldn't have owned a super sweet BDSM club if it wasn't
for you two. Thank you!

ALSO BY KATEE ROBERT

The Wicked Villains Series

Book 1: Desperate Measures

Book 2: Learn My Lesson

Book 3: A Worthy Opponent

The Island of Ys

Book 1: His Forbidden Desire

Book 2: Her Rival's Touch

Book 3: His Tormented Heart

Book 4: Her Vengeful Embrace

The Thalanian Dynasty Series (MMF)

Book 1: Theirs for the Night

Book 2: Forever Theirs

Book 3: Theirs Ever After

Book 4: Their Second Chance

The Kings Series

Book 1: The Last King

Book 2: The Fearless King

The Hidden Sins Series

Book 1: The Devil's Daughter

Book 2: The Hunting Grounds

Book 3: The Surviving Girls

The Make Me Series

Book 1: Make Me Want

Book 2: Make Me Crave

Book 3: Make Me Yours

Book 4: Make Me Need

The O'Malley Series

Book 1: The Marriage Contract

Book 2: The Wedding Pact

Book 3: An Indecent Proposal

Book 4: Forbidden Promises

Book 5: Undercover Attraction

Book 6: The Bastard's Bargain

The Hot in Hollywood Series

Book 1: Ties that Bind

Book 2: Animal Attraction

The Foolproof Love Series

Book 1: A Foolproof Love

Book 2: Fool Me Once

Book 3: A Fool for You

Out of Uniform Series

Book 1: In Bed with Mr. Wrong

Book 1.5: His to Keep

Book 2: Falling for His Best Friend

Book 3: His Lover to Protect

Book 3.5: His to Take

Serve Series

Book 1: Mistaken by Fate

CHAPTER 1

MEG

*O*nce upon a time, a woman fell in love with a man. He wasn't a good man. Men never are, I've found. But this woman hadn't learned that hard lesson yet. She still had stars in her eyes and the kind of innocent love in her heart that the world delights in setting aflame.

When the man asked the woman for a favor, just a tiny little favor to prove her love to him, because she did love him, didn't she? Of course she said yes. Of course he left her to pay the price for his sins. Of course he never once looked back.

And the woman?

The woman lost her innocence in the flames of his betrayal.

She rose from the ashes, a goddess in her own right, second only to her new master.

It's a good story, as such things go. Far more romantic than the reality: I loved the wrong man and made a deal with the devil to save him. That kind of man doesn't cleave to innocence lost, no matter what lies he spilled to bargain me away, and he left me as soon as the price was paid.

It's just as well.

The devil suits me better anyway.

The devil in question sits next to me in a corner booth in a restaurant that's unfamiliar to me. He's wearing his usual suit that always seems a tiny bit rumpled in the sexiest way possible and his salt-and-pepper hair is styled to perfection. Add in the thick black-framed glasses, and it's enough to have me clenching my thighs together in anticipation. Or it would be if I didn't know him better.

Nearly ten years at his side and I know what the gleam in those dark eyes and the tiny smile pulling at the edge of his sensual lips means. Nothing good. Not for me. Not for whoever he has his eye on.

I idly stroke the stem of my wine glass and sigh. Another day, another game of manipulation. Sometimes, I swear Hades pulls shit just to keep boredom at bay. When one rules his little sliver of Carver City and has every *other* ruler in town simpering at his feet, boredom is the only real danger he faces.

I wish my life were that simple.

I contend with boredom. Of course I do. I'm Hades's right hand, his queen, the second most powerful person at the Underworld. No one would dare touch me. To do so is to court his wrath, and if there's a single person in this world who holds a grudge better than I do, it's Hades.

None of that protects me from the harm a decade together can cause. The kind of drifting that sets two people at odds despite their best efforts. I don't know where we went so wrong, and I can't begin to fix something so broken on my own. Hades doesn't even seem to notice the distance between us that grows more and more uncrossable with each day that passes.

"How would you like to play a game, love?"

If he were the real Hades, or whatever creature rules the afterlife, he couldn't be more tempting and dangerous than he is in these moments. I look away. I have to. I'm not the green twenty-three-year-old girl who bargained away her life for a man who'd forget her before the day had passed. I know better than not to play a game with *this* man.

No matter how much I love him.

"I'm really not in the mood."

"My dear sweet Meg, always determined to play it straight." His smile never wavers, but some of the warmth leeches out of his eyes. A warning, that. "You should know better by now."

Yes, I should. I very much should know better by now. There was a time when I'd happily dance to any tune he set, wanting to please him for the sure happiness he shone down on me in those perfect moments. Now our love is more cruel edges and the kind of cut that one doesn't even notice until hours later.

I lean back, putting as much distance between us as he'll allow. "Like I said, I'm not in the mood." I sound cold and uncaring, but I can't seem to stop myself.

"Jafar's baby girl is rubbing off on you, I see." He studies his wine glass, still half-full despite our ordering before the meal arrived. "How is the darling Jasmine these days? For reasons unknown, Jafar seems disinclined to respond to my calls."

For reasons unknown.

It certainly doesn't have to do with Hades orchestrating her kidnapping a handful of months ago. "Pride a little hurt? Maybe you should have taken care of Ali before he damaged the Underworld's reputation." I smirk. I can't help it. We know each other's buttons too well, and even though it hurts, we can't help dancing on them as it suits us.

"We're nothing without our reputation," he muses, but I can tell he's already moved on. Whatever he's thinking of now, it's not the events from a few months ago. Hades reaches over and clasps my wrist in a deceptively gentle grasp. He flips it over and runs his thumb over the tattoo there, a blue flame. It marks me as his.

Forever.

My body goes tight, readying in fight or flight, my breath stalled in my lungs as I wait to see what he'll do. Hades. My Sir. My owner in every sense of the word. I might dominate others in his club, might have what appears to be free rein over everyone there as I choose, but he is the only one who holds my leash. With Hades, there is no give and take.

He dominates. I submit. The end.

It used to be enough. We were in this together, true partners, true *equals*. These days, it feels like we're going through the motions with each other. Coming to this quaint little restaurant with its faux romantic lighting and expensive wine list might be out of our ordinary, but this game just proves that Hades isn't really trying to bridge the gap. He simply wants a new setting for a new scene.

Exhaustion rolls over me in a wave. I am so incredibly tired of playing. I should part my lips and tell him exactly where I stand, tell him I'm not happy and haven't been for a long time, beg him to *see* how wrong things are between us.

I don't. Even with this man, I've learned my lesson too well. The trust we built so painstakingly between us is weathered and beaten. I can't be sure that he'll meet me half-way, and because I can't be sure, I am incapable of taking that first step to reach out.

Instead, I resign myself to another night of pleasure that will hold the pain at bay, at least for a little while. "Heavy-handed, don't you think?" I keep my tone dry as I pull against his grasp. "After ten years, do you really think it will have magically disappeared if you don't check it daily?"

"It's a reminder, Meg. For both of us." He brings my wrist to his lips and presses a devastatingly sweet kiss there. The contacts shoots straight to my core. When he starts gently, he ends the cruelest, and even as I resist him, I crave what only he can give me. Barbs. Thorns. The kind of heat that scars. His words echo in my head. *Let's play a game.*

I shiver, something going soft inside me despite my best efforts to hold steady. "What kind of game?"

"Your favorite kind." He traces my knuckles with his thumb. "I'm going to pick a person in this restaurant… and you're going to fuck them."

I twist and look out at the room. We've never been here before, but it's packed on a Friday night. The main room is small enough to create an intimate feel. With the low lighting and soft music filtering through hidden speakers, it's the kind of place that invites a couple to lean in, to speak softly in each other's ears, to buy into the romance that exists simply by being here. And it is almost exclusively couples in here in pairs or on double dates. The food was an eclectic mix and though I was too on edge to eat my fill, the smells from neighboring tables have my mouth watering. I'll come back here again someday alone, when I can enjoy the meal without anticipation putting off my appetite.

I study the tables I can view from my spot, but I don't see anyone I recognize. That's a warning in and of itself. Hades might break my heart over and over again in a thousand different ways, but he would never put me in a position where I could truly be harmed. He may be careless with my heart, but he would never make the same mistake with my body.

Sending me to fuck some stranger? There are so many

variables. There's no way he can control it. No way he can guarantee that I'll be safe. He's bluffing. He has to be.

I relax back into the seat and turn back to face him. He is so handsome, his face the subject of so many more good memories than bad, I can almost pretend that nothing has changed. That we're still fresh in this relationship and nothing has had a chance to sour. I squeeze his thigh with my free hand, letting my fingers drift higher. "You want me to fuck someone here."

"I'm not in the habit of repeating myself."

"Unless it suits you."

His small smile has me shifting closer. He picks my hand off his thigh. "Unless it suits me." Hades repositions me so that I'm leaning against him, his lips brushing my ear with each word. "Do you see the waiter?"

"*What?*" Is he serious? He wants me to fuck a *waiter?*

"The blond."

I see who he means immediately. Truth be told, I clocked the man when we walked in, the same way I clock anyone who catches my eye. There are half a dozen people in this room who got a second look, but he's the only one wearing the same white shirt and black pants as the rest of the staff.

He's old-world movie-star handsome. The chiseled jaw, the easy smile, the big body that is athletic without being over-the-top muscled. Young, too. Not just in age, though if he's older than twenty-five, I'll be surprised. No, this guy is almost…

I jerk when I recognize it.

He's an innocent. There's something shiny and new about him that will make people like Hades want to tarnish it. I used to be the same way, once upon a time. Now, I'm the one who does the tarnishing. "I don't play with babies, Hades."

"Come now, Meg." He nips my earlobe. "Look at how eager he is to please. He'll probably come in his pants the second he tastes your pussy. All that enthusiasm in such a fetching package. You should thank me for giving him to you."

I shouldn't.

I really shouldn't.

Whoever this man is, I know better than to take this at face value. Hades didn't pick him randomly. He has a plan, has some manipulation going on. If I agree to this, I'm playing a part, and I don't get to cry foul later when it all comes to light. I lick my lips. "Thank you, Sir."

"Anything for you, love."

I have to laugh a little. Trust his gift to have more strings than Pinocchio. "You're hardly giving him to me. I'm assuming I'll have to seduce him?"

Hades's chuckle in my ear makes my nipples peak. "Give yourself a little credit. Crook your finger, and he'll be eating out of the palm of your hand."

There's a catch. There must be.

I close my eyes and force myself to relax. "You don't usually send me after the vanilla. In fact, you *never* send me after anyone unless we're in the club." The club where there are safety measures in place. Cameras in every room, a full staff of security to dissuade anyone from stepping out of line, and Hades himself who rules with an iron fist.

Not that I think I can't handle this guy, but I've been surprised before.

"Meg," Hades murmurs. "You're mine, are you not?"

It takes me a few seconds to form my reply. It *hurts*. It hurts so much to speak these words that mean a mere shadow of what they used to. "Yes, of course."

"Do you trust me?"

"Most of the time."

The amusement dissipates from his voice. "Do you trust me?"

I lick my lips. "Yes, Sir."

"Good girl." He releases me and gives me a little nudge. "There's a private room at the top of the stairs that belongs to the owners. The door is unlocked. Take him there." He touches me with a single finger beneath my chin and raises my face to press a devastatingly gentle kiss on my lips. Bargains are sealed with less, and I can't help feeling like I've sold my soul yet again for his pleasure. "You'll be safe. I'll ensure it." He waits until I scoot to the edge of the booth to say, "Don't disappoint me, love."

I work up a little bratty glare, but I know better than to argue with *that* tone. "I wouldn't dream of disappointing you, Sir." I grab my purse from under the table and stalk away from him.

It takes three steps for reality to catch up with me. If I were a better person, I would use my safe word to get out of this little game. One little word and Hades calls a stop to everything. My very own emergency brake, though I'm too stubborn and too into everything we do together to use it often. That's the crux of the matter. If I were a better person, the thought of seducing this bright-eyed waiter wouldn't heat my blood. It wouldn't send a downright delicious curl of desire through me. I want him, and I never would have taken him if left to my own devices.

Hades knows.

Hades always knows.

In this moment, it doesn't matter that he undoubtedly has ulterior motives. He's given me a new toy to play with, and the thrill is all I can think of as I slide up to the bar and order a whiskey straight. I can feel Hades's attention on me. A languid weight at the back of my neck. If he's got a room already picked out, then there will be measures in place to ensure it all goes according to plan. He'll remain close by.

He always did like to watch me work.

I turn and survey the restaurant. People have ⌐
clear out as the clock winds later. I frown. Where di⌐
waiter go? Several minutes tick by before the truth settles
over me. "Shit."

He's gone.

CHAPTER 2

*M*y feet drag as I clock out of a long shift in a month of long shifts. I need the money, so I can't afford to say no when my coworkers call in, but damn... I am so tired. I duck into the break room to change my shirt before I head home. It started raining sometime after I got here, and this uniform costs too much to risk ruining with something as mundane as rain water.

I snort at the thought.

A couple of months ago, I could have bought enough of these shirts to wear every single day of the year without doubling up. I wouldn't have done it, of course, because while they're top end, they aren't the kind of clothing I was used to when I lived in my parents' house. Considering how tight the budget has become in such a short time, I should have brought more clothing I could pawn. In another month, I'll be on a strict diet of ramen.

I check my phone, and though I'm not surprised that I have no notifications, my stomach sinks all the same. Leda hasn't responded to my texts in weeks, and it's not like she's going to suddenly do it tonight. She washed her hands of me and I can't even blame her. I tried to help her, and all I did was make it worse.

It doesn't stop me from wanting to check on her, to make sure she's okay. To offer her the protection I have no business offering. I might have fancied myself strong enough to play that role, but my father outmaneuvered me. Again.

And Leda got hurt in the process.

I carefully fold my shirt and stick it into my backpack. Thinking dark thoughts seems to be all I'm good for now. It doesn't help that I'm exhausted from the sheer energy it requires to smile and be polite no matter how shitty the restaurant customers act—or the fact I haven't slept through the night in longer than I care to remember. I close my eyes and press the heels of my hands to them. I'll get through this. What little suffering I'm experiencing now is nothing compared to what Leda went through, and though she would never say I deserve this, I can't help thinking that maybe I do. Compounding her hurt, even unintentionally, doesn't mean it's okay.

I sigh and let my hands drop. Plenty of time to play whipping boy to myself once I get home. The last thing I need is one of my coworkers wondering what the hell I'm doing hanging out in the break room instead of booking it for the door the second I clock out. No one else is in the room, so I allow myself to stretch, something in my back popping as I reach my fingertips toward the ceiling.

"Sounds painful." A woman's voice, low and throaty and full of promise.

I jump. "Sorry, I thought I was alone."

"No need to apologize. I was enjoying the show."

I face the woman and go still. She's easily the most captivating person I've ever seen. Not beautiful, exactly, but the sharp lines and equally sharp smile root my feet in place. Her dark brown hair is pulled back from her face, as if she knows how starkly beautiful her perfection is and plays it up for all it's worth. I can't look away from her blue eyes, and I have the most insane desire to go to my knees before her. To run my hands up her lean legs. To… *Get a hold of yourself.* "Ma'am, is there something I can help you with? You're in the employee break room."

"Ma'am?" She looks a little horrified. "I cannot believe you just ma'am-ed me."

It's the only appropriate response when greeting a woman. And this stranger is all woman in a way that has me fighting my body's attempt to respond. "I'm sorry?"

"You should be. Very sorry." Her tone drops, and she takes a step into the room.

She's nearly my height in her heels, but significantly smaller than I am. It doesn't seem to matter, because she takes up all the space in the room simply by breathing. Her smile widens. "Would you like to make it up to me?"

Surely I'm reading this wrong? No way did this woman come back here to find *me.* I glance around the room. The understated luxury in the main floor of the restaurant doesn't extend to the employee break room. There's a secondhand couch that's probably older than me up against one wall and a folding table with a stained microwave perched precariously on top of it. A few months ago, I wouldn't have fit into this place, but I don't have a choice now. This woman? She *definitely* doesn't fit in. "It's against the rules." I mean for the sentence to come out strong, but I sound more like I'm requesting confirmation.

"Rules were made to be broken, don't you think?" She lifts a dark eyebrow. "What do you say? One drink and you can send me on my way."

I frown, trying to think past the spell she seems to weave with her proximity. Spending time with guests on restaurant property is a firing offense. I really, really can't afford to lose this job. "I'm sorry."

Something flares in her blue eyes, and she moves closer. "My date left me."

"What?" I'd seen her on the restaurant floor, of course. She seemed to own the room the second she walked into it.

I'd noticed the older guy she was with too. He wore an extremely expensive suit in the careless way of someone rich beyond measure. But it was the way he studied the room that drew me, the kind smile and cold eyes. He was just as attractive as she is, the deep lines around his mouth and eyes speaking of plentiful smiles for those he deemed important enough to bestow them upon. There was power in the way he moved, in the way he drew every eye in the room even though it appeared he only had eyes for this woman.

Apparently appearances can be deceiving.

I've always had shit taste in who I was attracted to. This couple seems like they're no different. What kind of man leaves his woman behind after a dinner date? I should offer to call her a car. *That* is the reasonable thing to do. Not offer to take her to my place around the corner.

She gives me a slow smile. "I'm going to call a cab, but would you mind waiting with me?"

"Of course." I know even as I agree that I'll regret this. I grab my backpack and follow her out of the room. But instead of heading for the door like I expect, she takes a right turn and moves up a set of stairs that are strictly off limits. I stop short. "Employees aren't allowed up there."

"The owners and I are old friends." She must see my hesitation because she motions to herself. "I'm not exactly dressed for the weather."

She can say that again. She's clothed in a sheath dress that stops a full three inches shorter than polite dinner wear, and the white fabric looks delicate enough to tear if I so much as touch it.

Not sure what it says about me that I want to rip it in half, but I'm the one in control. Not my darker impulses. "Okay," I finally say and follow her up.

She leads me into a small loft apartment that the owners must use when they stay over in town. I step over the threshold, and I can't shake the feeling that I've passed some point of no return. I try to shrug off the foreboding, but I can't quite banish the weight of it.

The woman drops her purse on the couch and kicks off her heels. She shoots me a look. "I hope you don't mind. I have a twenty-minute wait, and these heels are killer on my feet."

It's not like I have more than a shitty bed waiting for me at home. I gingerly sink onto the couch next to her. I'm a big guy, and there are times when it's smarter to make myself smaller so I don't freak people out. Women, especially. Women alone, extra especially. She asked me to wait with her, but I'd hate for her to regret it.

She doesn't look anything but intense. She crosses one of those long, long legs over the other, causing her dress to slide higher up her toned thighs. I try to drag my gaze up to her eyes, to keep things polite, but I can't quite manage it. There's a tattoo there, something small and intricate. I think it's a skeleton key. Part of me wants to push her dress higher to find out.

To discover if she's wearing panties.

Damn it, I'm ogling her like some kind of creep.

"What's your name?"

I manage to sit back, though now I'm battling the cock-stand of the century. I look anywhere but at her, finally focusing on the truly hideous abstract painting across from the couch. "Hercules."

"Someone's parents had high aspirations."

The last thing I want to do right now is talk about my parents. Even though I'm not living in the same city they rule anymore, it's hard not to feel like I'm existing in the shadow of their disappointment. "Something like that."

"I'm Meg." She circles my wrist with her hand, her nails lightly pricking my skin, and it's everything I can do not to moan. What the hell is wrong with me? This lady needs help, not some horny idiot who has half a dozen truly impolite thoughts running through his head.

I want to kiss her.

I want to push up that dress and see exactly what she has on underneath it.

I want to trace that tattoo with my tongue, to taste her.

Hell, I want to fuck her.

What the fuck is wrong with me? She needs help and I'm panting after her like some piece of shit guy who only sees tits and an ass instead of a person.

I'm acting like my *father*.

The thought is a bucket of ice water poured over my head. In that moment of clarity, I pull back, but she tightens her grip on me. I'm stronger than her. I can get free if I pull hard enough, but it means grappling with her and maybe hurting her. I go still. She raises an eyebrow. "I'll give you a dollar if you tell me what you were just thinking about."

No way in hell am I subjecting her to that. "That's not a good idea." If this was a different situation, if she wasn't stranded, I might be willing to believe all signs pointing to her hitting on me. But it *isn't* a different situation, and I can't afford to assume shit.

"Try me." Meg smiles and traces her nail across the inside of my wrist. It feels like my whole body narrows down to that single touch. "I might surprise you, Hercules."

I clear my throat, trying to focus past the way her touch

zings through my body. I feel drunk on her, even though I haven't had a drink since I left Olympus. Maybe that's why I tell her the truth. "You're beautiful." I look down at where her paler hand brackets my wrist. "That's what I was thinking. That you're beautiful." Not the full truth, but then I just met this woman. I would have to be out of my fucking mind to tell her that I can't stop wondering what her pussy tastes like. There are lines. There have to be.

"Oh, Hercules." She sighs a little like I've said something that pleases her greatly. "You really are too pure for this world, aren't you?"

If she only knew how quickly my thoughts had gone dark and filthy. "No. Not really."

Her smile goes sharp. "I'm afraid I haven't been perfectly honest with you."

"What?"

Another of those sharp smiles that has my cock throbbing in response. What is she *doing* to me? I'm no inexperienced virgin. I've had plenty of fun with both girls and boys through my late teens and early twenties. I know attraction when I see it, when I feel it. But this is... different. She touches me like she can see the desires beneath my skin and takes great enjoyment plucking them one by one. I have the strangest suspicion that she could make me come without ever touching my cock.

The idea excites me.

Fuck. Everything about her excites me.

"I didn't call a car." She keeps up that movement against my wrist. Back and forth. Back and forth. "I was hoping to seduce you."

My thoughts stumble over themselves as I try to make sense of what she just said. "You want to seduce *me?*"

"Is that so surprising? I mean, look at you. You're practically a walking wet dream." She casts a meaningful glance to where I've tried and failed to hide my erection. "I saw you, and I wanted you."

Now is the time to stop this. Even if what she's saying is true, she came to dinner with another man. A man who touched her with familiarity and stirred things inside me even more uncomfortable than what I'm feeling right now. If she's using me to get back at him... Does it matter? It shouldn't. I don't know him. I doubt I'll see her again after she's through with me. I should just take the offer she's making and enjoy myself for once without overthinking things.

Too bad I can't.

I gently extract my wrist from her hand, hating the way I miss the heat of her skin against mine the second her touch is gone. "You'll regret it if you sleep with me to punish him."

Her blue eyes go wide. "Are you for real?"

"I try to be."

She gives herself a shake. "Look, you seem to have gotten the wrong idea. He and I are... complicated. He's not my husband. He's not my boyfriend. He's..." She hesitates, clearly fighting for the right words. "Complicated." For half a second, her barriers dissipate, and she looks vulnerable and lonely and more than a little sad.

"I don't use women. Or men, for that matter."

"Even when they're asking to be used?" She looks away and then back, her gaze sharpening. "Even when I'm *telling* you I want to be used."

I should stand up. Should walk out that door and down the stairs. But that vulnerability calls to me in a way that has me closing the distance between us. "I'm lonely too."

"I didn't—"

I kiss her. I don't mean to, but then I never mean to get myself into trouble. Whatever her story, whatever put that look in her eyes, if I can take it away for a little bit and

17

leave her better off than before, aren't I obligated to at least try?

She tastes like wine and something spicy, and her mouth goes soft beneath mine almost immediately. And then her tongue is there in a brief stroke against mine, a query I answer in kind. Kissing her feels as natural as breathing.

As natural as breathing?

Ha.

More like as natural and dangerous as a free fall.

CHAPTER 3

MEG

I had a plan going into this, but Hercules has smashed it to pieces. This man with his kind eyes and sweet smile... He's nothing like I expected. He kisses me like it's the main event, as if we never have to go farther than this because he can't get enough of my mouth on his. And through it all, I can feel Hades's presence, even if he's not in the room.

Hercules. What a fucking name. *Hercules*. Fitting in its way, because he's built like a Greek statue. His golden hair is cropped short and his eyes are so blue they take my breath away. Especially with how he's looking at me now, like he can't believe this is happening and he must be the luckiest man alive. His shoulders flex beneath my grip, and I can't wait to get him out of his shirt to see if he's as defined as he seems. In fact, that seems like an excellent idea.

I nip his bottom lip hard enough that he gasps, going a little melty against me. I spare a thought to wondering if Hades knew this man had a masochistic streak. It wouldn't surprise me. Hades always seems to know when someone around him is harboring a kink or twelve. I tug on Hercules's

19

shirt and he allows me to pull it over his head. I sit back and just look at him. "You call me beautiful, but you're the beautiful one."

His golden cheeks go a little pink and he bites his bottom lip in the same place I did just now. Oh, this guy is too much. I lean in and soothe the spot with my tongue. "Tell me what you want."

"I…"

He's going to hold back. I can already tell. I grab his wrist and press his hand to my thigh, right over my tattoo. "Not the polite version. Not what you think I want to hear. Tell me what you want right now, in this moment, more than anything else."

Hercules's gaze drops to my mouth and then lower to where his hand brackets my thigh. "I want to taste your pussy."

My whole body goes hot and tight. He says he's not pure, but there's something almost innocent in the way he allows me to lead this. Submissive, yes, but more than that. I want to dirty him right up. I guide his hand beneath my dress and catch my breath as he palms me between my thighs.

He makes a sound suspiciously like a growl. "No panties, Meg?"

"I don't like them."

"Fuck, neither do I."

He doesn't try anything, letting me lead this. *Submitting.* All the tangled feelings from dinner with Hades burn to ash in this moment. Damn him, but he's right. This is exactly what I need tonight. I lean back against the arm of the couch. "Take what you want."

He looks at me for a long moment as if he's sure this is a trap. I roll my hips a little, rubbing myself against his palm. It snaps him out of it. He moves down my body so he can shove my dress up to see my pussy.

The look on his face.

I would pay an absurd amount of money to have a picture of this moment, to keep it locked away and bring out whenever I needed a bump. He looks at my pussy like he's just found a treasure he's spent his life chasing. And then he's on me, dragging his tongue down from my clit, over my pussy, spreading me to get lower yet, and then moving back up to flick my clitoral hood piercing. Hades is rarely wrong about these kinds of things, but I'm still almost shocked by his enthusiasm. He fucks me with his tongue, growling against my flesh even as he drives my pleasure relentlessly higher.

Not quite high enough yet.

"Hercules—"

He shifts gears, moving up to my clit and sucking hard as he shoves two fingers into me with enough force to lift my hips off the couch. "Oh *fuck*." I look down and find him watching me closely, gauging my reactions. He holds my gaze as he does it again, fucking me with his fingers and giving my clit long pulls that have my toes curling and my eyes rolling back in my head.

How did this get so out of control?

When did I become the seduced, rather than the seducer?

"Wait, wait, wait."

He immediately lifts his head, though he doesn't remove his fingers, the dirty boy. "Did I hurt you?"

"No, nothing like that." I prop myself up on my elbows and try to think through the pleasure of that pulsing thing he's doing with his fingers against my G-spot. "I need…" God, that feels good. It would be the easiest thing in the world to let him make me come like this.

But I know how to read a man, and this one will make me orgasm hard enough to see stars, then he'll fix my dress, call me a car, and send me home. He's got that kind of selfless martyrdom written all over him. Not tonight.

I push on his shoulders until he sits back and then crawl into his lap and claim his mouth in another kiss. I can taste myself on his tongue and hell if that doesn't make me hotter. I've always loved this shit.

"Meg, you don't have to take care of me." His hand is between my thighs again, parting my pussy and delving deep. "I want to make you come."

"You will." I'm doing a bit of delving on my own. Normally, I pride myself on my seduction techniques. I can have a person on the verge of orgasm just by undressing them when I'm feeling inspired. I love to hold off and tease until pleasure becomes pain becomes pleasure again.

I have none of that finesse tonight.

I need him inside me and I need it now. My hands actually shake as I yank open his pants and reach inside for his cock. And, oh god, he's even bigger than I anticipated. "I need you."

He catches my wrist, a frown marring his perfect blond brows. "You don't have to."

"Hercules." I fight his hold to give him a rough stroke that makes a muscle tick in his jaw. "I want to ride your cock. I want you deep and hard inside me, and I want us both to come like that." When he doesn't release me, I go in for the kill. "Let me fuck you, Hercules. *Now.*"

Just like that, he's mine.

He manages to get his pants off without totally dislodging me, but it's fine because I'm too busy yanking off my dress to care about the awkwardness of this. Ten years of playing with Carver City's sexual elite, and I'm fumbling over myself like a teenager.

I dig through the decorative cabinet next to the couch and find a condom. He raises his brows at that but doesn't comment as I rip the packet open and roll it onto his cock. "Hurry, hurry, hurry."

"We don't have to rush."

"Speak for yourself."

His low laugh has my whole body clenching. Hercules catches me around the waist and pulls me closer with one arm while he uses the other hand to position himself at my entrance. "I'll go slow."

"I don't want you to." I slam down on him and, holy shit, maybe I should have given myself a little bit to adjust to his size. I rock and writhe, but he bands an arm around my waist and seals us together completely.

"*Meg*." He sounds just as desperate as I feel.

I run my hands up his chest and meet his gaze. His blue eyes have darkened to near-black, as if his iris swallowed all the color up. Gone is the sweetness that attracted and repelled me in equal measures. This creature is all man, and he's more than a little smug as he takes in my expression. I can only begin to guess what he sees written across my face, but it pleases him.

"I want you to fuck me." My command comes out a little breathy, but I can't help it. Not with him filling me so perfectly.

"I *am* fucking you."

I roll my hips, managing a tiny bit of delicious friction. Not enough. Not for what I need, not for what I suspect we both need. I take his chin and hold his gaze. "Fuck me, Hercules. Hard. I promise I won't break."

The words are barely out of my mouth when he pulls me off his cock and all but tosses me down onto the couch on my stomach. Then he's between my thighs again, urging my ass up and guiding his cock back into me. I start to rise up, but his hand on the flat of my back stops me.

Dirty boy.

He grips my hips and gives a few experimental thrusts, testing me. If only he knew. I shove back against each one,

23

until he's so deep, I'm half sure I can feel his cock in the back of my throat. "*Yes.*"

That's when I realize he's been holding back. Because when he starts to move, there's no mercy for me. It's fine. I don't want it. If I wanted something soft and sweet... but then, I never do. This is neither, and it's perfect in every way. Just down and dirty fucking, each stroke hitting me exactly where I need it. It's been so long since I had anything resembling vanilla, I had almost forgotten I can get this need met without kink involved.

Except kink *is* involved.

Hercules might not know it, but he's Hades's proxy in this. Fucking me because my Sir commanded it.

And just like that, I'm coming. My orgasm draws a cry from my lips, and Hercules shoves deep, fucking me in short pumps that draw it out for long seconds. When I think I can't bear any more, when I'm about to beg for mercy, he follows me over the edge, my name on his lips.

He flops down next to me on the couch. "Damn."

"Damn is right," I murmur. I can't think past the racing of my heart. I didn't expect this. I never could have anticipated it.

"Did I hurt you?" I can actually feel his hesitance trying to take hold again.

I press back against him with a grin. "Not even a little bit."

"But—"

I turn and drape one leg over his hip. He dwarfs me, and his big hand settling on my hip makes me feel almost dainty. It would be the easiest thing in the world for him to dominate me physically, but he has this unsure look on his pretty face, as if he expects to be kicked. And not in a fun way. I run my hands up his chest and cup his face. "Hercules, you followed orders beautifully."

Something in him relaxes at that and he pulls me closer,

though it almost feels like I'm a teddy bear that he's using for comfort, rather than the woman he just fucked hard and dirty. I don't mind. Aftercare is part of the process, even if it was an almost-vanilla scene. I let him cuddle me and allow myself to enjoy this moment for what it is.

A beautiful man just made me come and now is looking to me for comfort. No games on his part. No walls. The sheer simplicity of it soothes me in a way I couldn't anticipate. I stroke my hand down his arm. "No regrets?"

"No regrets," he breathes. "I just kind of can't believe this happened."

I laugh and arch against him, feeling more relaxed than I have been in ages. "Oh, it happened. And it was good."

"Meg," he says slowly.

"Yes?"

He reaches between us and drags his hand down the center of my body. "I could call you a car." He traces me with a blunt finger, pushing inside and dragging my wetness up around my clit.

"You could." I'm practically quivering as he does that move again. It's nowhere near enough to get me anywhere close to orgasm, but it feels good. So freaking good.

"Or…" He licks my ear in almost the exact same spot Hades did earlier tonight. "Or I could eat your pussy again. You stopped me before I was finished with you."

I shouldn't… Then again, I shouldn't do a lot of things I really enjoy doing. "That's quite the decision to make." I roll onto my back, taking him with me. "I suppose it's a reasonable request considering how much I enjoyed you fucking me like I asked."

"Totally reasonable." He urges me high on the couch so I'm sitting and he's stretched out between my spread thighs. He gives me a wicked grin that has butterflies with razor sharp wings erupting in my stomach. "I like you, Meg."

"I like you too, Hercules." I can't resist sifting my fingers through his light hair as he dips down and gives my pussy an open-mouthed kiss. I can't get enough of the sight of the sheer bliss on his face as he explores me with his tongue. Now that we've both taken the edge off, he's got a little better control, but it couldn't be clearer that he's thoroughly enjoying himself. Pleasure winds through me, and I tug on his hair to guide him back to my clit. "Make me come again."

This time, he doesn't tease. He follows my order fucking beautifully, working my clit skillfully as he brings me closer and closer to the edge. He doesn't slow down, he doesn't stop, simply goes after me with a single-minded determination I might find frightening if my pleasure wasn't his aim.

"Yes, Hercules, just like that."

Movement out of the corner of my eye has me lifting my head, but Hercules is too wrapped up in licking my pussy to notice. That's why he doesn't see Hades walk into the room. Only the heat in Hades's eyes gives away how affected he is by this, but I can't begin to say if it's fury or desire or some combination of both.

I open my mouth, but he shakes his head. He simply gives a small smile and mouths a single word. *Come.*

Just like that, the spell is broken. I begin to move again, grinding against Hercules's mouth as Hades looks on, held helpless by my Sir's gaze. My orgasm hits me with the strength of a freight train, a thousand times stronger than the one when it was just Hercules and I. It bows my back and draws a scream from my lips. The entire world goes fuzzy.

Not fuzzy enough to prevent me from hearing Hades say in his mildest voice, "And what do we have here?"

CHAPTER 4

I do so love it when a plan comes together.

The joy is downright orgasmic as I watch this boy scramble to cover Meg and himself at the same time. As if I haven't seen her in every stage of undress, in every moment of unbecoming. As if she isn't mine the same way my right hand is mine, an extension of myself.

Even though I know better, I allow myself to drink in the sight of them together. I could have waited longer to interrupt, but Meg had her instructions, and she let things get away from her. She always did have a sentimental streak. It's her one downfall, and I'm only too happy to exploit it for our mutual benefit.

And what a benefit.

Hercules is perfectly made. Part of me wishes I didn't notice that, didn't react to it, but denying myself is never something I bothered to learn how to do. He's all golden muscles and golden hair and a righteous indignity I will take great joy in snapping into pieces at the first opportunity.

"What are you doing here?" He's managed to find a shirt

to ball up over his cock, but it acts more as a tease than anything else. I've already seen it in all its glory, after all.

I raise my eyebrows. "I'm claiming what's mine." I meet Meg's gaze. Just as I expected, even with the interruption, she's loose and relaxed in a way she hasn't been in a significant amount of time. It confirms what I already knew. Hercules is a bridge and he will serve his purpose well.

But only if I trigger the proper pressure points. I snap my fingers and point to a spot next to me. "Come, Meg."

Hercules's confusion becomes something akin to horror as Meg slips out from beneath him and walks toward me. "No. What are you doing? Stop it."

She looks almost guilty as she sinks to her knees by my side, but while Meg might entertain herself with fighting me, she loves being mine. Even with how complicated our relationship has become, how tangled our history. I lay my hand on her dark hair because I know it will infuriate him and incite every protective instinct he has. "Good girl."

Hercules still looks like he's been hit by a train. "I'm going to need you to explain what the hell is going on." This man was built for what knighthood was supposed to be hundreds of years ago. A paragon of self-righteousness, a force for good. I monitored him for months before making my move. When faced with a helpless creature, he will invariably turn himself inside out in order to offer protection.

The trick is convincing him that Meg is helpless, a trait she's never possessed.

"A mere game, I'm afraid." I keep stroking her hair. "It amuses me to send my Meg to fuck other men and women, and so I sent her to seduce you. Really, I would think the situation is self-explanatory."

"You *made* her fuck me?" The betrayal in his eyes is a living thing, quickly followed by fury and... Ah, there it is. The desire to save her from the devil who stands over her.

Really, it's too easy, as simple as lining up the dominoes and tipping the first one over.

I ignore his question, because I know it will infuriate him further. "Get dressed, love." I turn my attention to the boy. Oh, he's not *really* a boy. He's a man, even if he still has an aura of innocence about him. He has the look of his father, both in coloring and in features. I wonder what Zeus would say if he knew my plans, and I barely hold back a smile imagining his rage. A rage that will be his undoing.

All in good time.

Meg dresses quickly and runs her fingers through her hair. She still looks like she's been fucked within an inch of her life, but she's halfway presentable by the time she rises and takes my hand. I bring our laced fingers to my lips and press a soft kiss to her knuckles. "You please me."

Her smile is pained, and she can't help shooting a look at Hercules. Does she even realize how much this man calls to her? There are submissives aplenty in the Underworld, but innocents are a far rarer occurrence. When this is all over, my Meg will thank me for the lengths I go through for her. If there's another reason in the mix? Well, I am who I am.

She finally drags her gaze back to me. "Thank you, Sir."

I lead her out the door and down the stairs, and she follows like a good obedient little sub. I know it's coming, and I almost relish the way she lays into me the second we slide into the back of the town car.

"What the *hell*, Hades?"

"You're welcome for what appears to be a most satisfying gift."

Her glare can't completely diminish the way she practically glows after her time with him. "What was that little song and dance about? You acted like you own me. You rubbed it in his face."

I'm not ready to discuss my plans. "I *do* own you."

"Hades, you're such an asshole sometimes."

I grab the back of her neck and tow her over my lap. "I give you leeway, Meg. I indulge you."

"Damn it, let me go!"

I shove up her dress and deliver two hard smacks to her ass. "Tell me your safe word." When she doesn't immediately respond, I shove two fingers deep into her pussy. She's still drenched from her orgasms and Hercules's mouth. If I spread her wide, will I taste him there? My cock hardens even further at the thought. I have to close my eyes and fight for control. *Soon. Very soon.* "Tell me."

"Cerberus," she mutters.

"That's right. Cerberus." I press hard on her inner wall, just like she loves, and she writhes for me. "The safe word you neglected to use once during our little game. You wanted to fuck the golden boy, and you wanted me to watch, and when I told you to come, you orgasmed all the harder for how dirty it made you feel. I *know* you, Meg. I know your body and your soul. You may play the martyr for the public, but you don't get to play it with me."

"I hate you," she sobs even as she spreads her thighs wider to give me better access. It's always like this with us. Always a fight to the finish, and even in the soft aftermath of fucking, we still jostle each other with power games.

"No, you don't. I give you what you need. Remember that, even when you're getting starry-eyed over a *waiter.*" Hercules is hardly just a waiter, but that fact is immaterial in the face of this conversation. We've taken our first step to reclaiming what we once had, even if I have to drag Meg along with me inch by inch. "Tell me 'thank you' for the spectacular gift I gave you tonight."

She pants and writhes, but she's not really fighting to get free. She's struggling solely so I'll hold her down and bend her to my will. I spank her again with my free hand. Once. Twice. A third time. "Now, Meg."

"Thank you, Sir." The words come out as if a curse.

"Good girl." I topple her onto the back seat and move to kneel on the floorboards. "You performed marvelously. Would you like your reward?"

She bites her bottom lip like she wants to tell me to fuck off again out of sheer perversity, but desire overcomes all else. At the end of the night, I've given her exactly what she needs and she knows it. Meg pulls her dress up higher. "Yes, Sir. I would love my reward now."

"That's what I thought." I smooth a hand down her stomach and part her pussy with my fingers. She's pink and swollen from what she's done. I pin her in place and drag the flat of my tongue over her. Meg lets loose a whimper and reaches behind her to grab the headrest.

I can taste him on her skin. I can *smell* him on her skin.

I wedge my hands beneath her ass and lift her closer to my mouth, devouring her with a ferocity bordering on frenzy. Even as she screams her way through an orgasm, even as I replace her on the seat and she opens my slacks to withdraw my cock, even as she rides me in slow, decadent strokes…

I can't say for certain if it's jealousy of Hercules that spurns me on.

Or desire for him.

CHAPTER 5

HERCULES

I can't let it go.

Every time I close my eyes, I see Meg forced to sit at *his* feet. I see the graceful curve of her body as she bends like she was created to occupy that position. I see the possessive way he strokes her hair—possessive and controlling. No matter that he walked in on us, no matter that he apparently *wanted* her to have sex with me, no matter that I don't understand anything about what the fuck happened in that room.

No, that's a lie.

I understand the triumph written across his beautiful face when he called her away from me and she obeyed.

I understand the frustration and anger on *her* face too.

She's trapped. This guy has some kind of hold on her, one I recognize right down to my bones. I know all about being stuck in a place that slowly strangles the life out of a person, about what pieces of yourself you have to cut off in order to gain your freedom. I left parts of myself back in Olympus, but I count the cost worth it. I'm free, after all.

Unlike Meg.

Unlike Leda.

Impossible not to conflate the two, even though their situations are hardly similar. Leda was attacked. Meg is... I'm not really sure what's going on. All I know is that a powerful man holds her leash and orders her to do things like fuck strangers. I *thought* she enjoyed what we did, but knowing the context I can't be sure. If he forced her, can she even give consent?

The thought that I might be more like my father than I could have dreamed haunts me. I can't sleep. I can't focus on work and keep making stupid mistakes. I even go so far as to type out a text to Leda, though I have enough control left not to send it. It's not fair to look to her to make me feel better. I promised not to contact her again, and I will keep that promise.

Again and again, my mind goes back to Meg. If she's as trapped as I fear...

Smarter to leave it alone. If I couldn't make a difference as Zeus's son, can I really make a difference as a nameless waiter in a city that's not my own? I don't even have money to offer as a payout, though I suspect no amount of money would make a difference. I've seen that man's type before. I used to know plenty of men like him. Ambitious and cruel and willing to trample over anyone who gets in their way. People like me.

People like Meg.

It takes me all of two days to figure out who he is—Hades, the owner of an exclusive club called the Underworld. I spend far too long looking at his picture on the website, the distinguished silver in his hair and the classy black-framed glasses. He's attractive. Really attractive. His mouth, curved in the same soft smile he'd worn when he caught me eating his woman's pussy, makes my stomach clench in a way that's not altogether unpleasant. Like he knows a secret that I don't and finding out will either please me greatly…or be something I regret for the rest of my life. There is no middle ground there. I shouldn't crave that any more than I should desire Meg, a woman who only fucked me because she was ordered to.

Yet when my day off rolls around, I find myself pushing through the doors into the building that houses the Underworld. I half expected some Victorian house that looks haunted and full of secrets, but it's a skyscraper in the middle of downtown. The lobby is like a thousand other lobbies—tile and neutral colors and elevators. That's it.

I check the directory and head to the correct elevator bank. It's only when the doors close me in that it hits me how out of line I am. Whatever game Meg and Hades played, it was obviously between them. I didn't ask for an audience, but it's not like I would have objected, given the right circumstances. I don't mind being watched. Hell, I like it.

Charging in here to save Meg is high-handed at absolute best, and deliriously misguided at worst. I should turn around and walk out and move on with my life.

I should…but I don't.

The doors open, and I walk straight to the desk situated in the middle of an empty room. It houses a Black man who is possibly the most beautiful person I've ever laid eyes on. His dark skin is so flawless, I'm half convinced he doesn't actually have pores, and he wears a suit that's worth about six of the one on my body.

He gives me a similar rake of his gaze and then presents a wide smile. "What can I help you with, handsome?"

"I'm here to see Meg." If we could have a conversation, maybe it will dial back the protective impulse that drove me to this lobby in the first place. If I can reassure myself that she's not trapped, that maybe I misunderstood what happened after we had sex in that apartment… Maybe then I can let this whole thing go.

His face snaps into coldly professional lines. "I'll see if she's available. Sit, please."

I turn and find a cleverly hidden bench in the same stone as the floor. A waiting room can be its own kind of defense, its own kind of weapon. It sets up the power dynamics before an audience is ever granted. I recognize that, but I don't have a choice to do anything except play this game. I settle down to wait.

In the end, it doesn't take long. Ten minutes after I arrive, the man clears his throat. "You may go in."

"Thank you." I move around the desk to the large black door. It's meant to intimidate and it's successful. My nerves try to get the best of me, but I shove them down deep and fall back into my old habit of masking my expressions. A vital survival tactic in what my father likes to call his court. I wonder what Hades calls his inner circle, but that thought has no place here.

I push open the door and walk into the next room.

I'm not sure what I expect. With a name like the Under-world, it could go a number of ways. Instead, it looks like any bar in some high-end spot. Booths line the walls, each tucked back into the dark gray walls and shrouded in shadows except for a single small stylized chandelier that hangs over each. They're all different shapes and styles, but each is made of silver and has either glass or crystal pieces muting the light. It's a startlingly classy effect considering I know what goes on in this place.

The rest of the floor is much better lit with the circular bar acting as the main attraction. It showcases a wide array of alcohol options that border a giant marble sculpture that's… I blink. It's almost abstract, but I'm certain that it's depicting an orgy.

What catches and holds my attention is the man lounging against the bar, his black-on-black suit somehow making him look ever more distinguished than the last time I saw him.

Hades.

What the hell?

He arches a brow at me. "Don't look so confused. You honestly think you can come to my front door and ask after Meg and I wouldn't know about it?" He gives me that same half smile that's haunted me for days. "I think we both know you're smarter than that."

Maybe I am.

Maybe I knew it would come down to seeing him again.

I don't know. My stomach is twisting in on itself, a toxic combination of anger and self-righteousness and desire making it hard to think. I clear my throat. "I'd like to see her."

"So intent on my Meg." He motions and a tall, curvy Latina woman appears behind the bar, deposits two drinks, and moves away. There's no one else in the room, so she must be trying to offer some privacy. Hades picks up the glass, and I can't help noticing the elegance of his hands, the graceful way he moves. He crooks his finger. "I promise I won't bite. Unless you ask nicely."

My blood rushes to my cock, and I don't fucking understand it. I should want to knock this guy out, but something about him has my instincts misfiring. There's no fight or flight. It's flight or fuck, and even in my current confusion, I know better than to play into the latter.

I *should* know better than to play into the latter.

Hades sighs. "Fine, I'll take on the role of the bad guy. Either you sit, have a conversation with me, and I decide whether or not I want my Meg around you, or I call in Allecto and she escorts you out. It's really that simple."

I don't know who this Allecto is, but I'm too focused on

the first part of his sentence to worry about her. "Meg is a person, not a pet. You don't get to decide who she does or doesn't talk to."

"Meg is both a person and a pet." There goes that smile again, the one that seems to say he's enjoying a private joke that I have no access to. "Sit, Hercules."

My body snaps to attention, obeying the sharpness in his command before I can decide if I want to. I stride to him, and his smile widens. "What a good boy you are." He tilts his head to the side, studying me in a way that makes me feel like he can see beneath my clothes. "I wonder… Would you kneel if I told you to?"

"No," I snarl to cover up the truth. I'm not sure what I would do. I can almost feel the bite of the floor through my jeans. The weight of his hand on my head the same way he touched Meg that night. It makes my chest ache, and I don't understand why.

Another of those shrugs that means everything and nothing at all. "I suppose we'll find out."

"I want to see Meg."

He takes a sip of his drink and raises his eyebrows. Reluctantly, I pick up mine and do the same. It's scotch. Very, very expensive scotch. I lick my lips, going still at the predatory way he watches the movement. "I want to see Meg," I repeat.

"Yes, yes. All in good time." He leans back against the bar. "Let's be honest between the two of us, shall we? You don't want to see Meg. You want a whole lot more than that."

How can he know that when even *I* don't know what I want? I take another drink to cover up my mixed responses. "Why do you think that?"

"I have many talents. Reading people is one of them. You, my dear boy, got your head spun around by Meg's pussy. I can't blame you. She's divine, isn't she?"

"Don't talk about her that way." Even if I dream about her

pussy. Even if I wish I hadn't dicked around the first fifteen minutes of our acquaintance so I got more time with her taste on my tongue. It's more than that. He's making it sound cheap and dirty.

He's making it sound like what happened that night is exactly what I'm afraid of.

He leans close, and I realize that he's actually an inch shorter than me. He seems so much larger than life, it's strange to look down into those dark eyes. Hades smiles slowly. "For such a smart boy, you're awfully dense. I can talk about Meg however I damn please. She's mine, Hercules. I *own* her. I told her to fuck you that night, so she did. If I stripped her naked and set her on this bar and lined up every member of the Underworld and let them fuck her one right after the other, she'd thank me for it just like she did after she fucked you." He lowers his voice, still so close that our chests damn near brush. "I can do every single dark and twisted thing I want to our Meg, and she has no choice but to comply."

Anger finally derails my attraction to him. If what he's saying is true, and what little evidence I have supports it, then she truly didn't have a choice that night. My stomach lurches and I clench my fists. "I won't let you hurt her again." I can't go back in time and take back what happened between us, but I will do whatever it takes to ensure she's not put in that position again.

Something flashes in his eyes, there and gone too quickly for me to identify. "I won't let her go. I suppose we find ourselves at an impasse." He finishes his drink, and I try my best not to watch the way his throat moves when he swallows. "What a shame." He starts to turn away.

"Wait."

"Yes?" Is he holding his breath? I can't be sure.

I down the remainder of my drink, letting the alcohol

buzz through my veins, though it doesn't give me nearly as much courage as I'd like. "I heard you make deals."

Hades turns fully back to face me and steeples his fingers. "You heard correctly."

"I'll make a deal with you to free Meg."

He taps his fingers against his lips. "Meg is very dear to me, Hercules. I'm not sure what you could possibly offer that would make me give her up."

I don't possess anything of worth. Not anymore. If I were still in Olympus, I'd have access to resources and more money than even Hades could bring to the fore. Hades. Olympus. I stop short. I hadn't even made the connection before now. Surely it's not coincidence that Hades goes by *that* name. The one shared by the bogeyman in Olympus. *Be a good boy or Hades will get you.* It's not a threat I've been on the receiving end of since I was a small child or I would have made the connection sooner. Hades isn't supposed to be a real person, for all that he's technically one of the Thirteen. If he existed, I would have known about it. "Hades."

He seems to sense the change in me and raises his brows. "That is my name."

"Do you have some connection to Olympus?"

Just like that, he goes as icy as he was the first moment we met. Cold. So fucking cold. "If you're afraid of making a deal, then stop wasting my time. I have more important things to be doing at the moment."

I have nothing to offer him. Not really. My trust fund is long gone, and even if it wasn't, Hades doesn't seem the type to be swayed by a series of commas and zeroes. No, he'll want something more. Which is a damn problem. I *have* nothing except...

I take a deep breath. "You can have me."

"I can...have you." He studies me. "The devil is in the

39

details, my boy. I'm going to need you to be significantly more specific."

I clear my suddenly dry throat. "I mean you can have me. However you want to take that." It's only right. A way to balance the scales of the wrong I've done. The mistakes I've made. Penance. There's a sweet relief in that, in giving up control so completely. I don't really understand it, but in the end my feelings don't matter. Helping Meg does.

"You mean, I can fuck you." He circles me slowly, a predator going in for the kill. "I can shove my cock between those pretty lips of yours. I can do whatever I please to *your* cock. I can take your ass whenever and however I like." He stops in front of me again, seemingly unaffected by the words he just launched at me like daggers. "Is that what you mean when you say I can have you?"

"Yes." It takes me two tries to keep speaking. "If that's what it takes."

"A better man would turn you away. Forced consent is hardly consent." He smiles suddenly, a full smile that rocks me back on my heels. "You're a terrible negotiator. Truly awful. I accept your terms—you're mine, and I no longer force Meg to follow my commands against her will."

I swallow hard, trying to think. "That's a very specific sentence."

"Yes, well, *I* am not terrible at negotiating." He raises his voice. "'Tis, another round. We're sealing a deal with a drink."

The woman appears again, this time with the bottle. She pours a healthy splash into his glass and then mine, gives me a sharp look, and disappears around the curve of the bar again. I reach for my drink and pause. His words *seem* fine on the surface. I do this, and he can't force Meg anymore. She won't have to fuck strangers unless she wants to. She won't have to follow Hades's orders anymore. Surely she'll be happy to be free?

I can't think straight. Not with the scotch in my system, though Hades's presence is more to blame for the muddled way my thoughts run together than the alcohol. I frown at him. "Do you *want* to fuck me?"

He gives me that blinding smile again, as if I've done something to amuse him greatly. Hades sets down his drink and reclaims the final step between us. He grips my neck, the strength in his fingers surprising. So is my reaction. My cock goes hard, and I have to fight back a moan.

What the *fuck?*

"Poor baby sub. You don't even know what you are, do you?" He tsks. "Don't worry. I'll teach you."

"Teach me what?"

"Everything."

I don't even know what that means. Not really. I just know that I suddenly want it. "Okay."

"We'll seal it with a kiss then," he murmurs against my mouth. But he doesn't follow through like I expect.

I belatedly realize he's waiting for confirmation. I nod as much as I'm able to with the way he grips my neck. "Yes. Seal it with a kiss."

"Good boy." There is no teasing touch of his tongue. He simply takes my mouth as if it has been his all long. He forces me wide open for him and plunders me with his tongue. I lift my shaking hands and fist them in his perfect black shirt, though I can't say for certain whether I'm clinging to him to steady myself or trying to get him closer. In the end, it doesn't matter.

He releases me and steps back, leaving me swaying on my feet. Hades smooths down his shirt and then fixes his glasses where they've been knocked off-center by our kiss. "'Tis will get you set up in your new room. One of my other people will give you the tour."

That snaps me out of my haze. "What?"

Hercules gives me a pitying look. "Come now, Hercules. You didn't think you'd bargain away yourself to me and then go back to your sad little life, did you? Call in and quit your job. My people will gather your belongings and see to your apartment. The Underworld is your home now."

CHAPTER 6

MEG

"*D*id you hear about the new guy?"

I look up from the spreadsheet detailing the Underworld's income last month. I wasn't sure what the disruption of Balthazar's territory would do for our bottom line. Coups in Carver City make everyone nervous, and nervous people will either drop mad cash or button it up completely.

Judging from the accounts list I have, they went with the former.

Thank fuck.

I drag my attention back to the present to find Tink standing in the doorway to my office. She's victim to one of the many deals Hades has made over the years. I don't know the terms of this specific one—I rarely know the details unless he feels I need to—but she's fit right into life here at the club while still running her stylist business during the day.

She's also a delicious little plus-sized blonde with a taste for pain, bondage, and group play. Add in snark and total disrespect for most authority, and she's my kind of girl.

It takes a moment for her words to penetrate. Even then, I don't comprehend them. "What did you say?"

"Hades has a new guy starting tonight. From the gossip Tis had, hot from the source, he doesn't even *know* he's a sub and I'm expected to give him a crash course in BDSM before the club opens." She crosses her arms under her breasts. "I don't get paid enough for this shit, Meg. I really don't."

"Why does he have you training instead of one of the Dominants?" Instead of *me*. I don't handle every new sub we hire, but if they're important enough to be brought in because of a deal, then I should be.

"She said Hades is handling that part of his training personally."

What? "We can negotiate hazard pay once he's up to par and working," I say absently. A new hire from Hades means one of his deals. Normally every employee who the Underworld hires goes through me, whether they're dominant, submissive, or just looking to bartend. It's one of my most important functions as the person who manages this place.

BDSM in all its flavors requires an incredible level of trust from all participating parties. If the wrong person were to become involved... Well, it hasn't happened since I've been here. We get assholes sometimes, but no one who actively ignores the rules, both explicitly stated and generally understood. Anyone who plays here is guaranteed a consensual good time, no matter what they're looking for.

Which means I need to check this guy out before tonight. Hades wouldn't actively undermine our operation, but he often plays deeper games that make my life difficult. Sending a submissive who doesn't realize they're a submissive even out into the lounge without the proper preparation is a recipe for disaster.

Training them himself...

He hasn't been that hands on in training since *I* was new here.

What the hell is going on? I blink to find Tink still watching me with her pretty green eyes. "Was there something else?"

"I'm coming up on the end of my contract." She props her hands on her hips, drawing my attention to her floral romper and black strappy heels. A black cropped jacket pulls the outfit together just like Tink always seems to. She makes my suits and slinky dresses feel mundane sometimes, but no one can pull off fashion the way she does.

I lean back. "Two months. You're not quite there yet."

"Compared to the last four years and change, two months is almost the end." She considers me. "Is staying on an option?"

I blink. Tink hates Hades. Actively loathes him. I can't imagine she would be content to work for him unless under duress. "Do you *want* to stay on?"

"I don't know yet." She shrugs. "I'm exploring my options."

If I were a better person, I'd guide her out the doors and tell her never to look back. Tink was meant for greater things than working as a combination assistant manager, costumer designer, submissive, and general fire-put-outer.

I'm not a better person. She's worth her weight in gold, and I'd be a fool to let her go. "Of course. You'll always have a place here."

"Oh. Okay, then." She nods a little too fast. "My shift starts at eight, but I'm going to give this dude a run-down at seven."

"Does he know that?"

"He's staying in the building."

I'm not expecting *that*, though I should. Tink also lives

45

here, courtesy of the terms of her deal. Of course this new toy for Hades will be under our roof. "I'll talk to him now."

"Thanks." She turns and disappears through the door.

I stare blindly at my office. I've put this room together over the years. It's the one place in the Underworld that's mine. That I *earned* through actions and time and trust from my employees. I indulged myself with the pretty teal color on the walls, the one that makes me think of the trip Hades and I took to the Maldives on our first anniversary. I don't like clutter overmuch, so all the important information is filed away in the classy cabinets that have locks on each door. I keep my desk clear, which isn't a positive right now, because my hands itch to fiddle with something and there's nothing but my computer marring the smooth mahogany surface.

There's no help for it. I'm not going to be able to focus until I've gotten to the bottom of this particular mystery. I could ask Hades directly, but I can't guarantee he'll tell me the truth. Beyond that, I'm curious.

Sure. That's it. It's simple curiosity.

As I push to my feet, I take a moment to be honest with myself. I'm a little jealous, too. It doesn't make sense, and it's not something I'll ever admit, but I like there only being Tink and me in here as permanent deal-related employees. As Tink said, she's up in two months. I can't imagine what that would be like. Mine is a lifetime contract. There's no end in sight, and I made my peace with that a long time ago.

No use thinking about it now.

I make sure to lock my office door before I head down the back stairs to the employee floor. It houses a dozen apartments, though only five were in use until today. I step through the door to find Allecto leaning against the wall.

She raises a dark brow and pushes her long black braids over her shoulder. "That didn't take you long." She's a beauty like all

Hades's Furies are—me, Allecto, and Tisiphone. Her dark brown skin is flawless, and she wears a sports bra and high-waisted workout pants. Obviously she's on her way to the gym.

I could play it cool, but she and Tis are as close to sisters as I've ever had. I lean around her to look down the empty hallway. "Don't act like you're not curious too."

Allecto gives me a sly smile. "You should go introduce yourself. He's in number six."

Near-sister or not, I don't trust that look on her face. "What do you know?"

"Nothing much." She bypasses me and heads down the stairs to where the gym is located. "More than you."

I wait a full three seconds and then stalk down the hallway to the door with the stylized six on it. I raise my hand and then reconsider. Something about this whole situation sends warning bells tolling through my mind. It doesn't make any sense.

Surely I have nothing to be afraid of?

I knock briskly before I can stall longer. I listen to the heavy footsteps approach from the other side and find myself holding my breath. And then the door opens and the very last person I expect to see stands there, his blond hair a little messy like he's been running his fingers through it, his blue eyes going wide at the sight of me, his mouth curving into a smile. "Meg."

"I… *Hercules?*"

He barely seems to register my shock, grabbing my hands and towing me into the apartment. It's decorated like all the unoccupied ones are—tasteful neutrals and welcoming furniture that's just as comfortable as it looks. Hercules releases me almost instantly, but I can still feel the imprint of his hands on mine. More than that. I can still feel his tongue rolling over my clit. His cock filling me. His strong hold keeping me in place as he fucks me just like I commanded him to.

He looks at me like I'm the greatest gift he's ever been given. "He followed through on his promise. I honestly wasn't sure he would."

Surely I'm misunderstanding this. Surely Hades didn't do what I'm beginning to suspect he did. "His promise?"

"Your freedom."

I stare. He looks so incredibly proud of himself, a golden retriever expecting to be praised for his good behavior. Did I really think this guy might be a good one? I really should know better by now. I take a careful step back and cross my arms over my chest. "Let me see if I have this straight. You decided to bargain yourself away for a woman you just met—"

"Yes—"

"—*without* talking to her first and figuring out what *she* wanted."

He's starting to realize he might have misjudged things. Hercules flushes. "I saw the way you were with him. You both admitted what he made you do with me. I had to do the right thing."

The right thing.

The right thing.

I shake my head slowly. "You are an idiot."

Hercules's blue eyes go stormy. "Don't talk to me like I'm a stupid teenager."

"Then stop acting like one!" I have to turn away to regain control of my tone. Screaming at him might feel good for a few moments, but he truly doesn't understand. In the end, it's like kicking a puppy, and I'll feel worse for doing it. I press the heels of my hands to my eyes. "How long?"

"What?"

"How long did you give him? A year? Three? Five? Seven?"

His silence gains weight. I turn back to find him staring at me as if he's never seen me before. "I gave him forever, Meg. A full trade. Me for you."

My breath leaves me in a whoosh. *A lifetime*. Who is this guy that Hades was willing to lay out those terms? I don't know. There was a time when he would have told me his plans, would have sketched them out in all their intricacy and filled me with wonder at how devious his mind was. No longer. The distance between us is too great these days, both of us moving about our lives separately with deliciously painful clashes that hurt more than they help. Even with that, I thought we were still partners. Dysfunctional ones, yes, but equals in our own way. Silly me. I should know better than to trust anyone at this point. Even him. *Especially* him. "You should have talked to me first," I say weakly. "You don't understand."

"Help me understand." He cautiously takes my hand and tugs me toward the couch. As if *he* is going to comfort *me*. This man makes absolutely no sense. He's the one in more trouble than he obviously understands. He's the one Hades has just conned. *I'm* the one who should be comforting *him*.

But I didn't beg for him to save me. He didn't ask. He just took one look at us and assumed he knew a single damn thing about how our lives work. He's a fool, and I don't suffer fools, even when they're pretty enough to make me temporarily lose myself.

"Oh, *now* you're willing to slow down long enough to actually consider my opinion?" I jerk my hand out of his. "Does my damsel in distress roll allow for a speaking part?"

"I don't get why you're pissed. Shouldn't you be happy? You wanted out from under Hades, and now you can be."

I laugh. A broken, sad sound. "You have no idea what you're talking about."

His confusion shifts to anger and his mouth goes tight. "How the hell would I know what I'm talking about when you didn't *talk* to me? You say I didn't consider what you wanted, but you did the exact same thing to me. If you're telling the truth about not wanting to be saved, then stop for a second and think about how that night looked from my perspective. He said he *made* you fuck me, Meg. As in forced."

I understand what he's saying, but I'm reeling too hard to sympathize fully. "So you *talk* to me! We have a conversation. You don't jump headfirst into a deal with Hades because you made assumptions and didn't bother to fact-check them before acting." I hold up my hand when he starts to speak. "I… I can't do this right now. I have to go." I turn and walk away. I have to. Hercules might have fucked me, but he doesn't know me. He obviously doesn't want to know me either. Not the real me. He's looking for someone to save, and he assumed I fit the bill. It never occurred to him that he should ask first.

I close the door behind me and take a slow breath. Anger is so much easier than guilt. I *knew* Hades had something else going on when he sent me after Hercules, and I did it anyways. I hadn't realized the misleading conclusions Hercules would draw from the whole situation, but I should have. I knew he wasn't part of our world, and I was too lost in my own experience to make sure he understood. Part of this is on me.

But not all of it.

It takes fewer than five minutes to climb the stairs to the level above the club to Hades's office. He keeps a room that's vaguely office-like on the club floor itself, but it's all for show —and play. As secure as the Underground is in general, it's not secure enough to leave vital business information where someone could just walk in, locked doors or no. Our clientele specialize in being where they shouldn't.

So Hades gives them a decoy office. No one has thought to question it yet. They see what they want to see, and they leave it at that. Hades is too powerful to fuck with.

For them.

I'm too angry to heed the warning. He and I are going to have words, and we're going to have them right fucking now.

CHAPTER 7

She comes through my office door like a gale-force wind. Even after all these years, my Meg steals my breath when she gets riled like this. She's out for blood, and mine will do just as well as anyone's. We both know it won't happen, that I will never yield, but Meg never hesitates to charge onto the battleground when she's decided it's worth her while.

She's decided it now.

For *him*.

I study her as I sip my scotch. She looks as divine as always in her carefully tailored suit and sky-high heels. Her hair is mussed, and I know she's been to see Hercules. A tiny flame of jealousy flares, but I'm not interested in feeding it. Meg may be mine in every way that matters, but she's not built for monogamy. Begrudging her that is like begrudging a falcon its need for the sky. After all, I brought Hercules here for her, at least in part.

Meg narrows her eyes. "You played him." She breaks the silence first. Point to me.

"I played him." Fuck if it doesn't feel good to *finally* be putting this plan in motion. Decades' worth of anger with no outlet, no recourse, and the method of my revenge walks right into my web like a lamb to the slaughter. Whether or not Hercules is guilty makes no difference to me. Neither does his knowledge—or lack thereof—when it comes to his father's sins.

Thinking of Zeus has me tightening my grip on my glass. Some things don't go away with time, and my rage at the man is a live thing in my chest, snapping and snarling and demanding payment in blood.

Meg clenches her fists. "What happens when he realizes I'm not leaving?" She froze, her blue eyes going wide. "Wait a damn minute. Are you kicking me out? Is *that* what this is about? You needed an upgrade?"

I straighten, and she instantly takes a wary step back. My Meg knows me well, but apparently not well enough. She's the most priceless thing in my life, the one person I could never replace, not even if I searched the world over. I knew she was unhappy, but for her trust to have broken down this far stalls my breath in my chest. I will reclaim our relationship. Hercules will help me, whether he realizes it or not. He's helping even now, lancing a wound that we've both spent years pretending didn't exist.

I set my glass on the table and meet her gaze. "Strip."

"Damn it, Hades."

I love the way her mouth forms my name, even in anger. I raise a single brow. "Was my order unclear?"

She considers arguing. I can see the battle in her expression. It doesn't matter. We will have this conversation one way or another. If I have to pin her down and rip each piece of clothing from her body first, then I will. Finally Meg reaches for the button of her jacket. "No, Sir. Your order wasn't unclear."

I can actually see her coming back to herself as she loses

each piece of clothing. Meg may enjoy dominating, but with me, she's the perfect submissive. Not in a well-behaved sort of way—the term doesn't apply to her—but in the way she inspires me to step to the line every single time. I don't have to hold back with this woman, because she can take everything I give her. More, she loves it.

Once she's undressed, I snap my fingers, and she drops to her knees. An instinctive response, and one she no doubt resents. I allow myself a moment to appreciate the picture she creates on her knees, all sharp angles and bottled-up fury. Some days I think she hates me more than she loves me, but she is one of the few constants in my life. We were made for each other, two twisted trees that grew to lean on each other to the point where they won't survive alone.

Meg has no plans to leave me. I would know it if she did. That doesn't change the fact that she's unhappy. She's withering with every day that passes, and I want to see her bloom once more.

"That's better. Shall we try this again?" I push slowly to my feet and move to her. I don't touch, not yet, but I circle her, letting the anticipation build in both of us. Finally, when she's practically quivering, I reach down and draw my fingers through her hair.

Meg leans into it, though her mouth tightens as if she didn't mean to. "You used me as bait. You tricked him into coming here. You *trapped* him with a lie."

"Yes." No need to deny it. Not here. Not with her. "Though one could argue that there's a very fine line between a lie and the truth. The man is a white knight in search of a damsel. It's not my fault that he saw what he wanted and ignored the reality. You are no damsel, love. You never were." I wind her hair slowly around my fist, increasing the tension as I force her head back.

So beautiful, my Meg. So sharp and brittle and broken. I

cup her jaw and drag my thumb over her bottom lip. "He doesn't see you, love. Not like I do." A slip, that. I have no reason to be jealous. Meg is mine. Hercules is as well, though he isn't aware enough to realize it. Not yet.

She blinks up at me, vulnerability crawling through her eyes for one breathless moment before she shuts it down and her walls go back up. "Hades... Sir." She swallows, and I can feel the movement against my palm where it rests on her throat. A reminder of who truly owns her. She presses her lips together and then seems to decide to continue questioning me. "*Why?*"

I allow my lips to curve a little. It's not beyond me to yell and rage, but I learned a long time ago that soft words and gentle sentences inspire fear and obedience just as easily. More so in some cases. Meg sees and shivers in my grasp. I could tell her my plans, could lay all the details out in a neat little row. But, knowing her, she'll balk at the idea of using Hercules; both to heal our relationship, and to construct my revenge. No, there's plenty of time for pure honesty later, once we've come out the other side.

I speak softly. "I don't want you to fuck him again. Anything else is up to your discretion, but not that. Not yet." Not until it serves my purpose.

She frowns as if I can't see the conflict written all over her body. "I don't want to fuck him."

"Yes, love, you do. And you can... but not yet." I give her bottom lip another slow stroke. "Do you think I'd deny you anything, Meg? You want him. I'll give him to you."

The line between her brows deepens. "You didn't do this for me."

It stings a little, her lack of faith in me. It's nothing more than I deserve, but after ten years together... No use in following that thought any deeper.

"Why?" she finally asks.

"Because, love, we're going to seduce him. Together." And, in doing so, we're going to bring all of Olympus to its knees.

CHAPTER 8

HERCULES

*T*his isn't going at all how I expected.

I spend the rest of the day looking at this mess from a thousand different angles, and there's no getting around the truth: I fucked up. I'm just as much a fucking idiot as Meg accused me of being. I let my desire to protect her get the best of me. After what happened in Olympus, I should know better. Protecting other people only leads to trouble, and in the end I don't make a single goddamn difference. I can't seem to help myself, though.

Not before, with Leda.

Not now, with Meg.

The path seemed so clear before, but by the time someone knocks at my door, I'm a bundle of nerves. I have no idea what I really signed on for. Fucking Hades, sure. Something that I shouldn't want, but there's no denying the anticipation that zings through my veins. He's nothing like the guys I messed around with in high school and college. He's got an edge about him that says he wants to hurt me. I'm afraid I'm going to like it.

I open the door to find a cute, curvy blonde standing

there. She's wearing a short skirt and a cropped lace top thing, and I blush at the sight of her pale pink nipples showing through. In the second it takes to pull my gaze to her face, she's started laughing at me. She props a hand on her generous hip and smirks. "God, you're precious. They're going to eat you up with a spoon." She turns and starts away, which leaves me scrambling to shut my door behind me and keep up.

I finally catch her right before she hits the elevator. She's fast for such a little thing. "I'm Hercules."

"I'm aware." She punches the button and gives me another look, finally settling on my jeans. "First up is wardrobe. *That* will not do."

I follow her into the elevator, feeling like a kid tagging behind an adult. "What's your name?"

She sighs like it's an intrusive question. "Tink. I'm handling your training, because obviously I've pissed off the big guy in recent weeks."

"You mean Hades."

"I mean Hades." The elevator slides to a stop, and she leads the way down the hall and through a door into another, smaller hall. Tink doesn't wait for me to gawk. She just opens yet another door and strides through. Inside is the largest closet I've ever seen. Or maybe it's a store? I honestly can't tell as she moves to the right side and starts sifting through the racks. She shoots me another look and frowns. "Take off your clothes."

"I'm sorry?"

"I can usually eyeball measurements, but the baggy T-shirt is throwing me off." She made a vague motion. "Strip. We don't have a ton of time, so save the bashful virgin act for the customers."

Customers?

Somehow, in all this, it never occurred to me that I'd be

dealing with *customers*. I'd braced for Hades. Had prepared myself as much as was reasonably possible. Nothing could prepare me for *this*. "I'm not sleeping with people."

Tink pauses and gives me a long look. Whatever she must see on my face makes her sigh. "Wow, you really are a baby. Look, Hades isn't a pimp. I mean, I guess technically he could qualify since some of us like to fuck the customers. But it's not part of the contract. Submission or domination, depending on our terms, but not fucking."

It's like she's speaking a different language. "I don't understand."

She mutters something about hazard pay and comes to stand before me. She's so short, she barely hits my chest, but that doesn't make her presence any less intense. Tink taps my chest. "Strip."

There's enough snap in her voice that I obey without thinking, pulling my shirt over my head with one hand. She snatches the fabric from my hands and tosses it to the side. "That thing you just did, how you felt so right in obeying me? That's submission."

"I know what submission is." I'm not an idiot, no matter what she obviously thinks. "I know what Hades is, too." King of the Underworld. Someone with his hands in all the right pockets, because from what I could glean in my rudimentary research of this place, the clientele is the elite of Carver City. They're what the Thirteen are back in Olympus. Powerful and rich beyond measure, with a total lack of morality.

"Then why are we having this conversation?"

I try to articulate the strange feeling inside me. "When I made the deal, he acted like he now owns me."

"If you made a deal with him, then he *does* own you."

That's what I thought. "Then why…" I motion at the room.

Understanding flares and she rolls her eyes. "Hades

doesn't fuck anyone but Meg. I mean, he does scenes with others sometimes and he enjoys watching, but just because you sold yourself to him doesn't mean he's going to like make you his sex slave or something."

Except that's exactly what Hades implied when we sealed our deal with a kiss. I barely manage to keep myself from asking how Tink sealed *her* deal. It's none of my business, and she obviously doesn't like me that much already. "So we all just work in the club?"

"Pretty much." She moves back to the racks and pulls out a pair of shorts. "These should work. Put them on."

This time, I don't bother to argue. I'm obviously not going to get much in the way of explanation, and I gave my word to Hades. I won't let something as mundane as modesty get in the way of keeping it. I strip out of my jeans and pull on the shorts. They're smaller than I expected, barely covering my ass in the back and hugging my cock and balls so snugly that they create an obscene bulge in the front.

And, except for the front panel, they're made of see-through mesh.

"Hades can be something of a traditionalist, so he likes us barefoot." She considers me a full second longer and shakes her head. "I can't really blame him for taking the deal now that I see what I'm working with. You're pretty."

The way she says it makes it sound like it's a bad thing. "Thanks?"

"This way." Tink leads me deeper into the room and through another door that takes us into what I recognize as an employee dressing room. She stops in front of an empty locker. "This will be yours. We don't use locks because nobody is dumb enough to steal from one of Hades's people." She opens the locker and pulls out a thick black leather collar. "We wear these while on shift." She dips back into the locker and pulls out a thick green circular ring and I have a horrified moment of wondering if she's going to demand I wedge it onto my cock, but she just snaps it into the hook at the front of the collar.

The one that looks like it attaches itself to a leash.

Just like that, I can picture it. Kneeling at his feet in this ridiculous fucking outfit with a chain attached to the collar, its leather handle dangling from his graceful fingers. My gut goes tight and I have to fight not to physically respond. It doesn't seem to matter. Tink sees it. She gives me a sad little smile. "Welcome to the Underworld."

Then she drags me along to training. In the next few hours, I get a crash course in BDSM, submissives, safe words, and what exactly is expected of me working here. The first couple of weeks will be observing and basically acting in a role similar to what I did back at my old job—serving drinks, working the front lounge. I'll also be doing more hands-on training… with Hades.

I don't know if I look forward to it or dread it, but I'm too nervous right now to know the difference.

Tink glances at her watch. "It's time." She surveys me. "No one will touch you without permission, but that won't stop some of those assholes from messing with you verbally. Don't play into it, because if you snap, Hades will punish you and he'll do it publicly. Just keep your eyes down and mouth shut. And *listen*. We do a recap at the end of each night with the information gathered, so pay attention, even if you don't recognize the players."

It's too much and too little all at the same time. I don't know what I expected when I said yes to him, but this isn't it. He's throwing me in the deep end, and there isn't a single person who will help me if I drown. Tink might feel a little bad, but honestly, I can't get a good enough read on her to know for sure. She might just as easily shrug and move on to the next new recruit with the same amount of crankiness.

But as I fall into the familiar rhythms of taking drinks orders and moving through the tables and bar, things start to unwind for me. This is familiar. I know how to do *this*, even if it's a relatively new skill. The rest of it will figure itself out, but I can get through tonight.

Or so I think, right up until I catch a familiar profile out of the corner of my eye.

I turn to find Meg standing near the bar. She's wearing a pair of tailored slacks and a deep purple bra-like top that I can *almost* see through. Why is she here? She should be well on her way to freedom. Not haunting this place where I'm currently trapped.

Unless...

Unless she came for me?

My chest feels tight as she strides toward me on wickedly high heels. There's no familiarity on her face, nothing to indicate her thoughts. The warmth she showed me in that apartment above the restaurant remains nowhere in evidence. This woman could be a stranger for the cold way she studies my body, lingering on my chest and cock before trailing down my legs.

"What are you doing here?" I don't mean to speak. I really don't. My intentions don't seem to make a difference. "If he broke his word..."

"Hades never breaks his word," she says absently. "I'm here because I want to be." Meg tilts her head to the side, causing her hair to cascade over her shoulder. I want to run my fingers through it, to tug her face up to meet mine, but I know better. I still have to clench my fists at my side to keep myself from doing it.

"He wants to see you." She turns and walks away, leaving me to follow in her footsteps.

As I do, my confusion hardens to something significantly uglier. *I'm here because I want to be.* She does whatever she wants to do. No one is forcing her into anything. That's what her words translate to, before in my new suite and here on the floor. Several truths settle over me, each a jagged shard in my throat.

Hades isn't forcing Meg to do anything. He didn't force her to fuck me. He didn't force her to her knees. He isn't keeping her like some princess trapped in a tower. She consented to the entire thing. If she didn't, then my deal would have set her free and she wouldn't be walking through the lounge like a queen moving through her subjects.

He played me.

Meg played me.

By the time she leads me through a tall set of doors into a monochromatic gray office, I'm furious. I stop just inside the door. "You screwed me over."

"I didn't even know you were here until you'd already made the deal." She keeps walking, moving to stand at the shoulder of the man sitting at the desk.

Hades steeples his fingers and watches me with deep, dark eyes behind the black frames of his glasses. He's wearing his customary black-on-black suit, and I hate that I respond to him. To them. He leans forward as if only casually interested in this conversation. "Are you going back on your word?"

"Why shouldn't I? You went back on yours."

"Did I?" He still sounds so fucking distant, I can't stand it. He glances at Meg. "I gave my word that you wouldn't do anything you didn't want to, love."

Her mouth twists, but she smooths out her expression almost immediately. "I have my safe word for a reason."

"I don't respect many rules, but that one is sacred." Now Hades focuses all his indomitable will on me. "Time for you to pick a safe word, little Hercules."

Little Hercules. As if I'm not several inches taller and

significantly heavier than his slim frame. Somehow, it doesn't matter. Even across the room, even so furious and betrayed that I can barely draw a breath, I have to fight not to hit my knees for him.

I want to tell him to fuck off. That I didn't sign up for this. That I never would have given him this power over me if I wasn't stupidly playing the hero for a woman who wasn't interested in being saved. In the end, all my assumptions don't matter.

I gave my word.

I'll keep it.

My honor is the only thing I have left, and I can't let something as stupid as my own mistake get in the way of it. If that were an option, I'd still be enjoying my pampered life back in Olympus. I've already turned my back on so much. Why not turn my back on my fucking freedom too?

"Olympus," I grind out. It's as good a safe word as anything.

"Good boy." He pushes slowly to his feet. "Then we can begin."

"What?" That shakes me out of my anger. "But I'm in the middle of my shift and—"

"Tink can manage without you." He moves around the desk and toward the couch situated on the left side of the room. "Meg."

She follows him, and with each step, she loses some of the dominance that drew me to her in the first place, shedding it like a second skin until she's a single step behind him with her eyes downcast. It's the exact same transformation I witnessed in that apartment after Hades showed up, but I have a term for it now.

Switch.

Both Dominant and submissive, all wrapped up in a package I still desire even though I know better by now.

"You're overdressed, love."

That's all it takes, and she kicks off her heels and slips out of her pants, leaving her in only the cropped bustier and a lace thong. Hades merely raises his brows, and Meg rolls her eyes and strips the rest of the way down. Not a hint of shyness in the fact that she's standing naked before us, but did I really expect there to be?

"Show him how it's done."

She sinks gracefully to her knees, her back perfectly straight, and lowers her eyes. She's so beautiful, it takes my breath away. I don't get much time to enjoy the view, because Hades steps in front of her and gives me a look like he can divine my thoughts right out of my head. "Your turn."

I hesitantly reach for my shorts, but he shakes his head. "Keep them on for now. Consider this your first lesson."

I'm nowhere near as graceful as Meg. My body feels strange inside my skin as I lower myself to my knees and reluctantly bow my head.

I don't expect his gentle touch at the back of my neck, and I can't stop my flinch. Hades chuckles as if he enjoys my response. "This won't work if you don't watch, little Hercules. The show is just for you."

I know it's a trap. I'm not a fucking idiot, though at this point all evidence of my actions say otherwise. I still lift my head and watch him circle Meg.

She doesn't look up, doesn't flinch when he bestows the same touch along the back of her neck that he did to me. She simply sits there, the very picture of a perfect submissive. I have the strangest desire to see her with a whip in her hand and cruelty in those blue eyes.

Hades pulls a necklace from his pocket. No, not a necklace, a collar. It's a gorgeous piece of work, weathered black leather with diamonds sewn into it to look like the night sky. An oversized buckle rests at the back of her neck to keep it in place. "Do you know how to keep a woman like Meg happy, little Hercules?"

Yes, this is definitely a trap.

I swallow past my suddenly dry throat. "I'm sure you're going to tell me."

"Smart boy." The words don't sound like praise coming out of his mouth, and heat rises to my cheeks in response. Hades reaches down to run a finger along her collar. "You give her everything she could possibly need."

There it is again. That flash in Meg's eyes that betrays her. She might be here of her own volition, but there's something else going on. Something deeper. It might be as mundane as dissatisfaction, but I honestly can't be sure.

"Submission," he continues, moving his touch to her jaw. His touch still seems light, but he guides her head back, arching her spine. "Spread, love."

She does as he commands, spreading her thighs wide. I can see...all of her. Her breasts that I palmed less than a week ago. Her stomach that I bracketed with my hands as I fucked her exactly like she commanded. Her pussy where I buried my face and licked her until she came. She's pink and wet, and somehow I didn't expect that. No matter what lurks in her eyes, she likes what Hades is doing to her, though it seems precious little at the moment. He's putting her on display, all but tattooing his name on her ass.

Claiming her.

He releases her and walks to the couch to resume his position. "Come here, little Hercules." When I start to rise, he shakes his head slowly, his lips quirking into a small smile. "Crawl." The instruction is gentle and no less cruel for it.

My whole body goes hot and tight as I move onto my hands and knees and crawl across the distance between me and the couch. There, I hesitate. Am I supposed to join him there? Kneel here? Something akin to panic wells inside me, but it doesn't get a chance to gain momentum because Hades catches the back of my neck in the unbreakable grip and guides me to kneel at his feet facing away from him.

"Don't move. That is a command, by the way." He sifts his fingers through my hair and it feels like he's touching me in a thousand different places. "What happens if you break my command?"

I lick my lips. "You punish me." My cock is so hard, it's creating a gap in the top of my shorts, like it can punch its way to freedom.

"That's right." He moves behind me, and my breath catches in my throat as his legs come down on either side of my body. His thighs brush my arms, and even though he hasn't bound me, I feel like I'm locked in place. He squeezes my shoulders, and I jump as he whispers in my ear. "Tell me your safe word."

"Olympus," I breathe.

"Good boy." He lifts his voice. "Meg, you may begin."

here's nothing quite as satisfying as watching the son of my enemy submit. He's beautiful at it, even when he's fighting his basest impulse. Hercules wants to kneel at my feet, to obey my commands, but he thinks he shouldn't so he fights me. He won't win. I could tell him that now, but spoiling the ending takes the fun out of the game.

Seeing Meg's reaction to him is almost as satisfying. She's so angry with me, my Meg. It doesn't seem to register that her anger is a pure thing, untainted by so much baggage we carry around. An anger that only drives her desire higher.

I continue kneading the tight muscles in Hercules's shoulders as Meg stalks naked to the door and opens it. The woman who walks through is one of my personal favorites of the submissives on staff. Aurora. She's sweet and gentle and cries so prettily. She's beautiful in the way priceless art is beautiful. Her light brown skin all but shines in the low light and her hair—pink this month—falls in waves that are almost curls around her narrow shoulders.

She smiles at Meg, and I give a smile of my own as

Hercules's breath catches. "She's very beautiful, don't you think?"

"They both are."

It amuses me how loyal he is to my Meg, little though she deserves it. He wants to play knight in shining armor to her princess in distress, and he still hasn't quite realized that she's as much dragon as I am. More so in certain situations.

Meg takes Aurora's hand and pulls her farther into the room until they stop in front of the chair directly across from us. It's just high enough to bend someone over if you want to fuck them, and Hercules and I are low enough that we won't miss any details.

He won't miss any details.

Meg looks at me askance. "May I, Sir?"

Anyone else might miss the hint of disrespect that flavors those three little words. I raise my brows, and she has the grace to flush. On another night, I'd make her eat those words while she eats Aurora's pussy as I flog her until she sobs. That's not on the agenda right now and she knows it, the little brat. "Yes." I wait for her to start to turn before I put a little snap in my voice. "But first come give our little Hercules a kiss."

Her brows slam down, and it takes her visible effort to recover. I'm not playing fair, but then she should expect it from me at this point. A punishment is still a punishment, even if it doesn't appear to be one on the outside.

This boy got under my Meg's skin. A mutual feeling if the way he tenses beneath my hands is any indication, but I knew that already. He wouldn't have effectively sold his soul to me for anything less than blinding lust. Meg kneels gracefully in front of Hercules and, after another arch look in my direction, leans forward and presses a kiss to his lips. Because I'm still touching him, I feel him gravitate toward her to deepen the kiss.

69

I'm not surprised when she lets him. Meg is drawn to this man in an entirely different way than she's drawn to me. It's part of the reason he's here.

I count slowly to fifteen, allowing them this, if only so I can be the one to take it away. "That's enough, you two," I say mildly. "You're making poor Aurora feel left out."

Aurora, at least, isn't disobedient enough to contradict me. She stands exactly where Meg left her, gaze downturned and her hands clasped before her. All of my submissives have a style, and I allow them that freedom within certain boundaries. Aurora wears a short silk slip that might appear virginal if it weren't short enough to barely brush her thighs and didn't have thin straps that appeared as if they'd break under a harsh exhale. The Dominants who contract with her eat that sort of thing up, and she's become one of my biggest moneymakers as a result. She also has a schoolgirl crush on Meg, so this scene serves to reward them both.

Meg rises gracefully to her feet and pads to Aurora. She uses a single finger to lift her chin, and I don't have to see Meg's face to know she's smiling warmly down at the woman. "We'll keep it simple today, okay?"

"Okay," Aurora whispers.

"Safe word?"

"Thorn."

"Good girl."

As Meg begins, I turn my attention back to Hercules. He's so tense, he might as well be marble carved on the floor between my legs. That won't do. That won't do at all. I knead the tight muscles in his shoulders. The man may be nothing more than a pawn, but he's no less beautiful than my Meg, albeit in a different way. Hercules has the coloring and bearing of someone used to walking in the sun. Whether he'll wither living here in the dark remains to be seen.

I lean down until my lips nearly brush his ear. "First, you

learn by watching. Then you learn by participating. You belong to me, and I won't allow anyone else to hurt you."

"Anyone else?" His voice had an edge of growl.

"I'm going to hurt you, little Hercules. And you're going to enjoy every moment of it." I dig my thumb into the trigger point at the top of his spine. Unsurprisingly, there's a knot there, and I work it ruthlessly until he lets out a little pained sound. I exhale carefully against his ear, enjoying the way it makes him shiver. Does he realize he's leaning back into my touch, ever so slightly? I doubt it. "Meg is a woman of varied tastes. She's also one of the best Dominants working in the Underworld. Aurora is one of the best submissives."

While I spoke to Hercules, Meg guided Aurora to bend over the arm of the couch and brace her forearms on the cushion. She's a little shorter than Meg, so her toes barely touch the ground. Meg runs her hands up the other woman's legs, starting at her ankles and working her way up to her thighs. She slides Aurora's slip up over her hips, baring her ass. "Paddle or the flogger?"

"Paddle, please."

"Good girl." Meg smiles, and it's as if we're not in the room. I've always loved watching her work like this. There's a reason why every single submissive in Carver City will crawl over broken glass to her the second she crooks her finger. Hercules will be one of them. He already is if the avid way he watches the scene unfold is any indication.

Meg walks to the chest behind my desk and comes back with a wide wooden paddle. It could possibly break bones in the wrong hands, but she's a master of our craft. She gives it a few experimental swings, building the anticipation.

I murmur in Hercules's ear, "Do you see the way Aurora's toes curl? She wants that first strike." I glance down Hercules's chest and allow myself a smile to find his cock standing at attention. "Meg will warm her up with pain, and then if she's a good little submissive, she'll allow her to come."

"How?"

I doubt Hercules realizes that he's voiced the question, but I answer anyway. "Knowing my Meg, she'll eat her pussy. She's got a taste for it, and Aurora is so pretty when she comes through her tears."

Meg delivers the first strike across the lower curve of Aurora's ass, right where it meets her thighs. The other woman jumps, but then obviously fights to hold still, to obey. Meg smacks her again, falling into a rhythm I recognize intimately. I force my attention back to Hercules, who's breathing hard as if *he* is the one being beaten. "I'm going to touch you now."

He gives a shaky nod, his gaze glued to the swing of the paddle. It won't take much to send him into subspace when we begin to play, not if he's dancing on the edge of it simply from watching. He's like a child who's never seen Christmas, and the sheer splendor of it overwhelms him. At least at first.

I slide my hand down his chest and delve into his shorts. I've seen his cock, of course, hard and wet with Meg's desire. I still take a moment to enjoy the way he fills my fist. I give him a hard stroke and then lift my hand. "Spit."

"What?" He's hoarse as if he's been screaming for hours.

"I won't repeat myself."

It takes him a moment to respond, to obey, to coat my palm with his saliva. Against my better judgment, I'm moved by the purity of him. I want to break him into a thousand sharp pieces, to drag him down into the dark with the rest of us, but I can't help appreciating the very thing I want to ruin. I take his cock again. There will be a time to tease, a time to torment. Tonight's not it. He needs to know exactly who he belongs to.

I jerk him roughly, relentlessly, until he's lifting his hips as best he can and fucking my hand. His gaze is pinned to where Meg beats Aurora, and while I appreciate the sentiment, that won't do. I dig the fingers of my free hand into his hair and turn his face to mine. "I own you, little Hercules. Say it."

His blue eyes are glazed as he licks his lips. "You... You own me."

"Now be a good boy and come for your master."

One stroke. Two. And then he gives a guttural curse and does exactly as commanded, coming in great spurts across his own chest. I give him a few more pumps before I release his cock. I don't move back. Not yet. I simply maintain my position, bracketing him in as he shakes, allowing him to lean on me while he finds his balance again.

It won't last.

I won't allow it to last.

But I can't quite help running my fingers through his hair and guiding his face to lean against my thigh as I settle back to watch Meg work.

CHAPTER 10

MEG

I'm so furious, I can barely think straight. All my attention should be on Aurora, and Hades is sitting there, fucking around with Hercules within my line of sight. It feels like a punishment, because that's exactly what it is. He never comes at something from the front when he can flank the problem instead. I don't know why *I'm* being punished for Hades's machinations. I obeyed his commands, every single one of them, even when I knew it would hurt Hercules to leave him and kneel at Hades's side.

I did it all, and yet I'm the one on the outside of their little scene with my face pressed against the window.

I toss the paddle to the ground. My headspace isn't right to keep up the pain play. I won't lose control. I won't *allow* myself to misstep like that, but it's not fair to Aurora to do this when my darker emotions are riding me so hard.

I step to her and run my hands up the backs of her thighs and squeeze her ass. Even with the shortened beating, she'll be a little bruised tomorrow, just like she adores. "Spread."

She eagerly spreads her legs, balancing on her toes. I press one hand against the small of her back and slip the other between her thighs. She's so wet, she soaks my fingers as I explore her. "You've pleased me, Aurora, and I'm in a giving kind of mood tonight." A lie, but it doesn't matter. She has nothing to do with the ugliness going on in my head. "You can choose your reward."

"I want…" She twists just enough to look up at me from beneath her curtain of pink curls. "I want to make you come."

God, this girl is a gift. Whoever she lands with when she finally settles down is one lucky asshole. I keep stroking her pussy, pretending to consider it. As if I'd deny her anything. As if I'd deny *myself* this. "I'll consider it." I push two fingers into her and fuck her slowly. She whimpers and writhes, but I hold her steady as I work her toward orgasm one agonizing stroke at a time. This moment, right here, is one of my favorites when I top. I love seeing someone come undone and knowing I'm the cause behind it. Knowing that I'm giving them exactly what they need.

I sink down onto one knee and pull her hips back away from the couch arm. She spreads her legs even more, anticipating me. "Good girl," I murmur. I reward her with a long lick, but really I'm being selfish. I want to lose myself in this girl, to forget for a little while that my life is off the rails, and has been for a long time. To stop thinking about the two men watching us right now. To avoid any fear about what the future will bring. Not to worry about anything but making this beautiful girl come apart.

I take my time, enjoying this, enjoying her. But even in the midst of this, I am still all too aware of the two men on the couch watching. Or are they even watching anymore? Have they gotten distracted with each other until they've completely forgotten I'm in the room? The thought shouldn't hurt as much as it does.

Aurora's breath sobs out every time I circle her clit, and suddenly I'm done playing. I want her there, and I want her there now. I work her pussy with my tongue until she's thrashing and I have to tighten my grip to hold her down. Aurora loves that shit. She always has. She comes with a breathless cry and rolls her hips, fucking my mouth as much as I'll allow. I bring her down gently and press one last kiss to her pussy before I rise and help her off the chair.

She's all sunshine and soft smiles as I smooth her hair back from her face. I kiss her forehead. "You did well."

"May I have my reward?"

I laugh, a little of my dark mood filtering away. It's impossible to be completely morose when I'm spending time with this girl. "You know, most people just want more orgasms."

Aurora looks at me with those big brown eyes. "I like what I like."

"Don't we all?" I take a step back, make sure she's steady on her feet, and then sink into the chair. "Very well, pet. Come get your reward." I spread my legs.

She shoots a look at Hades and Hercules, and against my better judgment, I do the same. The sight of them steals my breath and muddies my thoughts. Hercules is languid in the way only a recent orgasm can bring—and the evidence of it is right there on his chest. He's slumped between Hades's legs, his head on his thigh. For his part, Hades appears completely relaxed…as long as I don't look into his dark eyes. They're all predator as he takes me in. My scene with Aurora might end once she's received her reward, but the scene going on with Hades isn't over. Not by a long shot. This was just warm up.

They haven't forgotten me, after all.

Aurora runs her hands up my thighs and smiles in a happy way that warms my heart. My life would be so much easier if I had fallen for someone like her instead of someone like Hades. She is light and springtime and sweetness. She might even make me a better person just by virtue of loving me.

Or at least that's the fairy tale.

I sink my fingers into her pink hair. "You're teasing."

"Sorry." But she doesn't look the least bit sorry. That's okay. I'm not either. Aurora presses a prim little kiss to my pussy, and then she goes after me with abandon. She gives herself completely, unabashedly.

I wish I could enjoy this for what it is. If it was just us in the room, I would. Aurora and I have played plenty of times before without Hades present, and I've never had a problem focusing everything on her. But now? I should feel powerful in this moment. I've made my submissive feel good. She's driving me closer and closer to orgasm. I should be walking on top of the world.

Instead, I look at Hades and Hercules, and I feel my reality fracturing in a way that has nothing to do with plea-sure and everything to do with unwelcome pain. Change always hurts. Always. Hades might think he has control of this situation, but I don't. *I'm* out of control and spinning out.

Hercules shifts, drawing my attention fully. He's hard again. I might laugh if there was more air in the room. His attention seems to be everywhere at once—the curve of Aurora's back, her mass of pink waves as she licks my pussy, my flushed body bared on the couch. His finally meets my gaze and sticks. Those blue eyes are wide and hot, and he looks like he's been led into hell and only now realized that there's no going back.

Welcome. Plenty of suffering to go around.

Aurora sucks my clit hard, setting her teeth against the sensitive bundle of nerves. My orgasm surges, and I don't know where to look, Hades or Hercules, Hercules or Hades. In the end, I close my eyes and shut them both out, letting Aurora tease me through the waves. My body finally gives way, and I slump down on the couch. "Well done, pet."

She makes a happy sound and climbs up to cuddle against my side. This is as important as the rest, the opportunity to bring us both down. I stroke her hair idly, letting her warmth sink into me. I don't want to open my eyes yet. I truly don't. The second I do, the next stage begins, and I don't know if I'm ready for it. I don't know if I can survive whatever Hades has planned, tonight or in the future.

There once was a time when I didn't even question it, when I knew beyond a shadow of a doubt that I was first in Hades's world. First before the Underworld, before all who patronized the place, first even before his ambition. I would walk into a room and it didn't matter what he was doing; he would level that intense focus on me and smile. We'd talk for hours, and fuck, and talk again. He built up the trust that had been fractured with Declan, the asshole who convinced me to bargain myself away.

Some people looked at us and assumed that Hades built me into the woman I am. It's not the truth. He simply gave me the platform and freedom to figure out who I was meant to be. To explore the dominant nature I dimmed for past partners, for the world itself. To lose myself in the freedom of submission.

We plotted and planned and together we boosted the Underworld into the hub of power in the center of Carver City that it is today. No one fucked with us, and that was partly because of my role, my plans, my help.

Until it all changed. Not at once. I didn't even notice at first. Our conversations shortened and eventually stopped almost completely. Hades started shutting me out, and I didn't know what to do but shut him out in return.

I know this man better than any other person in this world, but right now he feels like a stranger to me.

"Meg."

I obey the command and look at him. So cold, those dark eyes behind his black frames. As cold as they were when I first came to the Underworld, before he let me in. It takes everything I have not to tense. "Yes, Sir?"

"It's time." His expression thaws as he looks at Aurora. "You did well."

I can actually feel her blooming under his regard. I don't blame her for it. Impossible not to feel like the sun has turned in your direction when his smile is warm and genuine. She sits up a little. "Thank you, Hades."

"Would you like to watch what comes next?"

Aurora nods quickly. "Yes, please!"

"Meg." A snap of command in his voice in response to my reluctance. I bite down a sigh and slide out from my spot. I round to the cedar chest on the other side of the chair and pull out a blanket. I take my time wrapping it around Aurora, partly to spite Hades, partly because I don't want her to feel anything but warm and fuzzy about our scene.

I press a kiss to her forehead. "You good?"

She cuddles the blanket more firmly around her shoulders and beams at me. "I'm good."

I take a deep breath and turn to face Hades. I don't allow myself to look at Hercules, though I can feel his eyes on me. Hades raises an eyebrow, and I sink to my knees, my body obeying before my mind has a chance to catch up. I press my palms to my thighs and spread my legs the way he likes, keeping my gaze down.

He shifts out from behind Hercules and stands. Anyone else would struggle to their feet after sitting like that so long, but Hades is perpetually graceful. One of the many things that used to fill me with awe, but now is simply part of *Hades*. He circles me slowly, building anticipation. Building the smallest bit of fear. I know he'll never harm me, not on purpose, and I have absolutely no doubts that he'll respect my safe word. Hades might bend and manipulate and make deals with the worst people in existence, but he won't cross this line. Not with me. Not with anyone.

He finally stops in front of me. "I think the cane."

Even though I know better, shock has me raising my gaze. "What?"

"The cane, love." He takes my chin in a gentle grip, his expression contemplative. "I think we both know you've earned it."

I suck in a harsh breath. He means I've earned my punishment, though I honestly don't know if he's punishing me or Hercules. Canes are no joke. "Hades—"

He lifts a single brow, and I swallow my words back. I hate this. I hate that he's using me as a way to bring Hercules down...

But a part of me unfurls in sheer joy at what comes next. I'm not a true masochist, but pain brings something extra to fucking that's always delighted me. Canes are different, yes, but in my heart, I don't think for a second that Hades will simply beat me and leave it at that, no matter what else he has going on in that wicked brain of his. First the pain, then the pleasure. Sometimes the two intermingle, but maybe this is as much test as punishment. How far can he push me while we're both dancing on the edge of something truly devastating?

Only one way to find out.

I lick my lips. "I would love the cane, Sir."

"Good girl." His soft touch urges me to my feet. I already know our destination. There's a stylized St. Andrew's Cross tucked in the corner, the dark wood shiny and smooth. Hades waits for me to step up to it and then cuffs my wrists so my arms are extended on either side of my head. He gives my ankles the same treatment. I don't have to look over my shoulder to know that both Aurora and Hercules have an excellent view. The room was arranged this way on purpose, after all.

Hades moves away, and I have to fight the urge to try and twist to follow his movement. It won't work, and it will only drive my fear and anticipation higher. I press my lips together and focus on breathing.

Hades moves to the same chest I got the paddle from and takes his time going through the options. Drawing out the moment. "There are a thousand ways to beat a submissive, little Hercules. You saw one with Meg and our lovely Aurora. A paddle gives that nice meaty smack, that delightful shock of pain. Floggers are a personal favorite of mine as you'll find out soon." His voice drifts behind me, and I know he's pacing, probably fondling that fucking cane while he does. "Canes are something special. I'm going to stripe our Meg's ass, and you're going to sit there without moving, no matter how lovely her cries are. Do you understand?"

"But—" Hercules sounds hoarse and worried.

"Do you understand?"

Silence for a beat, two. Finally, Hercules grinds out, "I understand."

"Good."

I jump as he smooths a hand down my spine. "Your safe word, love."

"Cerberus." Always, always reminding me that this is my choice, that I have an emergency exit if I need it. Some days I relish that power, of knowing I can put a stop to our play whenever I damn well want to. Some days, *today*, I wish he wouldn't remind me that this is as much my choice as it is his. I choose this. I choose *him*. I helped damn Hercules to a lifetime deal, whether I meant to or not. It doesn't matter. I didn't ask questions. I was too intent on playing the game, of taking my pleasure out of it, to worry about consequences.

81

Maybe Hades is right. Maybe I do deserve the cane tonight.

I resent him more than a little in that moment, for knowing what I need even before I do.

The only warning I have is the whistle of the cane before he lands his first strike. The impact shocks my breath from my lungs and for one weightless moment, there's no pain at all. That's how I know it will hurt. I inhale and then the pain comes, washing my vision in red.

Hades doesn't give me a chance to recover. He lands another strike and another, and I know without a shadow of a doubt that he's striping my ass with perfect precision, marking me as his as effectively as if he's tattooing his name there. I try to be silent, try to hold out, but I've never been able to before. Tonight isn't enough to magically change that. A whimper slips past my lips as he hits the curve where my ass meets my thighs. Hades doesn't stop, doesn't relent, doesn't do anything but strike me again.

As the next strike lands, I begin to beg.

CHAPTER 11

HERCULES

I don't know what's happening to me. I watch Hades beat Meg with a long, thin cane, leaving a stripe of red welts down her pale ass and down her thighs, and part of me wants to rush in there and rip him away from her. The other, more confusing part of me, imagines what she's feeling, and I crave it with a strength that leaves me breathless.

The other woman, Aurora, moves from the chair to sit next to me on the floor. She gives a happy sigh. "I love to watch them."

Them.

This isn't something Hades is doing to Meg. No, this is an intricate dance they're doing *together*. Meg's broken her composure, and she shakes and writhes, and Hades never lets up, never hesitates, never strikes anywhere but exactly where he intends. He shifts, and I see the look of utter concentration on his face that has my cock hardening to painful levels. He is entirely focused on Meg, and it's so hot, I can barely stand it.

He finishes halfway down her calves and then drops the

cane and runs his hands roughly over her newly welted skin. Her whimper turns into a throaty moan that makes my gut clench, but I can't tell the source. Concern or desire. Some combination of both, maybe.

Up until this point, I've lived my life with very clear lines. Right and wrong. Yes and no. What I like and what I don't. I feel like the moment I met Meg propelled me into this world of gray where there are no boundaries aside from a safe word, where everything can be negotiated and things that should be terrifying are actually sexy as hell. I don't know myself in this world. I don't have a clear path. I don't know what the fuck I'm doing.

Hades uncuffs Meg and keeps her steady as he guides her to turn around. I expect him to do what Meg did, to bring her back to the couch, maybe cuddle her a little bit, offer some kind of aftercare. He doesn't. He cuffs her wrists back to the cross, pressing her hard enough that she lets loose another of those desperate moans. Tear tracks mark her face and her entire body is flushed and shaking. She looks like she's been through a war, but there's something in those blue eyes that stills me. A peace I've never seen on her face before.

Hades wipes her tears away with his thumbs and kisses her softly. When he lifts his head, he doesn't look away from her. "Come here, little Hercules."

It takes a long moment for it to penetrate that he's talking to me, and another long moment to climb to my feet and walk to him. I can't hide my giant cockstand, and considering Hades jerked me off not too long ago, I don't bother to try. He motions me forward with an imperial gesture, still not looking to ensure I obey. Why would he need to, though? I've already promised him obedience. In this moment, it feels like I've promised him a whole lot more.

He catches my wrist and pulls me the last foot forward. This close, I can see that Meg's nipples are hard points and that the flush in her skin isn't solely from pain. Hades shoves my hand between her thighs and presses two of my fingers deep inside her. "Jesus," I breathe. She's so fucking wet. She clamps around my fingers, and I can't help pumping a little.

"You have a choice, little Hercules."

I can't drag my gaze from Meg—her face, her body, her pussy wetting my fingers. "What choice?"

"You can continue to observe." His pause holds legions. "Or you can join."

If I'm smart, I'll retreat to the couch. These two are masters who have already proven that they won't hesitate to manipulate me to further whatever their endgame is. I'm in over my head, and there isn't a life raft in sight. I find myself nodding. "I'll join."

"Perfect." He strokes a possessive hand down my spine, stopping at the top of my shorts. "On your knees."

I have to stop finger-fucking Meg to obey, and she makes a little keening sound that punches me right in the chest. I want more than anything in that moment to give her the orgasm she's obviously aching for. I take a step forward, but Hades catches my shoulder. "Ah-ah. Obedience is the first rule." He moves to stand at my back, pressing his entire body against me. The feeling of him clothed while I'm standing naked makes every muscle clench. His voice in my ear only heightens the feverish desire in my blood. "On your knees."

I slowly sink to my knees between them, Hades's hand still clasped hard on my shoulder. I lick my lips and fight the impulse to lean in and lick her.

"Remind me of your safe word." His thumb brushes my neck, a touch I'm half sure I've imagined.

"Olympus," I breathe.

"Don't move." He gives my shoulder one last squeeze and then his heat at my back is gone.

I obey. I can't help but do exactly what he says. Some

85

awareness has filtered back into Meg's gaze, and she watches me with the kind of anticipation that makes me have to fight not to close the distance between us. Hades doesn't make me wait long. He reappears next to us with a flogger in his hand. "This is where we start you, little Hercules." He flicks it against my chest. It stings a little bit, but I'm not sure I'd call it actual pain. Whatever Hades sees in my face satisfies him, because he moves to stand behind me again, though this time he doesn't touch me.

His next command lashes me with more force that the flogger did. "Make her come." I open my mouth to ask Meg what she wants, but Hades anticipates me. "Now, Hercules. You both belong to me, and me alone. My Meg deserves a reward, and I've decided that your tongue will do nicely. Do try not to come in your pants."

Anger rises, and I welcome it. Just a game. This is all just a game to both of them. I move to Meg and wedge my hands under her thighs, lifting and spreading her. She's helpless like this, in a way she wasn't the last time we were together. It feels like we're on equal footing for the first time since I met her.

On our knees before Hades.

I lean down and drag my tongue over her. Meg gasps, and I can't tell if it's the feeling of my mouth or the pain of her ass pressed against the cross. I start to back up, but freeze when pain sparks along my shoulders. I already know what happened. Hades struck me with the flogger. A reminder to obey, maybe. Or maybe he just wants to beat me the way he beat Meg. The thought sends sparks down my spine. I want it. I don't give a fuck if I shouldn't, I *want* it. I hold Meg's gaze as I begin fucking her with my tongue the way I was commanded. An instrument of Hades's will. With every thrust, he whips me, driving me higher, sinking into the pleasure of her taste even as pain melts into a hot, dark blanket at my back.

Meg moves as much as she's able, rolling her hips to grind against my mouth, her blue eyes glazed with something more profound than pleasure. Something deeper. Her breath comes in gasping inhales that I begin to match without having any intention of it. It's like Hades and Meg strip down some instrumental human part of me, leaving only beast.

I suck on her clit hard, setting my teeth against the sensitive bundle of nerves, and her head falls back as a moan slips free. She's close. I'm afraid that I'm closer. The burning across my back and ass settles beneath my skin, drawing my balls up and sawing my breath in my lungs. "Fuck."

"Make her come, little Hercules." The snap in Hades's voice brings me back to myself, just a little. Meg tries to reach for me, but her cuffs hold her immobile. It's so sexy, I can barely stand it. I growl against her skin.

"Problem?" This time, Hades's voice is closer. I tense the barest fraction of a second before he kneels and he's pressed against my back again. This time I can't hold back a moan. The friction of his clothing against my smarting skin is almost too much. I clench my jaw and fight to keep from orgasming on the spot. Then Hades's voice is in my ear again, making it worse. "If you needed help making Meg come, you should have just asked."

Humiliation lashes me more intensely than the flogger did. Somehow that makes everything hotter. I want to please her, to please him. I can make her come with my mouth. I *know* I can. She's close even now.

But I'm not in charge.

Hades is.

He reaches around me and presses his hand to Meg's pussy. I watch him push three fingers into her hard, already knowing exactly what she needs, and my strange shame burns hotter. Worse in some ways… as he presses his cock against my ass, I can't help resenting the clothing barrier between us. I can imagine him driving just as deep into me as his fingers are into Meg right now. No, better than that. I can imagine him fucking me as *I* fuck her, even if it'd really be Hades fucking us both.

"You're getting distracted, little Hercules." He switches hands, delving the one still wet with Meg's desire into my pants as he starts fucking her again with his other. He grips my cock tight and I can't fight back a moan. Hades's chuckle is cruel. "It would be a shame if you came before she does."

Just like that, I can't hold on any longer. I suck hard on Meg's clit and come into Hades's hand, and it's only his clever fingers that have her following me over the edge. The pleasure goes on and on, wave after wave until my body goes limp and it's only Hades's arms around me that keep me from slumping over.

I rest my forehead against Meg's stomach. "Fuck."

"Yeah," she whispers. She still doesn't sound like herself, but I get that now. I don't sound like myself in this moment either.

I don't know what I expect after that. I honestly don't. But nowhere in my realm of possibilities is it for Hades to take care of us. He eases me back from Meg and cleans up my stomach before I can dredge up the energy to do it myself. Another blanket appears and he guides me back to the floor next to the couch. At some point Aurora gets up, gives my shoulder a quick squeeze, and slips out of the room. That shame from before hasn't gone anywhere, and it only worms its way deeper as I huddle beneath that fucking blanket and watch Hades tend to Meg.

He leans down and says something in her ear and cups her pussy in a possessive way that raises a strange kind of jealousy in me. Jealousy because I want her, yes, but jealousy in the level of caring she receives from him. She means something to him, something special. I might not understand the many undercurrents of their relationship, but even I can see that.

Hades uncuffs her and scoops her into his arms. Meg always seems larger than life, so it's almost shocking to see how small she really is. He carries her easily to the couch and wraps another blanket around her while she's still in his lap. I don't know what to expect. Am I supposed to leave? The thought hurts. A lot. More than it has right to.

Somehow, he knows.

Hades taps the couch next to him with a single finger. "Up."

My legs shake as I obey. I feel both too light and too raw, as if he's ripped me open for his perusal. Maybe he has. I must take too long, because he grips the back of my neck and guides me until I'm leaning against them, my head in Meg's lap. She has to spread her legs to make room for my shoulders, and that could have been an invitation of sorts, but it doesn't feel like it. I close my eyes. One of them sifts their fingers through my hair, but I can't work up the energy to open my eyes to know who. Does it even matter?

I don't understand any of this. The actions, yes. Not the motive behind it. I can't shake the feeling they chose me on purpose, *trapped* me on purpose. My father has a long history of fucking people over, and sometimes those people want revenge. They can't get to him, so they target the people in his sphere. My mother has had no fewer than four assassination attempts since I was born. My older brother, the heir to the title Zeus, has had double that. Just because I've mostly be spared from that danger up to this point doesn't mean a single damn thing.

In absence of better evidence, the only thing I can do is draw a line between these two things. Hades has some connection to Olympus. All signs point to him targeting me specifically, which means he likely is using me to get to my father.

I almost laugh at the thought, might even do it if I had the energy. Hades might know a lot, might have some deep plans running, but he obviously doesn't realize how deep my hatred for my father goes. If he wants to use me against the man, he's more than welcome to.

None of that explains Meg, though. She was surprised by the turn of events, which means she has no idea what Hades is planning. The thought of *her* being inadvertently hurt by this... Yeah, I'll keep my mouth shut and pay attention until I know something for sure. If I think for a second Meg is in danger, then I'll fight Hades, strange attraction to him or no.

Until then, I wait.

I don't mean to fall asleep. I have every intention of getting up and making my way... somewhere. Back to my room, I guess. I'm in no shape to sling drinks right now. But the darkness behind my eyes gains new depth and pulls me down despite myself.

My last thought is how absurdly safe I feel right now, with two people who I most definitely shouldn't trust.

CHAPTER 12

MEG

"What game are you playing, Hades?"

He strokes a hand down the back of my thigh, directly over the welts he striped there. A comforting touch and still a reminder of his power. Everything is like that with him, always has been. Layers upon layers. There are days when I'd give my right eye for him to just speak *plainly*. Just once. I already know his answer won't satisfy before he says, "A deep one, love."

I look down at Hercules. His body has gone slack with sleep, the adrenaline drop knocking him out as surely as any drug. If we can't rouse him enough to get him down to his suite, he'll end up here on the couch. It won't be the first time something like this has happened, but my stomach twists at the thought of him waking up and thinking he's been abandoned. "He's an innocent."

"He's from Olympus. There are no innocents there, not in the circles he moved in."

Finally, a hint at the truth. I should have made the connection the second Hercules picked *that* as his safe word, but I'd been too busy wallowing in anger and self-pity. I lean back enough so that I can see Hades's face. "He's too young to be connected to your exile."

"Yes."

No elaboration, and why would there be? Everyone thinks that Hades talks to me, that he divulges secrets to me and me alone. He used to, but that was a long time ago, before he started shutting me out. Now, when I'm actually trying to reach him despite every instinct screaming at me to protect myself, he's *still* shutting me out. Frustration blooms in my chest, chasing away the last bit of buzz from the scene we just finished. "I wish you would just *talk* to me."

He strokes my jaw. For a moment, the barriers between us disintegrate, and I can see how fucking *tired* he is. Tired down to his very soul. An exhaustion that could swallow mine. It's only a moment, though. I blink and then he's the enigma again, a soft smile playing at his lips. "Trust me, love. You never used to have such reservations when it came to following my lead."

Hurt lances my chest, a deeper pain than the cane welts. Closed out yet again. A demand for trust that he stopped earning when he stopped talking to me. Did I really think this time would be different, that he would suddenly change his ways? I know better. A thousand times over. My throat burns, and I look away. "I'm very tired. I'd like to go to bed."

For the briefest of hesitations, I think he may actually change his mind and let me in. But Hades just nods. "There's a meeting with the liquor distributer at ten tomorrow."

Just business. Always just business. "I'm aware," I grind out. Stupid to let this hurt me. I slide out from beneath Hercules's head and it's only sheer force of will that keeps my knees from buckling when I stand. Hades may own me in every way that counts, but he's no longer my safe space. I'm not even sure if he ever was, or if those bright years were just a figment of my imagination, an illusion a desperate girl wove around herself and the man she viewed as her savior.

I let the blanket drop and walk on steady legs to my discarded clothing. It's not uncommon for subs to navigate the club in only a blanket—or naked—but I am not a normal sub. My clothing is my armor, and no matter how dazed I feel right now, I can't afford to let anyone see. The Underworld is filled to the brim with predators, and it's their nature to pounce on weakness. Even me. *Especially* me.

I'm almost to the door when Hades speaks again. "Megaera."

I stop. "Yes?"

"You pleased me greatly tonight."

I resent the warm flush his words bring. Pleasure at pleasing him. I walk out of the room without another word. Hades will see to Hercules. It's not my problem, and staying in that room a second longer is just asking for the emotional breakdown I can feel barreling down the tracks in my direction. I have to get out of here, but leaving the building isn't an option, not when I'm feeling so off-center. It takes me six minutes to make it down the back way to the living quarters and lock myself in my suite. Even then, it's not enough. I strip out of my clothes, but each step reminds me of the beating Hades delivered, of the way Hercules fucked me with his tongue afterward. If that's not a metaphor for the two men, I don't know what is.

Pain and pleasure. Pleasure and pain. Both will kill you in the end if you're not careful.

I need a shower, but I'm too fucking exhausted. Emotionally. Mentally. Physically. Take your pick. I drag my fingers through my hair. I already know I'm not going to be able to sleep. Even after the scene, I'm wound too tightly, my thoughts tumbling over themselves to circle, circle, circle. I yank on my hair, but the spark of pain along my scalp does nothing to calm the turmoil raging through me.

A knock on my door, three measured beats.

I know who it is even before I pad naked to the door and pull it open. Hades stands there, looking as perfectly put together as ever. Isn't that always the way? He's in control, and I'm spiraling out around him. My defenses are long gone, but I try to dredge them up anyway. "Can I help you, Sir?"

"Did you think I wouldn't notice?"

"What?" I take a step back, and he shadows the movement, stepping into my suite and closing the door softly behind him. He feels bigger the second I'm locked in with him. It's as if, without the outlet of the open doorway, his presence fills the room to the brim, leaving no space for anyone else. Part of it's the power he wields as easily as breathing. Most of it is just Hades.

I keep backing up. I'm not even sure what I'm doing at this point. I'm incapable of running from this man, but I'm acting on sheer instinct right now. My back hits the wall, and I can't keep my little gasp in. Hades keeps advancing until he's barely an inch away, until it would be more natural for him to close that last little bit of distance. "You're hurting, love."

Damn you. I swallow hard. "You striped my ass. I'll be hurting for days."

"That's not what I'm talking about."

I can't do it. I can't answer the demand in his dark eyes. I've already stripped myself bare again and again for him. To do it right now on command... I can't. No matter how much I need it.

I should have more faith in Hades. He never needed me to express myself in words before, though he demands it often enough. He takes a step back and holds out a hand. "You should have told me."

"I don't know what you mean."

"Yes, you do. You're always so strong, so fearless. It took me too long to realize what was going on beneath."

I have no answer to that, so I take his hand and let him tuck me against his chest, bolstering me with his strength, protecting me from everything but the two of us. Ironic, that. I inhale the subtle scent of him and something inside me starts to unwind. It doesn't matter that I know better, that this soft moment never lasts. It's enough that he's here and giving it to me right now.

He guides us to my bed and nudges me to lay down. I watch him strip. It thrills me, even now, *especially* now, to see him dismantle such a vital part of him. Hades's clothes are his armor the same way mine are. More so, even. Naked, he climbs into bed next to me and pulls me back into his arms. We lay like that for several long moments, and he lets out a quiet sigh. "I can't be anything other than what I am, love."

My eyes burn and I shut them tight. "I'm aware of that." I'm not a fool, though some days it certainly feels like it. He appears to be trying, and with the dark blanketing the room around us, I tentatively release some of my truth. "I can't help needing what I need."

"I know."

He can't change and neither can I. We fit so well… but it's not a perfect melding. It never will be. The thought brings sorrow too great to bear and I shift closer to lift my face to his. He catches my mouth, anticipating my kiss. Hades always seems to know what I'm going to do before I do it. That annoys me most days. Right now, it's a relief.

He rolls me onto my back, pressing me down hard against the mattress and sending pain flaring over my ass and thighs. I

KATEE ROBERT

welcome it. Every touch pushes my fears away and settles something inside me. I didn't realize how much I needed this grounding until he arrived to give it to me. He carefully pushes a single finger into me, testing for tenderness. As if he hasn't overseen me fucking for hours in the past and then bent me over the arm of the chair and driven into me until I begged for mercy. I lift my hips in silent invitation, but he continues at the same pace, building my pleasure in slow waves, piece by piece. He shifts his thumb against my clit, teasing me, and I break our kiss long enough to say, "Hades, please."

He shifts to settle between my thighs. A breath later and his cock is filling me in the most perfect way possible. He pins me to the bed with his hips, his weight not allowing for any movement. I cling to him, even as I try to fight for more space to slide along his length. The pleasure and pressure and pain is almost too much. "I need…"

"I'll always find a way to give you what you need, love. You know that." His low voice is pure sin in the darkness. It doesn't matter that we're having what appears to be vanilla sex. It's never vanilla with me and Hades. Not really. Not when every touch chains me to him more thoroughly, every word marks me as his.

Just when I'm sure I can't stand it any longer, that I'll start to beg and plead, he begins to move. He's cruel in his gentleness, cruel in showing me how things could be if we were different people. If we hadn't made the same choices to get to this place. I can't breathe past needing him. He locks his grip around my wrists and pins them to the bed on either side of my head, and I could weep over the need to touch him. "Hades, *please*."

He bites my bottom lip, and then I'm coming, fighting against his hold, fighting to take him in deeper, to hold him closer. It's a lost cause. It always has been. For once, Hades doesn't try to prolong things, he follows me over the edge, sharing this with me. He gentles his kisses and moves us back to our previous position—him on his back with me tucked against him. His hold around me tightens, as if maybe he needed this just as much as I did, but the moment passes too quickly for me to be sure. After ten years, this man shouldn't be such an enigma to me. Maybe he always was. Maybe I just thought I knew him with the rash arrogance of youth, and time proved me wrong. I'm honestly not sure anymore.

He smooths my hair back. "It's you and me, Meg. Forever."

Threat or declaration of love? I don't know. I've never known. I look into his dark eyes, and in this moment I can truly believe that this man loves me above all others. That it would hurt him beyond measure to lose me. That he would raze this city to the ground if it meant my happiness was on the line.

Then he blinks and I can actually see him retreating. Sorrow rises, a drowning wave that I have no defense against. I tuck my face against his chest, and he lets me hide this from him tonight, just like he always has in the past. Some truths are too difficult to bear. I close my eyes and let the relative safety of Hades's presence around me lull me into sleep.

When I wake, I'm alone.

Just like always.

CHAPTER 13

*T*hings are going according to plan.

I should be delighted beyond measure. Victory. Revenge. It all lies just over the horizon. This is the moment I've wanted ever since that bastard in Olympus declared my sentence all those years ago. Exile. A punishment I may have admired if it weren't leveled against me. Worse than the sweet oblivion of death. The moment you stop breathing, your heart ceases to beat... that's the moment you're beyond pain. Exile means to live with the agony of knowing you can never go home, that the people who you cared about the most continue to live on without you.

To know how replaceable you truly are.

If that was his only sin, I might have been willing to let it go. Not easily, but I know better than to waste time and resources chasing an old grudge. But no, exile wasn't enough for \Zeus. He had to take *everything* from me.

I aim to return the favor.

I unbutton my suit jacket and sit behind my desk. The last few hours have left me tired, but certain business is best conducted before dawn. This call is one of them. I pick up the phone and dial from memory. Some knowledge never leaves us. It rings for several long moments before a man answers. "It better be good to be calling me at this hour."

That tone reaches through time and space. For a moment, I'm that foolish twenty-year-old man-child who believes I'm immortal and that nothing bad could ever happen to me because I have *power*. I didn't know what power was then, not in any meaningful way. "Hello, Zeus."

The man who once proclaimed we were close enough to be brothers, even if no blood connected us, inhales sharply. That little sound pleases me greatly. I've managed to surprise him, which is a coup all its own. He finally says, "Hades. Have to say, you're the last person I expected to hear from. Surprised to find you're still alive."

I suspected that the scattering of attempts on my life over the years could be traced back to him. Now I know for sure. Anger rises in a steady beat, but I throttle it back. Rage has no place in this conversation, not when one misstep means defeat. "I think we both know nothing as mundane as a hired hit is enough to remove me."

"Maybe not you, but others aren't so lucky." Zeus laughs, the sound bright and happy. He's always been able to do that, to fill a room with his joy—and to flip it off like a switch. "Why call me now? Surely you've not gone senile enough to think I'll let you back into Olympus."

I would burn that city to ash before I set foot in it again voluntarily. "Hardly." I keep my tone light. So light. "I found something of yours that you've misplaced."

"What's that?" Caution now, as if he finally realizes that I'm still a danger to him.

I let the moment spin out for several beats, enjoying this. "I've hired a new employee. Someone I think you may know."

"Hades," he warns.

I ignore it. "He's rather beautiful. Blond. Strong. Piercing blue eyes that remind me of someone…" I chuckle.

"Hercules." Now all joy is gone from Zeus, leaving only the danger beneath. "What's to say I didn't exile him just like I did with you?"

"Come now. I know better, and *you* know better than to try that subterfuge with me. He may not be your heir, but he's your son. A traitorous son is still a son. You never release the things you own, Zeus." I smile. "He's rather self-right-eous, isn't he? All he needs is a shining set of armor to go with his hero complex. I imagine he doesn't approve of the way you do business and decided to try to muddle through on his own. He was doing a poor job of it. Truly, you should thank me for snatching him off the street."

"That boy is coming home, and I'll rip you to shreds if you think you can keep him from me." There it is. The fury and rage that make Zeus the force to be reckoned with. Once upon a time, I admired and feared the man in equal measure. No longer.

In my part of Carver City, *I* am the monster others fear. I am the spider in the web I intend to draw my enemy to. Hercules is nothing more than bait. "You can try. You can fail. He's mine now, Zeus. And when I'm through with him, maybe it will be enough to begin to atone for your sins." I hang up before he can respond. The phone immediately rings, but I ignore it. Let him stew in his rage the same way I have for decades.

Exile. For nothing more than stepping into the role that was meant for me from birth. There is meant to be a balance in Olympus. A Zeus ruling on high. A Poseidon managing the middle and mundane. And a Hades seeing to the shad-ows. When I was young and just as foolish as Hercules is now, I thought that balance would persevere despite Zeus's thirst for power. It never occurred to me that he'd break a treaty going back to the founding of Olympus and strike directly at the heart of me.

Banishing the feared Hades cemented his place when his younger brothers were looking at the role with hungry eyes. No one dared cross him once they knew what lengths he was capable of.

And yet it was me and mine who paid the price of his ambition.

I sit back in my chair and attempt to shrug off the weight of the past. He won't be able to stop from striking back at me over this. I'll be ready when he does.

In the meantime, I'll fulfill my threat of breaking Hercules apart piece by piece. The man may not exhibit the sins of his father, but no one grows up in that gilded hell Olympus without being tainted beyond words. Even if he fought against it at one time, he's not strong enough to hold out indefinitely. I can't guarantee that, even with Hercules's history, he won't come when Zeus calls. Meg would be hurt beyond measure.

No, it's time to start binding him to us in every way. Until he's happy on his knees. Until he never considers his other options. If I relish the challenge? Well, I'm only human.

The next step begins today.

CHAPTER 14

HERCULES

*L*ast night feels like a fever dream. I might believe it to be exactly that if not for the faint ache along my back where Hades flogged me. It's not bruised, but there are light marks on my skin. I stare at them a long time, conflicted. I wanted them last night. I *want* them now. It's not the craving for this lifestyle that makes me doubt myself, though.

It's the craving for *him*.

I find the gym without too much trouble and spend an hour working through my demons. Sweating always paves the way for clearer thinking, and I've been lax in my routine since I left Olympus. Gym memberships are expensive and hardly qualify as a necessary expenditure. Unsurprisingly, the Underworld offers the best of everything. High tech treadmills and bikes. Free weights that gleam in the bright light. Everything looks brand new and barely used, though I know better. It's an illusion, just like the rest of this place.

I head for the free weights and begin the process of going through my old routine. My body remembers the motions, allowing my thoughts to wander right back to Hades.

Wanting the man who manipulated and trapped me is the height of idiocy. He didn't pick me by random; his cruelty is too calculated for that. If I'd stopped reacting to Meg and *thought* for a few minutes, I'd have realized that a long time ago. All roads lead back to Olympus—to my father—I'm sure of it. Would it change my actions? I don't think so. Even knowing what I do now, I still want her. I should be smarter than this, but I've already proven that *should* has no place here.

I want him.

I want her.

They desire me—some things can't be faked—but they both have an agenda that hints at a deeper game. My thoughts last night might have been drugged on pleasure and exhaustion, but it doesn't make them any less true. In the light of day, they feel all the clearer.

Hades plans to use me to get to my father.

I can't say if it will work. My father hasn't tried to summon me home since I left, allowing his lack of attention to translate into a punishment. He's always been like that, giving and withdrawing love in turn. Except, with Zeus, love is an edged weapon even when he's effusive and happy. Even with family.

With anyone who *isn't* family? They don't have the slightest bit of protection to keep my father from taking what he wants, when he wants. I hiss out a breath and push the barbell away from my chest. The ridiculousness of the situation is not lost on me. If Hades had come to me and offered a plan to bring my father down, I would have agreed and gladly.

Instead, he'd used Meg as both bait and a strange kind of punishment. *That* is the part that doesn't make sense to me. What little I know of this man paints a picture of someone who does nothing without a reason. He wouldn't put together a messy plan that potentially hurts the woman he appears to care about without a damn good reason.

In the end, does it matter what Hades's endgame is? I gave my word. I'm his for life. If he was going to try to kill me, he would have done it by now. If my being here aggravates my father, I'm still furious enough to enjoy the thought of that. That anger isn't going away. Not ever. He hurts everyone he comes into contact with. He plucks them, uses them, and then disposes them like they're tissues instead of people. And Olympus lets him. Everyone looks the other way because he has power, and that's the only god anyone in that cursed place worships.

I tried and failed to change things, so I left rather than witness it happen again and again.

The door opens and Tink walks in. She gives the entire room a dirty look before settling on me. "There you are." She's wearing jeans and a T-shirt that has a picture of a skeleton holding a pair of eyes perfectly centered on each breast with the text *My eyes are up here*. Tink is… quite the character. She snaps her fingers. "Up here, Hercules."

"I like your shirt," I say drily.

"It's my day off," she snaps back, but her lips tug up a little at the edges. She might be mean as a snake, but I like her. She gives me a long look, lingering on sweat slicking my bare chest. "Hades wants to talk to you. You should probably, uh, shower first. I'll wait."

"You want to watch?" I don't know why I offer. I'm mostly teasing, I think, though Tink is gorgeous enough that if the situation were different, I'd make a real pass at her.

She raises her eyebrows. "What a cute little exhibitionist you are." She laughs. "But I know better than to play with the boss's toys without permission. Get your ass in the shower and be quick about it."

She follows me back to my suite and takes up residence

on the couch while I head into the bathroom. I shower quickly, telling myself that it's prudence causing me to do so, rather than anticipation for seeing *him* again. I'm a goddamned liar.

I walk to the closet situated off the bathroom and flip on the light. And freeze. Yesterday, I'd dropped my bag into the middle of it with the intention of hanging up my clothes once I had some down time. The bag is gone. Now the space is filled to the brim. On one side is apparently my work wear, an array of fabrics in very small packages. On the other are more clothes than I've seen in one place since I left home. Slacks in black and gray. Button-down shirts in a wide range of colors. They've even bought me fucking shoes.

I wrap my towel around my waist and raise my voice. "Tink!"

"I'm not watching you wank it."

Her response *almost* detracts from my growing irritation. "Get in here."

She walks through the door and frowns. "What?"

"My closet." I motion at it. "What the fuck is this? Where the hell are my clothes?"

She peers past me and gives me a look like I'm having one over on her. "Is this a trick question? You have plenty of clothes."

I feel like I've entered a completely different world all over again. I thought I had things down, at least a little, but I didn't expect something as surface level as this closet being filled to rock me. And yet it is. "Where did they come from?"

"Oh. That" Tink rolls her eyes. "I know you liked your beggar white-bread style, but you can't dress like that here. Hades and the Underworld have a reputation, and as employees of both, we are part of upholding that."

I point at her chest. "What about what you're wearing?"

"Look, I have seniority *and* I'm playing errand girl when

I'm off the clock, so how about we don't criticize my excellent taste in clothing?" Her humor is gone and she's glaring again. "Put on some clothes and let's go. We've wasted enough time and I have shit to do today."

This time, I don't argue. In the end, we all answer to Hades and expelling my frustration at Tink is a shitty thing to do. I pull on a pair of black slacks and a light gray shirt. There are ties, but I ignore them. A quick comb through my hair and I'm ready. Tink doesn't say anything as she takes me up to the top floor, and I miss her snark a little bit. She punches the button to keep the elevator door open when we reach our floor. "Only door in there. That's where you're headed."

"I'm sorry."

She blinks. "What?"

"I didn't mean to put you on the spot about the clothes. I was just surprised and you were there so I took it out on you."

Another of those slow blinks. "Hercules, you barely raised your voice."

Her shock at my apology doesn't make me feel better. In fact, it makes me feel worse. "I'm sorry."

"Uh… consider it forgiven." She motions for me to get the hell out of the elevator. This time, I obey.

This isn't the same office from last night—or even the same floor. I'm not sure what I expect when I push open the door, but it's not the room I find myself standing in. Aside from the big windows overlooking Carver City, the walls are filled with black bookshelves from floor to ceiling, and the shelves are *packed* with books. Not just filed neatly. They're stacked as if the occupant ran out of space and couldn't bear to sacrifice even one. I barely notice the desk and overstuffed chairs across from it, or the thick patterned rug beneath my feet as I wander to the nearest shelf. Again, I'm surprised.

The books are genre fiction, each spine weathered as if they've been reread countless times. Mystery, fantasy, romance, science fiction.

"By all means, feel free to look your fill."

I jump and turn to face the desk. Hades sits behind it, watching me with an amused expression on his face. As I'm coming to expect, he's wearing black-on-black again. He's as put together as ever, and the exhaustion weighing me down after last night seems to roll right off him. He motions to one of the chairs across from him. "Sit."

I consider standing just to make a point, but it's a silly hill to choose to die on. I walk to the closest chair and sink into it. It's a rich emerald green that somehow fits in with the rest of the office, luxurious and sturdy and obviously well-loved. The whole room feels *comfortable* in a way I'm not prepared for. "Can I ask you a question?" I don't intend to speak, but I don't do well with secrets and bullshit. I'd rather just get this all out in the open so I can deal with it.

Hades raises his brows. "By all means."

"What did my father do to you to piss you off enough to target me?"

He studies me for a long moment, something like surprise written over his face. "You don't have a subtle bone in your body, do you?"

If I did, I wouldn't be in Carver City in the first place. I would have found a better way to fight my father, to help Leda, to make a difference. "I'd rather see the playing field clearly."

He sits back, still seeming to consider my question. Or, more likely, considering whether or not to answer honestly —or at all. "He took everything from me."

I was right. I don't know if that's good or bad at this point. I try to relax into the chair, but it's hard when I have Hades's full attention on me. "I'm not him." I don't hurt people the way he does. I don't hurt people *at all*. At least, not on purpose.

"Trust me, I'm well aware of that. You are, however, a possession that matters to him."

I was right. This is about revenge. I should have known I couldn't escape Olympus's politics even if I escaped the city itself. Carver City seemed like a safe bet for a place to settle down, but obviously Zeus's influence has spread to even here. "It must have been bad for you to go through this much shit to get back at him."

"A son for a son, little Hercules."

The implications hit me hard enough that if I weren't sitting, I'd be on my knees. A son... My father took his from him? But that doesn't make sense. I would have heard about it. I'm sure I would have heard about something like that. "When?"

"Before you were born." He waves it away with a flick of his wrist. "I have no intention of discussing it further. You wanted to know why; there's your why. Does it make you feel better?"

Since he sounds genuinely curious, I answer honestly. "No."

"There you have it." He shrugs. "I didn't call you here for that, however. I have a task for you."

My mind whirls with the implications of what he's told me. Within all the confusion and anger, there's hurt. No reason for his motive to sting. Did I really want to hear that he saw me across the room and couldn't rest until he had me as his own? That kind of shit only happens in movies and fairy tales. This is real life. Real life is ugly and brutal and filled to the brim with pain. I know this too well already. Of course he didn't want *me*. He has Meg.

Meg.

"Does she know about this?" There were a thousand ways

Hades could have accomplished this goal without involving her. I don't understand *that*. He wields cruelty with the precision of a surgeon with a scalpel. "It's really shitty that you'd hurt her just because you want revenge on my father."

"Hercules." The censor in his tone makes me flush. "The conversation is closed. I trust it will stay between us."

I open my mouth to argue, but his sharp look stops me. Instead, I swallow hard. "A task?"

"Normally Tink acts as Meg's assistant, but her contract is coming to an end. Regardless of whether or not she chooses to stay on at the Underworld, you'll be trained to take her place."

I swallow. "You want me to train to be Meg's assistant."

"Yes." His gaze doesn't leave my face. "Do *not* fuck her. Regardless of what else happens, that is a line you will not cross. If you do, I'll punish you both publicly." He leans forward. "And trust me when I say that you won't enjoy it in the least."

A thrill courses through me despite common sense whispering that crossing this man is a mistake, even in a game. I'm still furious at Meg. Last night changes nothing. But, like with Hades, I want her enough to cloud my judgment, and the protective urges that drove me to make this bargain in the first place haven't disappeared. Hades obviously knows that and plans to use it against me. Is Meg in on this particular game? I don't know. Our short history more than proves that I can't trust her. "Okay," I say slowly.

"'Yes, Sir' is the proper response."

"Yes, Sir," I immediately repeat. I have a lot to think about, but in the end it changes nothing. I gave my word. If I didn't know the reason Hades wanted me, that's on me. I charged in here, thinking I knew everything I needed to know, and ended up in over my head as a result.

Embarrassment heats my face. All I want is to do good,

but every time I turn around, I'm fucking things up worse than they were before I arrived. I can't keep up with the major power players no matter how hard I try. I don't even know if I'm capable of thinking about the long game the same way Zeus and Hades do. Every time I try to slow down, my instincts get the best of me and I jump without checking for water.

I need to change that about myself, and I don't even know where to start.

Hades studies me as if he can divine my thoughts right out of my head. "There's no shame in the impulsiveness of youth, little Hercules."

I try for a laugh, but it comes out bitter. "Are you a mind reader now?"

"I don't have to be when you wear your thoughts on your face for anyone to see."

"I don't know how not to." I don't know how not to do a lot of things.

He leans forward and braces his elbows on his desk. "Time and pain are the best teachers. You'll learn. Maybe not soon enough, but you'll learn."

I should end this conversation, but he's actually talking to me with something almost like compassion. I can't trust it—I know enough to know *that*—but I also don't want it to end. "Were you ever like me? When you were my age?"

"No." His smile is quick and bittersweet. "I was much, much worse. Or better, I suppose, depending on how you look at it. You had the self-awareness to realize all was not as it seemed and to look past your father's charismatic mirage. I didn't."

I can't imagine that, a Hades with stars in his eyes. It's possible he's lying to me about this, too, but my gut says it's the truth. I clear my throat. "I'm sorry for what he did to you."

He takes off his glasses and pulls out a black cloth to clean the lenses. It's such a mundane action, but it leaves me breathless. "Meg will be in her office. It's the next floor down." He glances up. "Tonight, we'll have another lesson."

That's a dismissal if I've ever heard one. I should be happy to leave this man's presence, but reluctance weighs me down. That was *almost* a full conversation without animosity or manipulation. Almost. I push slowly to my feet. "I'll see you later, then."

He lets me get nearly to the door before he speaks again. "And Hercules?"

"Yes, Sir?" I pause, but don't turn around.

"Next time you walk through that door, I don't want you wearing anything but your skin."

CHAPTER 15

MEG

*A*s much as I love the late nights in the Underworld, mornings are my favorite time of day. The entire building feels like it's a slumbering dragon, and I'm the only one around to witness it. The cleaning crew comes through before I'm up, so everything glistens and shines and feels brand new. Part of my job is ensuring they didn't miss anything, but I enjoy the quiet moments walking the empty lounge and back rooms. Without the bustling energies of people filling it to the brim it feels like…mine.

Mine and Hades's, though he stopped doing these quiet walkthroughs with me years ago.

It doesn't stop me from looking for him every single fucking morning. I should know better by now, but my stomach still drops a little when I don't find him waiting for me in the lounge.

I circle the bar that gleams in the low light, and then check all the booths. Our cleaning crew is the best, so this is mostly a formality. Next is the public playroom behind a locked door. When the Underworld is filled with patrons, this door is usually manned by Allecto or one of her people. I push through, putting my disappointment into movement in an attempt to exorcise it from my body.

The public playroom holds a little bit of everything. There are spanking benches and St. Andrew's Crosses and various racks for suspension play. Scattered throughout the room, there are also couches and other furniture for people to sit on to observe or fuck or do whatever they want to. The only limit is consent.

Everything is as it should be. The room smells faintly of citrus and I inhale deeply. It doesn't completely banish the sick feeling in my stomach, but it dilutes it. All my complicated feelings for Hades don't make a difference when I'm in this room. Knowing I'm responsible for the people who work here, that they depend on me for guidance and safety. It's a heady feeling. Hades might have paved the way for me to take this position, but *I* earned their trust on my own.

Next are the back rooms. They're all themed, from a mundane bedroom to a study to a doctor's office to a stable. During the day, the viewing wall is transparent so I don't have to enter the rooms to check them. Clean. Perfect. Ready for tonight.

By the time I finish my walkthrough, I'm steady enough to focus on the office work that comes next.

First up are spreadsheets and the reports from the staff who worked the night before. Sometimes it's just a simple record of their scenes with clients. Sometimes they have gems of knowledge that were dropped during the equivalent of pillow talk. All are filed and brought to Hades. He likes to hold all the cards when it comes to negotiations, and one never knows who will want a deal, so he has files on every major player in Carver City.

There are a lot of them.

The city is carved up into slices, each ruled by a different faction. Some of them are stable. Some are significantly less so. All have the ability to endanger the careful balance we have if they go rogue. By creating a neutral territory in the center, we ensure that nothing will happen without us knowing about it first. While Hades doesn't intervene without a deal, knowledge is power. And power is everything in Carver City.

The door opens, and I speak without looking up, "What are you doing here, Tink? You have the day off."

"Tink *does* have the day off."

I freeze in the middle of typing. Even as I tell myself that Hades wouldn't be that much of an asshole, when I look up, Hercules is still standing in my doorway. "What are you doing here?"

"Reporting for training."

Oh yes, Hades and I will have words about his high-handedness. He may technically be my boss, but *I* am in charge of managing the club. Up until this point, he's allowed me to do that as I see fit. Forcing Hercules into my presence is a test, and I resent him for it. Why is he so determined to rub this man in my face? It's like he knows that Hercules got under my skin, keeps getting under my skin, and wants to… That's the problem. I don't know what Hades wants. I can't begin to guess.

"Did our dearest Dom tell you what he intends?" I don't have much faith in it, so I'm already turning back to my computer when Hercules answers.

"I guess I'm training for Tink's job?"

That bastard. I close my eyes and take a slow breath. It's not Hercules's fault that Hades continues to play games. Whether this one is aimed at me, Hercules, or Tink doesn't matter. All that does is display his willingness to use the club as his conduit. "Sit." I grab my phone before I can think better of it. This is probably best left to when we have some privacy, but if he's determined to shoehorn Hercules into every aspect of our lives, then he'll just have to deal with the man overhearing our conversation. I push the button to dial his office.

For once, he doesn't make me wait. "I trust Hercules arrived promptly."

"Hades, what are you doing?" I take in Hercules for the first time since he's walked into my office. He looks like a different person this morning. I don't know if it's the expensive clothes that appear tailored to him or that he's just more at ease in his own skin than he was the first night I met him. In the end, it doesn't matter. Hades's endgame *is* what matters.

And I don't know what it is.

He lets the silence spin out until my heart is beating too hard and I'm ready to scream my frustration down the line. Finally, he says, "Tink's contract is almost finished."

"Yes, it is. And she's considering staying on afterward."

"She won't." He says it with such confidence, I almost believe him.

Almost. "Funny, but that's not what she told me yesterday. Do you know something I don't?"

"I know a lot of things you don't. However, this is just a feeling."

Just a feeling. Right. I strive for patience, not to let my frustration show. "I don't deal in feelings, Hades. I deal in facts. Until Tink tells me otherwise, I'm going to operate like she's not leaving, which means I don't need to fill the position of her replacement." More silence, an invitation for me to back down. I won't. Most of the time, I will submit to his pleasure. Not in this. Not right now. "Just tell me why," I whisper.

"He's a gift, love."

He'd said something to the same effect the night he sent me to fuck Hercules. I frown. "What's that supposed to mean?"

"Report to me once you're finished with him today."

Click.

I take the phone away from my ear and stare at it. He just... He just hung up on me. I carefully set it back in its cradle and take an equally careful breath. This isn't Hercules's fault, but it *feels* like it's his fault. If he'd just shown a little more restraint, just *asked* me what I wanted, then we wouldn't be in this situation to begin with. "Apparently I don't have a choice." I don't realize I've spoken aloud until he answers.

"I'm sorry."

I glare. I want to shake him until something akin to sense blossoms in that pretty head of his. "It's not your fault this time. You're just a tool, Hercules, and a blunt one at that."

He blinks and then bursts out laughing. "Wow, Meg, tell me how you really feel." Just like that, some of the tension eases in him and he slouches back in his seat. "You didn't have a problem with me last night."

Of all the— "That was different and you know it. A scene is its own little world."

He shrugs. "I won't pretend I'm an expert in what a scene entails, but we have a connection. You can't fake that."

It's on the tip of my tongue to tell him that I can, in fact, fake that. I close my eyes and strive for control. Cutting him down might feel good for a moment, but it's like kicking a puppy. Unnecessarily cruel. He made a mistake in bargaining his life way. That's punishment enough without me verbally stabbing him every time he brushes against one of my many emotional wounds. "Just because we have a connection doesn't mean I want you underfoot."

"I won't be a burden."

I open my eyes. "Before you were a waiter, what was your job?" If Hades is determined to have him here, I suppose I should treat this as professionally as possible. As if I wasn't coming on his tongue a few short hours ago.

He looks away, a faint blush coloring his cheeks. "I, ah, didn't work. After I graduated college two years ago, I took a year off and then I was supposed to start in my father's business, but life got in the way."

Life got in the way. Likely the same life that resulted in him ending up in Carver City. I want to judge him for his life of privilege, to cut him down out of spite because I'm hurting, but he's trying. I can try, too. "Okay."

Hercules looks back at me, all youthful promise and hope. "I'm a fast learner."

I raise my eyebrows. "I suppose we'll see, won't we?" There's no point in fighting this. I might as well put him to work. I brace myself. "Okay, first things first. Work is work and fucking is fucking. When you're on the clock, especially during office work, I need you focused on paperwork instead of pussy."

He grins. "You mean you don't want me to climb under your desk and eat you out for hours?"

My body flashes hot, and I give myself a full three seconds to enjoy the fantasy. Despite my best intentions, I find myself returning his grin. "Maybe later we can play that out."

"All work and no play." His blue eyes shine with mirth. "You know what they say about that."

"That is why it's called *work*, Hercules." Though now that we're talking about it, it's sounding like one hell of an idea. I shouldn't start breaking rules the second I lay them out. I really shouldn't.

Before I can walk back on my declaration of keeping work and fucking separate, he says, "Hades told me I'm not allowed to fuck you so I suppose I'll have to follow at least some of the rules."

I blink. "What?"

"I spoke with him this morning. He was pretty damn clear that my cock isn't allowed anywhere near your pussy until he gives permission." He shrugs. "Though he left the rest of it up for interpretation."

I may have had the same order from Hades, but the idea of them negotiating what Hercules can and can't do with me has fury fanning deep inside my chest. All my amusement, all my desire, turns to ash inside me in the wake of it. I want to hurt them both, to do something to make them reevaluate how easily they trade me as a favor between them. It doesn't matter what Hades has said about us seducing Hercules together; in light of his actions, it couldn't be clearer that *he* means to seduce the man himself, using me as a tool when it suits him.

I've played the part of tool before. I have no interest in playing it again. Hades must know that. Surely he hasn't forgotten so much in his quest for his endgame. Surely...

But I can't be certain. Not anymore.

I sit back. "Why you, Hercules? That's what I don't get. He's had people who have caught his eye over the years, but nothing like this. I just don't understand."

He opens his mouth, but seems to reconsider his next words. "Why don't you ask him?"

"As if it were that simple." I give him a mirthless smile. "He won't tell me."

"Are you sure?"

Just like that, I realize the truth. Hercules knows exactly why Hades picked him out of the crowd. *Hercules* knows and I do not. I absently rub my chest, grinding away at the ache there. No reason to feel this hurt. It isn't as if being shut out by Hades is a new development. I should be used to it by now. I just assumed he wasn't willing to open up to *anyone*, so it didn't sting so badly that he wouldn't open up to me. Apparently it isn't the truth.

"Meg?" From the worried tone in his voice, Hercules has said my name more than once.

"I'm fine." I turn back to my computer, but I can't quite focus on the screen. It keeps blurring across my vision. I blink a few times, but it doesn't help.

"Meg." His voice sounds closer. He rounds the desk and, after the briefest of hesitations, takes my hand and pulls me to my feet. And then I'm in his arms and he's holding me tightly. "Don't cry, Meg. It's okay. Everything will be okay."

"I'm not crying." Even as I say the words, wetness trails down my cheeks. "I'm fine."

"Meg." He tightens his grip, practically crushing me to his chest. "Fuck, I'm sorry."

I should push away, should tell him I can stand on my own, but I don't. I just rest my cheek on his chest and let him hold me. "You have nothing to be sorry for."

"Yeah, it doesn't feel that way. I've been fucking up ever since I got here." He laughs harshly. "I've been fucking up a lot longer than that, if I'm honest."

"Hercules…"

He strokes a rough hand over my hair. "All I wanted was to help you, and it feels like all I've done is make your life harder."

He's not exactly wrong, but he's also taking all the blame when there's more than enough to go around. I shouldn't have seduced him in the first place as part of a game with me and Hades. Hades shouldn't have used us both as pawns without communicating his plans. A whole lot of *shouldn't*. "I guess I should apologize too." My voice is watery and rough, and I hate the weakness it represents. The crack in my armor.

"What a mess we are."

"You can say that again."

He lifts me and carries me back to the chair on the other side of the desk, sitting with me curled in his lap. Again, I know I should stop this. Again, I don't. I let him hold me, let him comfort me, even though I don't deserve it. "What did you mean before? When you said you've been fucking up a lot longer?"

He takes a careful breath, and I wonder if he's going to lie to me. But Hercules just rests his chin on the top of my head and exhales. "My father hurt a woman. I found out and tried to make things right. I just thought if the truth came out, then he would be punished for the harm he did her. I didn't realize I'd be putting *her* reputation on trial more than his. He traumatized her, but I'm the one who ruined her life. I told her I could protect her, and then I wasn't able to." I start to sit up, but he tightens his hold on me. "Please don't try to comfort me. I don't deserve it."

It doesn't take much to read between the lines and know what kind of harm his father delivered that would put his victim's reputation on trial. "You were dumb to think that it would play out any other way than how it did, especially if you father has any power."

He makes a choked sound. "Thanks, Meg. That's very helpful."

I lift my head. "But that doesn't mean you're to blame. You tried to make things right. It blew up in your face, but you tried and that counts for something."

He looks so goddamn upset. Those blue eyes hold horrors in a way they never have in the other times we've talked. "I appreciate you saying it, but it doesn't count for shit."

I know how I would have handled that situation. I know

how Hades would have. In that, we are too much alike, perhaps. No matter how powerful, we would have taken the bastard down. The only difference is that Hades would have required a deal to put things into motion. I don't know if telling Hercules that he should have sought justice outside of the system is helpful. Probably not.

I cup his jaw. "What happened to her?"

He looks at me, but he's not seeing me. "She ended up dropping the charges. She just wanted to get out of town, to break fully from everything connected to what happened. I gave her as much money as she'd take and promised never to look for her." Hercules shakes his head. "I should have done something more."

Easy enough to follow this to the next step. "So that's why you left."

"That's why I left."

Noble or stupid? I honestly don't know. Maybe he could have done more good back in that place, fighting against the powers that be. Maybe. I'm not about to judge cutting his losses and leaving. I walked away from my entire life and all my future plans for a man who threw me away like trash the second he got what he wanted from me. And after I fell for Hades, I never once considered leaving, not with any kind of intent. Does that make me a coward for being content to live in his shadow? I don't know. I honestly don't know. Because I have no answers, I do the only thing that makes sense.

I kiss Hercules.

He tastes like mint and something surprisingly sweet, and after a moment of shock, he returns the kiss with interest. The man might be submissive but he's all enthusiasm as he slips his fingers into my hair and tugs until he's able to deepen our kiss, to tease my mouth open. To claim me, just a little, just right now. To *connect*.

It's not enough. I knew it wouldn't be the second our lips

touched. I want that connection as much as he does, want the purity Hercules brings to every interaction. He hides nothing. It doesn't even occur to him to try. After a decade with Hades, it's refreshing in a way that goes straight to my head.

I straddle him and the new position makes my shift dress ride up. Hercules strokes his hands down my back and squeezes my ass, urging me to grind against him. He's hard, all thick and long and full of promise. Exactly what I need. I reach down to the front of his pants, but he catches my wrist. "No, Meg."

"Excuse me?"

"Hades—"

Oh, for fuck's sake. The reminder stings. I yank my hand away from him. "Do you always do what you're told?"

The guilt on his face confirms it even before he says, "This time, I do."

The reminder is a slap in the face. I was willing to suffer whatever punishment Hades dreams up for his command. Apparently the same can't be said for Hercules. He might say he came here for me, but he stayed for Hades. I see the way Hercules watches him, recognize it on a soul-deep level. He's caught in Hades's gravitational pull. He's not the first, and he won't be the last. There is absolutely no reason for that to sting. And yet it does. "So much for that shining armor you're so fond of. You're just as bad as the rest of us."

I climb off him, but he catches my wrist again. "That's not fair."

"No, it's not, but I'm not in the mood to be fair right now." The lost feeling from last night washes over me again. I'm just a raw nerve right now, not good company for anyone. That seems to be the rule, rather than the exception, these days. "Please leave."

"Meg." Now censure creeps into his tone. "We have a job to do."

The sudden urge to scream and throw things washes over me. I have to close my eyes and breathe through it. I am *Megaera*, Queen of the fucking Underworld. I do not indulge in petty temper tantrums. It takes far longer than it should to wind myself back into something resembling calm. A facade, and not even a good one, but it'll have to do.

I carefully put my desk between us and sink into my chair. Hercules is still sporting a cockstand for the ages, but I ignore it. The room feels too small with him in it, but I ignore that too. I've never been claustrophobic, but right now the entire city feels too damn small. There isn't enough air, enough space, enough *freedom.*

I turn my monitor so he can see it. When I speak, my voice actually sounds normal. "These are the numbers from last night. Tink—and now you—are aware of them, but ultimately the books are my responsibility." *For now.* I ignore the insidious little voice inside me and continue. "Most mornings, Tink and I meet to discuss the information the staff gathered the night before. We have files on all the major players in Carver City, and it's in everyone's best interest if we know as many of their dirty secrets as possible."

"Who are the major players of Carver City?"

I might laugh if I didn't want to strangle both him and Hades for putting me in this position. I'm not a goddamn kindergarten teacher, and I might resent it less without Hades's clear hand of manipulation in all this. If he'd just *talk* to me, instead of forcing me to backflip through his hoops.

I pull out a laminated map that I keep in my locked desk drawer. It's an archaic way to keep track of things, but Hades is old school and sometimes the lines shift enough that it's actually useful. I unfold it and point. "This is Carver City."

Hercules takes in the red lines I've painstakingly marked, finally focusing on the little square in the center. It's only a couple of city blocks, but it represents safety in a way I don't think he can comprehend. He points to it. "This is the Underworld."

"Yes. Hades's territory, but for all intents and purposes, it's neutral territory for everyone else. They can visit the club without worrying about power plays and murder attempts, at least for the most part. These belong to others." I touch each of the slice in turn. They were in varying sizes and shapes, marked out with blood and violence in some cases, with deals and threats in others. "You will see their leaders and generals in here at one time or another. I'll get you copies of the files on them, but it's important that you don't do anything to fuck with their coming here. We can't gather knowledge if it's not given within this space. We don't send our people into their territories. It *has* to happen in the Underworld, and it can't if they're not here. Do you understand?"

"Yes."

I don't know that I trust him with this. He's still so new, he practically shines. The fact that Hades wants him trained up under Tink would blow my mind if I let myself think about it too hard. Tink's skills are hard-won, and she had most of them before she was put in the position to make a deal with Hades. Training her was just a matter of refining them a little and pointing her in the right direction. Hercules is another creature entirely. "That's enough for now."

He blinks those big blue eyes at me. "What?" He has the audacity to sound hurt, and I hate that I want to smooth his pain away at the expense of my own. He's an adult, and his actions have consequences just like the rest of us.

"I'll have someone drop off the files. Study them like your life depends on it. It might." When he doesn't immediately move, I dig my nails into my palms, striving to keep my growing emotional bullshit out of my voice. "Hercules. Please leave."

He studies me for a long moment and finally nods. "I'll fix this."

I don't ask what he means. In the end, it won't matter. "Some things aren't capable of being fixed. The faster you figure that out, the faster you'll get ahead in life."

CHAPTER 16

HERCULES

J'm half expecting Tink when someone knocks a little while after I return to my suite, but when I open the door, it's a striking Black woman with a mass of braids piled on her head. She sweeps a look over me and shrugs. "You're pretty, but I don't think you're pretty enough to be causing all this drama."

"Thanks?"

"It wasn't a compliment." She shoves a laptop at me. "Don't take this out of your room. The sensitive material on it can't leave the property. I don't think I have to tell you what will happen if you try something."

Nothing good. So far, nothing about this situation has gone like I expected, but I don't think for a second that Hades would allow me to pass on privileged information without recourse. I don't know what *kind* of recourse, but it doesn't matter. I have no intention of sharing it. Even if I did, I have no one to share it with. "I'll keep it in my room."

"Glad we got that sorted." She points at herself. "Allecto. I run security. You have any problems, you come to me or one of my people. *You* become a problem, I deal with you. Got it?"

"Got it," I say faintly. Tink had mentioned security, but because I wasn't currently allowed into the back rooms of the club where the intense play went on, I had put it from my mind until later. It was enough to know that Hades protects his people.

"Then we shouldn't have any issues." She frowned at me. "Don't know what he was thinking bringing you in." She shook her head and walked away.

I step back into my suite and close the door. Allecto's thoughts aren't anything that haven't been echoed back to me by multiple people since I arrived here. I get it. I don't fit in. I have to be trained from the ground up in a way that none of the other employees seem to require. It didn't make sense before, the reason why Hades would drag me into a lifetime deal. Now that I have some distance—now that I know it's because of Zeus—I understand it a whole lot better.

Seems fitting that I should suffer for the sins of my father. Seems almost like penance after how things fell out with Leda. I couldn't save her, couldn't stand up to him no matter how hard I tried. If there were others…

I stalk to the couch and drop the laptop there. Of course there were others. My father has hardly been a paragon of virtue, only to break character with Leda. There were others. There must have been.

Thirty years ago, one of the victims of my father's sadistic nature was apparently Hades's son.

I wish I knew more. What happened in that situation. What happened in the wake of it. Did Zeus kill him? The thought makes me sick to my stomach. I wish I could rule out my father being a murderer, but he's a rapist and has no problem committing assault. Why not murder as well? Would knowing the truth even matter? As Hades said, it happened before I was even born. It has nothing to do with me.

Until now.

Then there's Meg. It's obvious Hades didn't tell her his reasoning or his plans, and the fact that I knew even part of it hurt her. She covered her reaction up quickly, but I saw it all the same. I had assumptions about those two when I first came here and now, less than forty-eight hours in, I'm having to question all of them. They present a united front, but the closer I get, the more the cracks in their relationship start looking like canyons. It's none of my business. I should know by now to stay out of shit that doesn't concern me.

But when I stood between them, things felt more stable, like I was fixing something broken. It might be all in my head, but I can't shake the feeling that there's something there beneath the games and bullshit and plotting. Or there could be if we gave it a chance. Maybe. I don't have answers now, and I likely won't anytime soon, not with Meg and Hades's respective walls built sky-high. Tormenting myself by playing what-if is a recipe for disaster.

To distract myself, I open the laptop and turn it on. Tonight will be another gauntlet to run, and knowledge is the only weapon available to me currently. It won't pave the way for me to have the upper hand—I'm not delusional—but it might mean I don't drown quite as quickly when faced with something outside my realm of experience.

The desktop is clear except for a line of six folders. I click through the first and find five more folders labeled *Gaeton, Malone, Hook, Beast, the Man in Black*. I blink. These must be pseudonyms. I click into the first one and find a list of Gaeton's alliances and enemies—he answers to the Man in Black and has a note that he and Beast can't be left alone together in the club without concern for damages to the property. There's also a brief history and a list of kinks and favorite submissives. I click through more files, finding similar information compiled in each. Some of them are significantly longer than others, but it's a lot of information to process.

I sit back. No wonder Hades is so formidable. He knows the secrets of all the major players in this city. Knowledge worth killing over and they had passed it along willingly because he's allowing them to play out their deepest fantasies within these walls. It's brilliant.

I manage a nap and wake up with plenty of time to shower again and grab something out of my closet for my shift tonight. All the work clothing is in line with the shorts from last night—light on fabric and tight enough to leave nothing to the imagination. I decide on a pair of black shorts that shine like leather but are made of some kind of stretchy fabric. There are little rhinestones in a row down each side and they wink every time I move.

It feels strange to walk mostly naked to the elevator and take it up to the club floor, but I suppose I'll get used to it given enough time. I walk into the employee back room and the first person I see is Aurora. She's wearing white again, an elaborate lingerie set that looks like something a bride would wear on her wedding night. She grins when she sees me. "Hey, Hercules."

"Hey."

"Since Tink isn't here tonight, you're with me for the first part of your shift. Then Meg will take over like last night."

My stomach clenches at the thought of seeing her again after how things fell out earlier. I have an apology to give, and I'm not even sure how to make it right. I thought I was starting to understand the rules, but with Meg the edges blur. This morning, I didn't want to stop until I had her bent over the desk and my cock sheathed to the hilt. I wanted to fuck her until she came, until we were so lost in each other that nothing else mattered. But it's not just us engaged in this dance, and it doesn't feel like something as

KATEE ROBERT

simple as breaking the rules to go against Hades's command.

I don't know. I just don't know.

"Hercules?" Aurora takes a step closer. She's tiny in a way that makes me feel like one wrong move would break her. The look on her face is anything but meek, though. She frowns up at me. "What's wrong?"

"I don't understand this." I have to swallow the words before I blurt out everything. What's going on between Hades and Meg and me is our business, but it feels like they're playing on a different game board than I am. Like they're playing an entirely different fucking game. I would ask Tink if she were here, but she's not. I scrub my hands over my face. "We're submissives, right?"

"Yes."

"So a Dom gives you an order."

Aurora holds up a finger. "A couple caveats before you keep going. We don't answer to all Doms. We answer to ours and the ones we're in a scene with. That's it. It's not a blanket rule."

Am I Hades's? It sure as fuck feels like it. But it feels like I'm Meg's too, and that's where things get confusing. "Okay. So *your* Dom gives you an order. Is breaking it really so bad?"

"Every relationship is different. Some subs—like Tink—are brats. They get off on pushing against the boundaries and breaking the rules and mouthing off. The Doms they partner with usually *also* get off on that sort of thing. That's not how I operate. It makes me uncomfortable to act out like that." She shrugs. "Your mileage may vary."

"That...doesn't really help." The deeper I get into this world, the more I'm realizing that there aren't any hard and fast rules beyond consent of all parties. That's it. The scope it is staggering if I let myself think too hard about it.

Sympathy flashes in her dark eyes. "Look at it a different

130

way. He gave you an order. You obviously thought about disobeying it, even if you didn't. What would it feel like if you *did* go through with it?"

My stomach turns even as my skin heats. I regretted rejecting Meg the second I did it. If I could go back… "Conflicted."

She smiles. "A lot of this stuff is feeling your way, especially if you're in something more intense than a single scene. Talk to him about it. Or her. Or whoever. Communication is everything."

"Thanks." I manage a smile of my own. "How long have you been working in the Underworld?"

"A little over a year now." Her expression dims. "Hades helped me out when I needed it the most."

Another deal on his part, though at least this one appears to have benefited the person working here. I don't ask her the details of it. Deals seem to be a private thing, and I'm not really willing to go into my reasons either. I take a deep breath. "Should we get out there?"

"Yeah." She starts for the door. "The others will be along shortly, but we can make the rounds and get drinks started."

Working with Aurora is as different from working with Tink as day from night. I enjoy her company quite a bit, but I find myself missing Tink's snark. We fall into a comfortable rhythm of transporting drinks from Tis at the bar to the various customers who filter into the club as the night goes on. I recognize several of the people from the file Allecto delivered, and I try to pay closer attention to them, but before long, the room is packed and it's everything I can do to keep up with the orders.

I'm firmly in my head as I move to clear a table that's been abandoned by two women who have gone through the door that leads to the public playroom and the individual themed rooms. Tink dragged me through there on my first day when it was empty, so I'm a little blurry on the actual details, but if this room is where people come to socialize, those rooms are where they come to play.

I turn around and nearly run into a man standing there. For a second, I forget I'm supposed to keep my eyes down and look directly at him. Hook. One of the people Meg and Hades keep a file on. He looks like a fucking pirate. His medium brown skin is broken by a diamond nose piercing and a trio of golden rings circling his upper ears on each side. His long dark hair is pulled back from his face in some kind of ponytail thing and he's got a perfectly groomed beard that parts as he gives me a wicked smile. I swear his dark eyes actually twinkle at me. "Look what we have here."

I remember to drop my gaze, which gives me a good look at his tattooed bare chest and the leather pants that are tight enough to leave absolutely nothing to the imagination. "Would you like a drink?"

"Nothing for me." He reaches out and gives the green ring attached to my collar a gentle tug. I feel it all the way down to my cock. Hook makes a humming noise. "How long until you're up for grabs?"

My skin goes warm beneath his gaze, and I know I must be blushing a brilliant red. "I don't know." It strikes me that Hades might order me to fuck other people the same way he orders Meg to fuck other people. Before coming here, the idea felt foreign and almost repulsive. Now that I'm beginning to understand the parameters and push and pull of their —our—relationship, my feelings are less concrete.

"Guess I'll have to keep my eye on you then." He gives me another flash of bright white teeth against his dark beard. "You're a pretty thing, little sub. And you blush so nicely." He doesn't touch me anywhere but the ring, which hardly counts as touching *me*, but it feels like he's run his hands all over my body when he uses that tone of voice. It's disconcerting to say the least. I can't stop fucking blushing. Hook chuckles, the warm sound somehow making this whole conversation more unbearable in the best way possible. "What's your name?"

"Hercules."

He gives the collar one last tug and drops his hand. I note that he's got three rings on his right hand and another two on his left. "Don't look now, but you're about to be rescued from big, bad me."

That surprises me enough to glance where he jerks his chin. I follow the movement to see the last person I expect to be bearing down on us. "Tink?"

"I told you to stay out of trouble." She's wearing a bra, panties, and a garter belt that attaches to thigh-high stockings, all in green. Her heels give her a few extra inches and she uses to them to her advantage to step between me and Hook. "And *you*. You know better than to terrorize new subbies."

"Hey, Tink." He's still grinning, but his eyes have gone intense with something like hatred. Or lust. I'm not really sure. Hook leans back and makes a show of taking her in. "Long time, no see."

"Not long enough." She points a finger at him. "Act right."

"Brat." He says the word like he relishes it. "You want to keep me away from your precious Hercules? *You* could come play."

"Pass." She laughs in his face. "I'd rather chew off my arm."

I tense, expecting him to... I don't know. React badly. Puff up. Some guys take rejection like it's a personal challenge. Tink might be my superior, but she's still a woman who's a good foot shorter than both of us. The Underworld's security is too far away to step in if this goes sideways.

But Hook surprises me. He laughs, a great booming

sound that turns heads around us. "One of these days, you'll say yes."

"Hold your breath. Please. It would leave more air for the rest of us."

Another of those big laughs and Hook tips an imaginary hat to both of us. "Be seeing you." He ambles off toward the other end of the bar.

Tink immediately turns to me and glares. "What the hell are you doing?"

"We were just talking." I sound defensive, but I can't help it.

"You were blushing when you were *just talking* with him and you're blushing now." She gives me a long look. "Hook is trouble."

I gathered that from the file, but meeting him in person is something else altogether. "He's more charming than I expected."

"Yeah, he is. When he wants to be." She pokes my chest with a single finger. "Go find Meg. It's about time for the first part of your shift to be over, and I'm not going to be able to relax and enjoy myself if I'm worried about you doing something stupid."

"Aw, Tink, I could almost believe you cared."

She glares harder, but her bright red lips curve up a bit at the edges like she's fighting a smile. "Don't let it go to your head."

"I won't. Promise."

She swats my arm. "Meg. Now."

"Yes, ma'am." I laugh a little at her responding curse and turn to survey the room. I know Meg is in here somewhere because I caught a glimpse of her earlier. She avoided me and I had drink orders to fill, so I haven't hunted her down to talk. I still don't know what I'm supposed to say. Hades gave an order, and I followed it. I don't understand her feeling hurt over that, but maybe it's all tied up in *him* more than it is in me. Either way, we have to talk about it, and now's as good a time as any.

I find her in a corner booth with a couple. I know these two too. Jafar and Jasmine. She's the head of one of the territories in Carver City, and he's her right-hand man and lover. Jafar has medium brown skin and a close-cropped beard, and he sits in the booth as if he owns the entire thing. His relaxed posture doesn't cover up the predatory look in his dark eyes, but you'd have to be paying attention to notice it. He watches Meg and Jasmine, but seems content not to participate.

Jasmine is gorgeous in a flawless kind of way that makes me almost uncomfortable. I never would have the balls to walk up to her if we met under different circumstances. She's got light brown skin and a mass of wavy dark brown hair. She's sitting between Meg and Jafar, and leaning hard on Meg, her lips are parted and her breasts about to fall out of her tiny red dress with each ragged inhale. Even before I reach the table, I know what I'll see, and sure enough, the proximity reveals Meg's hand up her skirt.

Meg barely looks at me as she keeps finger-fucking Jasmine. "Hercules."

I don't know where to look. It seems rude to ogle the movement of Meg's hand under the red fabric, but my gaze keeps dropping there despite myself. Meg makes it worse when she leans back and uses her free hand to tug down the top of Jasmine's dress a little, just enough that I can see her brown nipples. I clear my throat and jerk my gaze up. Right to Jafar's amused dark eyes. His lips quirk. "And they call me cruel."

For a second, I think he's talking to me, but Meg responds easily. "It's because you're a man. No matter what I do, they like to see me as nurturing."

"Silly them."

She gives me a sharp smile and then focuses on Jasmine. "Come for me, pretty girl. I have a long night ahead of me, and your pussy clenching around my fingers when you come is going to get me through it."

I'm blushing again, but it's not desire. It's a toxic combination of embarrassment and anger. Meg might not be putting this show on for me—I'm not delusional—but she's allowing it to be punishment in its own way. I cross my arms over my chest. "By all means, take your fucking time."

For the first time since I walked up to the table, she lets what she's really feeling filter into her blue eyes. Anger. Hurt. Desire. "Don't worry, *little Hercules*. I will."

CHAPTER 17

MEG

*T*he words barely leave my mouth when Jafar intervenes. He catches my wrist and carefully extracts my hand from between Jasmine's thighs. "That's about enough of that." He gives me a long look. "Go deal with your shit, Meg. She's not your toy to use to prove a point."

I start to protest that I know that, that Jasmine's special to me, even if it's a friendship that occasionally allows for insanely hot fucking. But ultimately, he's her Dom and he's right. I might have started this little tease with her at the center of my motivation, but the second Hercules walked up, everything shifted.

Jafar readjusts Jasmine's dress to cover her breasts. She makes a protesting sound, but he leans down and gives her a quick kiss. "We'll go to your favorite room in back."

"The study?" Just like that, she doesn't seem all that concerned that I left her hanging. She twists to face him fully. "Right now?"

"Yes, baby girl. Right now."

I scoot out of the booth and move so they can do the same. Something akin to jealousy sours my stomach as Jafar

137

takes Jasmine's hand and leads her to the door that will take them deeper into the Underworld. They're headed to the private room designed just like an upscale study, but if I know them—and I do—they'll allow for an audience. If Jafar is in the mood, maybe even some outside participation. He knows what Jasmine wants, what she needs, and he never hesitates to provide.

"Meg."

I forget, for half a second, that Hercules stands at my side. A living reminder of how little control I have in my own life, of how little my needs matter. Hades plays his games. Hercules obeys, no matter the cost. Where does that leave me? Scrambling to patch up the heart that Hades keeps shredding, over and over again. Every time he turns away instead of reaching out to me, it's like Declan abandoning me but a thousand times worse because I was infatuated with Declan. I love Hades. I love him so much I stay despite the tiny cuts he deals out during every conversation, unintentionally or not. I swallow hard, hating the burning in my throat. "Let's go."

Another night, another scene with Hades as he draws Hercules deeper. I shouldn't resent the man walking at my back for holding so much of my lover's attention, but it's hard not to feel like they're leaving me out in the cold. Maybe not physically, but emotionally. I should be used to it by now. Hades and I are too broken. We guard our jagged pieces like junkyard dogs with their dubious treasure. I can't remember the last time I let myself be truly vulnerable, so I guess I'm as much to blame as he is. That knowledge doesn't cheer me in the least.

Hercules doesn't speak until he closes the door to Hades's public office behind us. "You're mad at me."

Mad. Hurt. Too raw to admit to any of it. It's not fair to be angry with Hercules for being privy to a part of Hades that used to be mine alone. Maybe it's not even fair to be angry with Hades about it, either. Relationships change. Maybe I'm the one to blame, the one who's too stubborn and stupid to let go of something that's no longer working. The one hanging on when it's pretty damn obvious I'm being replaced.

I sound more tired than angry when I say, "Hardly. You're being a good little submissive. The best Hades could ask for. Who am I to complain?"

"Don't do that."

"Don't do what?"

He touches my shoulder. Of course he does. Requesting, always polite to the bitter end. Never grabbing, never demanding. I want to rail against him, but it's just who Hercules is. I allow him to turn me to face him, and then I can't help but drink in the sight of him. His body is sun-kissed carved stone, and it's revealed in all its glory by the tiny shorts that barely cover his cock and ass. The collar around his thick neck thrills me even as I tell myself not to feel that way.

He's not mine, not really.

He belongs to Hades.

I finally get to his blue eyes, and I rock back on my heels at the anger in them. Hercules drops his hand from my shoulder. "What the fuck was that?"

"What the fuck was *what?*"

"I know you're pissed about earlier, but shoving Jasmine in my face felt shitty."

A curious static rolls over my thoughts. I straighten. "What makes you think my finger-fucking Jasmine has anything to do with you whatsoever? I wanted her. End of story."

"Maybe it started out that way. But the second I showed up, you did it to punish me. To hurt me."

139

He's a little right, but I'm not about to admit it. "I hate to be the one to have to explain this to you, but not everything I do has the slightest thing to do with you."

But he's not listening. Hercules leans down, his expression intent. "You're furious at me."

Something snaps in my chest. All my years of learning to control my words and expressions and this man cuts through my efforts without even trying. Anyone else in this building would be content to let me have my masks. *Hades* is content to let me lie when it suits him, to lock away the messy emotions.

Not Hercules. He just keeps poking and prodding until I feel like I'm going mad with it. I drag my fingers through my hair. "Of course I'm furious at you, you asshole! You *rejected* me, and it hurt." The truth, stark and startling, colors the air between us.

"There you are." He doesn't move back, but some of his anger seems to abate. "I was following orders, Meg."

Now that I've let slip a little transparency, I can't seem to stop. "That's bullshit. You chose Hades over me. *That's* what you were doing."

He jerks like I've struck him. "Is that what you really think?"

"That's what really happened, so yes, Hercules, that's exactly what I think. Because it's the truth."

He studies me, suddenly looking steadier than I've seen him since we met. Hercules shakes his head. "You're upset about the rejection, but it's more than that."

Damn him. Damn him for seeing me even when I don't want him to. I take a step back, but I can't stop the words that are pressing against the inside of my lips. Words not meant for him, but that doesn't seem to matter. "He's replacing me."

"*What?*"

My damn eyes are burning again, but I won't let a single tear fall. "Hades told you what his plans are."

Guilt flares on his expressive face. "Not exactly."

"But he told you why he picked you."

"Yes."

It's nothing more than I already suspected, nothing more than he'd already confirmed, but each word is a blow to my crumbling walls. I feel like a fool for thinking Hades and I could fix our relationship while Hades was scouring for someone to fill the shoes I used to walk in. "It's been *years* since Hades told me even that much. He lets you in when he shuts me out. Hard to misconstrue that."

He's already shaking his head before the last word is out of my mouth. "You're wrong. He loves you."

"He used to." I take a step back. "I'm going to go. You and Hades can continue your little love fest without using me as a buffer."

A buffer. That's exactly what I am to them. A way for Hades to avoid admitting that he wants Hercules. A way for Hercules to keep his pride even though he wants Hades back just as much. As soon as they get past that particular hurdle, they won't need me at all and they'll discard me just like Declan did.

I. Am. Done.

I manage one step before Hercules's big hand closes around my upper arm. "Wait."

"Fuck off."

He hauls me to a stop. "You're not a buffer."

"Sweet of you to say, but that's bullshit." The burning in my throat is back, stronger than before. I have to get out of here, and I have to do it now. "Let go, Hercules."

"What's your safe word?"

The question shocks me to stillness. I look up into his face, but this man is nothing like the one I've dealt with to date. He's downright forbidding. Something in my stomach flips over in a way that isn't entirely unpleasant. "Cerberus," I whisper.

He jerks me to him, the momentum slamming me against his chest. There's no chance to catch my footing because he takes my mouth as if he has every right to it. There's no tenderness here, just a special kind of brutality that's so much better. He bands one arm across my lower back and drags me backward to Hades's desk. I barely get a second to register his intentions when he lifts me onto the desk. "Hercules, wait."

He hesitates, but seems to remember that no isn't really a no. Not when you play like we do. His expression goes wild and almost desperate, and he shoves up my short skirt and pushes my legs wide. "I want you, Meg. I fucking care about you. If you won't listen to my words, then you *will* listen to my body as I fuck you senseless." He steps between my thighs and stops. "Condom."

Now's the time to put the brakes on. To stop this before Hades shows up, because this is *not* explicitly sanctioned.

I can't remember the last time someone wanted me enough to lose control, to throw caution to the wind and ignore the consequences. It's a heady feeling, and I don't want it to stop. I don't want *him* to stop. I need this connection more than I can put into words.

I reach up with a shaking hand and cup Hercules's hard jaw. "Your tests came back today. You're good. I am too, and I'm on birth control."

His eyes go dark. "No condom?"

"No condom," I whisper.

I wrap a fist around his cock and drag him across my pussy. Teasing us both. Spreading my wetness around. I can't help making a frustrated noise even though I'm the one responsible. I wasn't sure I wanted to cross this line, but now that we're dancing across the point of no return, I want it *now*. Hercules seems to feel the same way. He covers my hand with his and notches his cock at my entrance. He holds my gaze as he pushes into me in a smooth, steady move. Not slow enough for my body to fully adjust, but not harshly either. My breath catches in my throat.

"I should thank Jasmine."

I blink up at him. "What?"

He pulls out just a little and catches the backs of my thighs. As he thrusts back into me, he jerks me forward to the very edge of the desk, sending his cock impossibly deep. "Playing with her got you ready for me."

I have no intention of indulging this thread of conversation, but somehow I find myself asking, "Does it bother you? Me with other people?" I don't want his answer to matter, but it does.

There's so much raw emotion on his face that I almost look away. It's too much. Too honest. "Only when you do it intentionally to hurt me."

My breath whooshes out, and then there's no more space for words between us. Hercules presses me back onto the deck and begins to move, fucking me in long, sure strokes. We should be all furtive movements and frenzied orgasms, but he seems intent on doing this on his own timeline and somehow that makes it a thousand times hotter. I reach over my head and cling to the edge of the desk, bracing myself so I can rise to meet his thrusts.

I don't even hear the door open. I don't realize we're no longer alone until Hades's low chuckle coats the space around us, constricting the office and threatening to suffocate me. Hercules freezes mid-thrust. His blue eyes go wide, and we both turn to find Hades leaning against the door with his hands in his pockets.

He raises an eyebrow. "Don't stop on my account."

There's no amusement in his tone. It's cold. So fucking cold. Retribution is coming, and my traitorous heart is thrilled by it. Maybe I shouldn't love these painful games with Hades, but I can't seem to help myself. His punishments are just as much proof of his love as his rewards are. No matter how angry I am at him in any given moment, I still crave his attention with all the ferocity of a flower craving the sun. It's a desperation I don't know how to banish. In my darkest moments, I can admit that I don't want to.

Hercules's hand spasms on my hip. "Hades—"

He pushes off the door, and my heart crashes in my chest at the sight of him stalking toward us. The warning is all in his smooth movements, in the way his dark eyes take in every detail of this scene, of the way we've both intentionally broken his command. "Hercules." He speaks softly. "If you don't finish fucking her, I'm going to take her out into the public play room and let anyone who's interested do it for you. Your choice."

He will. He's done it before, and I've loved every second of it. There's something so incredibly freeing in Hades choosing for me, in his allowing others to act the part of his will with their hands and mouths and cocks. Even when pleasure becomes too much, when I beg for it to stop, he takes me to the very edge before he brings me down. I know this game.

Hercules doesn't.

He grips my shoulder and drives into me again. Harder. Deeper. Fucking me just shy of violently. His expression is tormented and yet he watches my face with an intensity that has me sliding closer to orgasm. Punishing me the same way Hades will punish us shortly. I love it. I reach down with one hand and stroke my clit, a light touch that contrasts with his rough thrusts. Pleasure rises in a wave and I turn my head enough to see Hades too. He's taken a seat on the couch and watches us with a still expression that does nothing to mask the heat in his eyes.

I'm so close…

Hercules pulls out of me and yanks me off the desk. I have a moment of vertigo as he hauls me around the desk and bends me over it. I understand immediately. From this new angle, we can both hold Hades's gaze. Hercules kicks my feet wide and then he's inside me again. I moan and thrust back against him, taking him deeper yet. He runs a hand down my spine, hot and possessive, and I know without a shadow of a doubt that he's glaring at Hades as if he can truly mark his territory on me like this. It doesn't work that way. Hades owns both of us. But I enjoy being the bone between them, just in this moment, just in this scene.

Hades leans forward and props his elbows on his knees, watching closely. "Are you trying to prove a point, little Hercules?"

Hercules snakes a hand around my hip and strokes my clit, touching me softly there even as he drives into me. "Giving you a show, *Sir*. That's what you wanted, isn't it?" He sounds like he's speaking through clenched teeth.

Maybe I was wrong. Hercules didn't know how to play the game when he arrived a few days ago, but he's learning fast. My pleasure coils tighter and tighter. I want to hold out, to spin out this moment between the three of us forever so we never have to reach the other side and the pain that awaits us there. An impossible feat. Hercules presses hard on my clit and my orgasm hits me with a strength that leaves me breathless. My mind goes blessedly, perfectly blank. I cry out and slam back into him, determined to take him with me. Apparently he has the same idea. His strokes go short and rougher yet, and then he's growling my name and grinding into me as he comes.

"Now we can begin."

I lift my cheek from the desk, not even sure when I dropped my head to the cool wood. "Should I say sorry?"

"You're not sorry." Hades pushes to his feet and stalks around the desk to us. "My orders are not complicated, you two. In fact, I laid down exactly one instruction and you managed to disobey it within twelve hours. I would be impressed if I weren't so disappointed."

Hercules presses a kiss to the back of my neck and slides out of me. "It was my fault."

"Of that, I have my doubts." Hades snaps his fingers and Hercules moves to kneel at his feet. He barely looks at the man as he continues toward me. "My Meg is quite the troublemaker."

I force my limbs to move and shift to sit on the desk. "More like I'm just craving your attention." I don't mean to say it. Instead of coming out bratty, the words have a ring of truth that bares me to my very soul.

My dress is still up around my hips, and I know I look a mess. I hold Hades's gaze as he closes the distance between us. He gives me a small smile. "Have fun, love?"

Fun? This little tango I'm doing with the two of them is many things, but I wouldn't call it fun. A week ago, I would have smiled and made a biting response. I don't have it in me tonight. I lift my chin. "He gave me what I need."

Hades goes still at that. His dark eyes take in every bit of me, seeming to dig beneath my skin, though muscle and bone, to my very soul. "Did he?" he says slowly.

Alarms peal through my head, but I've gone too far to back down. "You've been focused on other things." Things he's not including me in. Plans that he no longer details out for me with relish. He's shut me out and we both know it. I want so desperately for that not to be the case. I can't quite manage to voice those words, but I tell him with my eyes.

Hades reads me better than anyone. He has to see all the things I can't make myself speak aloud. He *has* to.

"Ah, Meg." He smooths my hair back with both hands and lets them linger on my shoulders, caressing my collarbones. Something soft and warm flares in his gaze, there and gone so fast I'm half sure I imagine it. "Who do you think set Hercules on the path that ended up with him here, throwing caution to the wind for you and you alone?"

I expect him to say a lot of things. This doesn't number among them. "What?"

Hades's smile is more than a little bittersweet, but it's *real*. "I meant it when I said he was a gift, love. Your gift." He brushes his thumb across my bottom lip. "A peace offering, if you will."

The implications of his words have me shaking down to my very center. Emotions flick through me, too fast to settle on just one. "What are you saying?"

He reaches down to the hem of my dress and pulls it carefully over my head. "Tonight is yours, Meg. Just yours."

CHAPTER 18

HADES

*I*f I was a different man, I would have told Meg my purpose for Hercules from the very beginning. I've made more than a few mistakes with her in recent years. Such is the nature of life. Even the best of us, the ones with the farthest reach, are still bumbling through it as best we can. I've hurt her. She's carrying a wound that *I* dealt, unwittingly or not. A wound I'm incapable of healing on my own.

But I'm not on my own anymore.

I cup the back of her neck and bring her forward until her forehead rests against mine and our exhales mingle. "You know there's nothing I wouldn't give you."

"I used to know that. I'm not so sure anymore."

The raw honesty in her voice cuts me to the quick. Deeper yet because she's not wrong. She hasn't been this honest with me in years. If I hold a good portion of the blame for that, she's not completely innocent, either. I close my eyes and inhale. The room smells of her desire and Hercules's need and their commingled scent that is pure sex. I'll deal with him in a moment. Right now, she's has my entire focus. "You should have asked." I trail my fingers over her thighs. "You left me to figure it out for myself what you need."

She looks away, flushing. "I never had to tell you what I needed before."

"Communication goes both ways, love." Now isn't the time for recrimination and blame. It took me longer than it should have to realize she was unhappy, longer still to decide on a path forward. Already, Hercules's presence is helping, just like I'd hoped it would.

"COMMUNICATION." She pressed her lips together. "Would you have told me the truth about him and your plans if I'd asked?"

I am not an easy man to share a life with. I'm self-aware enough to know that. Our games have always held a darker edge, and I'm incapable of changing that, even if it's what she wants. For the first time, I wonder if I've left things too long. If we are too broken to truly fix.

"Hades." Meg gives a broken little laugh. "I suppose that answers that, doesn't it?"

"Jesus fuck, Hades, just *talk* to her." Hercules glares up at us. At *me*. "Can't you see that you're hurting her?"

"Hurting is what we do."

If anything, his glare intensifies. "It's not the same thing and you know it."

I do know it. His righteous fury makes me feel strange, and I dislike it intensely. I snap my fingers at him. "Eyes on the floor, little Hercules." He holds my gaze for a long moment and then deliberately drops his. Letting me know that he's choosing to submit. That I'm not forcing it. He's stronger than he realizes, and it's a mistake to enjoy that strength when he's only here for two very specific purposes, neither of which truly includes the long term. I've always been too self-indulgent when it comes to strong submissives.

Meg is just another example of that.

"We'll talk after," I find myself saying. Asking for the trust she used to give so freely. She either trusts me now or she doesn't. Black and white. Up and down. I don't know how to be anything but what I am. It used to be enough for her, though things shifted somewhere along the way. If she can't give me this, then—no. Meg is mine, for better or worse. There is no *finished* with us. Not while there's still something left to fight for.

She finally nods. "Okay. After."

It will have to be good enough. I stroke my hand down the center of her body. "Top or bottom?"

Meg arches her eyebrows, looking like herself for the first time since I walked into the room and found her on Hercules's cock. She laughs. "I was under the impression that you intended to punish us for fucking."

"I considered it." I spear her with two fingers, enjoying the way her eyes go half-lidded and she immediately lifts her hips to take me deeper. "I'll tell you a secret, love."

"What's that?"

"This pussy is mine." I give her a few rough strokes to demonstrate. "His cock is mine as well. My cock fucking my pussy is hardly grounds for punishment, don't you think?"

She licks her lips. "Even with the order involved?"

Now it's my turn to raise my brows. "Do you *want* to be punished?"

"No, Sir." She shakes her head. "I want to top him. Together."

"Together," I repeat slowly before nodding. It feels strangely right, though she and I don't usually top in the same scenes. In fact, I don't think we've ever done it before. Observing the other, yes. Together? No. Never. "By all means." I slowly withdraw my fingers from her and wipe them off on her mound. "Shall we begin by cleaning you up?"

"Yes," she breathes.

I scoop her up. I can't seem to help myself. Even if she's not playing the part of submissive in this scene, she's *my* submissive, and I want this moment of connection to remind us both that as I carry her to the couch and deposit her gently in the same spot I sat earlier to observe them. "Would you like another secret, love?"

"I want all your secrets."

I don't know if I'm capable of handing them all over, even to her. I've spent the last thirty years hoarding them close. Old dog, new tricks, and all that. I press a quick kiss to her lips. "I enjoy watching him fuck you. He's so...earnest."

Her mouth quirks and a thread of amusement lights up her eyes. "Hades, you're being mean."

"Am I?"

"Yes." She pushes a finger against my chest, urging me back a step. "I like it."

I move back enough to clear the way to her. Once again, Hercules is watching us, though this time I choose not to reprimand him for it. He's got a strange look on his face, something sweet and almost wistful. I don't understand it, but tonight isn't for him. It's for Meg. I open my mouth, but she beats me to it. "Come here, Hercules. Crawl, please."

There's something absolutely decadent about watching that big man crawl. He doesn't hesitate to obey her, moving on hands and knees until he's close enough to touch. Meg spreads her thighs. "You heard our Hades. Clean me up."

Our Hades.

As if they claim me as much as I claim them.

I allow myself to watch Hercules lick her pussy for several moments before I turn away and walk to the toy chest behind my desk. After some consideration, I take out

151

the strap-on and the nipple clamps specifically designed for male anatomy. It's a good place to start. I walk back just as Meg makes a small sound and comes, grinding herself on Hercules's face. She's so beautiful when she's like this, filled with wild abandon. It doesn't seem to matter whether she's top or bottom in the scene; she throws herself into the experience fully.

When it's clear that Hercules will keep eating her out until they're both puddles on the floor, I lean down and lace my fingers through his blond hair. "That's enough." I give his hair a sharp tug. "Up."

Meg lifts her arms over her head and conducts a full-body stretch from her pink-painted toes to her fingertips. She smiles at me. "You bring me all the best gifts."

"I enjoy watching you play, love."

Her smile dims a tiny bit, but she recovers almost immediately. "Good, because I'm just getting started." She climbs to her feet and gives another long stretch. I allow myself to drink in the sight of her. She's lost weight she can't afford to in recent weeks, another mark in my mishandling of our relationship. Meg's still beautiful, of course. She's always beautiful to me.

She takes the strap-on from me and nods at Hercules. "If you would be so kind."

"You know better."

She laughs, the sound light and free of whatever plagues her. "I suppose I do. If you would be so *cruel* and get our Hercules situated while I get this thing on, I'd appreciate it."

I step closer and snag the back of her neck. I don't care that she's topping in this scene. She steps into me even as I guide her to my chest. I kiss her and never has it been more of a battle between two equals than it is now. She won't submit. I don't know how to. I revel in her taste, in her strength, in the promise of things to come. Tonight will serve my purpose no matter how it plays out. I can simply ride the wave of her making. Or I could if I ever discover how to let go and relax into it. I'm no more capable of it than she is in this moment. When I finally lift my head, we're both breathing hard and her blue eyes have gone a little hazy.

I leave her to manage the strap-on and walk to where Hercules kneels. "Up."

He doesn't hesitate to obey, climbing easily to his feet. He's gloriously erect, every inch of him a perfect specimen of masculine beauty. I lift my hands so he can see the clamps and chain that connect them. "Nipple clamps and a cock ring, little Hercules. Can't have you coming all over my floor while Meg takes your ass."

He licks his lips. "Okay."

I close the distance and give his cock a rough stroke. Desire has been a low simmer in my blood ever since I walked into the office and saw him driving into her. Meg's kiss and Hercules's cock in my hand has that simmer boiling off. I hold his gaze as I work the cock ring over him and down to his base.

His sharp inhale catches in my chest. I have to stop, to remind myself that this man isn't for keeping. He's a tool that will serve his purpose and be discarded once we're finished with him. An instrument of vengeance against Zeus while simultaneously acting the part of a bandage for mine and Meg's relationship. At least until we're back on solid ground once more.

Knowing that doesn't stop me from dragging my fingers lightly along his length, from enjoying the way he watches my mouth and licks his lips again. "So eager."

"Play your games, Hades. Pretend you look down on me." He leans forward a little, thrusting into my hand. "We both know you're dying to get inside me."

It's the truth.

I force myself to release his cock, and I grab the back of his neck in a punishing grip. I bend him back just a little and lean down to tongue his nipples. First one and then the other and back again. I enjoy the way he shakes in my grasp so I play with him a little longer than strictly necessary. Every response as if he's being touched for the first time. It's not the truth. He's no virgin, which is a strange sort of relief, but he throws himself into every sexual encounter with an enthusiasm that seduces me. *He* seduces me.

"Boys." Meg's amused tone has me lifting my head. She leans against my desk, naked but for the strap-on. I've watched her use it before, of course, on both men and women, but something about seeing her with that giant red cock and her wicked smile conveys that tonight is special. It's set apart from before. A turning point, if you will.

She's wrong. It can't change anything. I've been set on this path for too long to abandon it now. Hercules serves a purpose now, but I can't imagine him in a permanent place in our lives. But I allow myself to smile back despite that. Would it truly be so terrible to allow one night to pass without the plotting and furthering of my plan? I suppose not.

She motions at the chains still in my hand. "Would you like me to?"

I almost tell her no. But topping Hercules together feels right in a way I don't want to deny. "By all means."

"So polite when you want to be," she murmurs and crosses to take the clamps from my hand. Meg strokes a finger down Hercules's chest and makes a faux pained sound. "Poor baby. His cock looks lonely down there, Hades." Her smile widens in a wicked way that has my chest aching in response. "Give him a little tease?"

I can't remember the last time I was on my knees, *truly* on my knees. But for this woman and this man, in this moment?

I sink slowly down and take Hercules's cock into my mouth. They're merged here as well, her taste and his. I take my time, exploring his length with my mouth as I watch Meg expertly fasten the clamps to his nipples. When he's bent over, the chain will weigh on both nipples and cock, creating a pleasure-pain crescendo.

Meg gives Hercules a quick kiss and I suck him hard, earning a groan from him. It's enough for now. I move back to sit on the couch, already knowing where Meg is headed with this. She lifts her head and gives Hercules a surprisingly sweet smile. "I'm going to fuck your ass."

His breath does that delicious catch again. "Okay."

"And while I do…" Her smile turned in my direction gains teeth and a little bit of meanness. "You're going to suck Hades's cock. When he comes, I stop." She reaches up and drags her thumb over his bottom lip. "So it's up to you how long this lasts."

Evil woman.

I love her.

CHAPTER 19

I end up kneeling between Hades's legs as Meg takes up a position behind me. She smooths her hands over my skin as if soothing a startled animal. I could tell her it's not necessary, but I can't stop shaking. The clamps on my nipples don't exactly hurt, but the strange sensation is so acute, it would consume me if I didn't have a ring clamped around my cock. I realize I'm clutching Hades's thighs and try to relax my grasp. It doesn't work.

"We're going to do this slow." She squeezes my ass. "Once we're good, you start sucking Hades off and the clock begins. If you need to stop for any reason, tap out." She leans over me and smacks the cushion next to Hades, demonstrating. "Do you understand?"

"Yes," I manage.

This scene feels different than the last one. Markedly different. Hades is still here, still dominating, but having Meg step more fully into that role? It feels like puzzle pieces have clicked together in a way I wasn't prepared for. It's *right*.

She presses an open-mouthed kiss to the back of my neck. "Try to relax."

Hades's chuckle makes me look up. He's got that amused mask on, but it can't cloak the heat in his dark eyes as he watches us. "He's too eager to relax, love. Don't pretend you're not enjoying it."

She gives a little laugh of her own, dark and decadent like the best kind of expensive wine. "Guilty." Then the weight of her is gone from me back. I hear a bottle being uncapped and she spreads lube down my ass crack and gently pushes a finger into me. The sensation makes me inhale sharply. I've done ass play before and plenty of it, but this feels different. Everything about this is different.

As Meg fingers my ass, Hades sifts his fingers through my hair. "Relax," he murmurs. "Let her do the work." He guides my head to his thigh, letting me rest there. It's impossible to miss his hard cock pressing against the front of his slacks, but he seems content to ignore it. I close my eyes and focus on breathing as Meg removes her fingers and the cool head of the strap-on cock nudges my entrance. She eases into me a little at a time, one hand constantly stroking my hips, my back, and my ass. Hades continues to sift his fingers through my hair, doing his own kind of soothing. It's...weirdly nice. In this moment, I feel like I'm the center of their worlds—or at least their formidable attention.

When Meg's stopped her forward slide, when I'm filled completely, she gives a happy little sigh. "There we go."

I open my eyes to find Hades watching me with an indulgent expression. "We've barely gotten started, little Hercules."

I know that. Of course I know that. Meg squeezes my hip. "Good?"

It takes me two tries to find my voice. When I speak, I'm hoarse. "I'm good."

"Remember, tap out if you need to." She gives me one last squeeze and a snap creeps into her voice. "Now, be a good boy and suck Hades's cock."

I lift myself up enough that I have plenty of room to undo his slacks and pull out his cock. It's the first time I've seen him, and, fuck, he's perfect. My mouth waters at the sight and I lick my lips. Hades has his hand in my hair again, urging me up a bit so I can take him easily into my mouth. His barely audible exhale as I suck him down makes everything go hot and tight. I try to focus on technique, to… I don't even know. My intentions last only as long as it takes Meg to withdraw almost fully and then begin to fuck my ass. The growing pressure in my cock and nipples… The penetration filling me an obscene amount… Again and again I take him deep, until some piece of my mind clicks off and I relax fully into everything they're doing to me.

They break me down to a baser version of myself, someone more animal than human. I suck Hades's cock with everything I have, giving myself over to the feel of him filling my throat as Meg fills my ass. I could come from this sensation alone, except the cock ring ensures that I won't be able to. I want this to last forever, to go on into time unknowable, but we are only human and the human body can only contain so much pleasure.

Hades's hands tighten in my hair and it's the only warning I get before he's coming, pumping down my throat in long strokes, the salty taste of him lingering on the back of my tongue. I keep sucking him, not wanting this to end, but he gently pulls me off his cock. "That's enough, little Hercules." His voice has gained a ragged edge, and I soak up the change just as much as I soak up the feeling of him smoothing his thumbs along my cheekbones, wiping away the tears I hadn't realized I shed.

Meg eases out of my ass. I'm vaguely aware of her cleaning us up, but now that they've stopped fucking me, all I can think about is my throbbing cock and nipples. I shift and the soft sound of the chain feels unnaturally loud in the room. They guide me to the couch and I realize that the strap-on is gone. Meg shares a look with Hades where he sits next to me, and together they begin removing the clamps and cock ring. Hades undoes the first clamp and the instant relief barely lasts a breath. Pain lances me and I curse as my back bows, my body trying to escape something that there's no escaping. He soothes the pain with his mouth, but my senses can't decide if it helps or makes things worse. Before I can figure it out, Hades repeats the process with my other nipple.

I'm so focused on his mouth, I don't even notice Meg carefully removing the cock ring until she sucks me down. "Fuck," I grit out.

"Relax," Hades murmurs, as if that's even in the realm of possibilities. "Let her reward you."

"Wait," I manage.

Neither of them stop. Of course they don't. I didn't say my safe word. I have no fucking intention of saying it either, but even through my haze of pleasure, I can tell this isn't quite right. "Meg." I can't quite catch my breath. "Ride my cock. Please."

She slowly lifts her head. Even through the scene, I can see the strange vulnerability in her eyes. Tonight hasn't quite fixed the missteps Hades and I have made along the way. Some wounds have to be healed with words and actions, not just fucking. I don't care. I hurt her, and the desire to make things right overpowers everything else. "Please," I repeat.

"Greedy boy." Hades's voice in my ear is more tempting than the devil himself. "Give him what he wants, love. He's more than earned it."

I'm not done, though. I look at him. "I want her to ride my cock. I want you to make her come."

His lifts his brows, but he doesn't give me a window to his soul the same way Meg does. Hades is an enigma. That's fine.

He can keep his thoughts to himself. This isn't about him. It's about *her*. Finally, he nods. "As I said, you've more than earned us honoring such a

pleasurable request."

Meg finally nods. "Okay. Lie down on the couch. Arms behind your back and clasp your elbows."

I obey and we all shift to accommodate. The new position arches my back and ensures I can't touch her. A perfect kind of agony. She moves to straddle me and Hades follows suit, straddling my thighs directly at Meg's back. Holy shit, I didn't think this through. It's one thing to be between them, overwhelmed by the sensations of them fucking me. It's entirely another to have Meg sinking onto my aching cock and Hades's fully clothed darkness behind her. Both of them watching my face, both of them predatory in the most delicious way possible.

Meg leans forward and presses her palms to my sensitive nipples as she rolls her hips, fucking me slowly in an entirely different way than she was not too long ago. Hades mirrors her movements, cupping her breasts and playing his long fingers along her nipples. "You did good work, love." He's not talking to me, not with his lips pressed to the spot behind her ear, not with her eyes sliding closed even as he shifts one hand down the center of her body to stroke her clit. It's as if I'm not here, as if my cock is just as much a toy as the ones in the chest behind his desk. It should infuriate me, but it's just as agonizingly sexy as everything else we've done tonight.

Use me. I don't say the worlds aloud. I don't want to break the spell that the three of us have woven tonight. If that requires my silence to begin to repair the harm done, to ensure that this is *Meg's* night, then I'm more than happy to oblige.

"I know," she breathes and her hands fall away from my chest. She sounds like a different person, some of her dominance bleeding away as she leans back against him, still grinding down on my cock. Fuck, but they're beautiful together. The brightest star and the darkest night, both made better by the presence of the other.

If only they realized it.

"Take him deeper." Hades urges her to slam down harder on my cock. Meg moans and lets her head fall back on Hades's shoulder. He keeps up those low words, winding her pleasure tighter and tighter around us. "Just like that. Such a pretty cock he has, don't you think?"

"Yes."

"I picked him just for you. Hercules and his pretty cock." He meets my gaze as he says it, and we have a moment of perfect understanding. Anything for her. We may go about it in different ways—we will *always* go about it in different ways—but the goal is still the same. Meg's pleasure. Her happiness. I don't fool myself into thinking it's Hades's only goal. He's admitted as much that it's not. But he loves her, no matter how strange their relationship is to me.

Not as strange as it used to seem. I can see the lines of it now, am beginning to understand exactly what it is they offer each other. Just like I can see the gaps neither one of them are capable of filling. I don't even know if they realize the lack. They must, at least on some level, or I wouldn't be here in this position, acting the part of their third. I could fill those gaps for them, I could be the softness to their jagged edges.

Hades nods once as if I've made the offer aloud. He takes Meg's hands and guides them behind her back, mirroring the same position I'm in. "Use his cock, love. Take exactly what you need." He resumes stroking her clit, a possessive touch that conveys the truth. My cock might be hers, but he owns everyone in this room.

Meg's strokes lose their smooth rhythm, and Hades is

there with his free hand, gripping her hips and forcing her to keep up the motion that will send her over the edge. I'm close behind, every muscle in my body coiling tighter and tighter as I fight off orgasm. She has to come first. She *has* to.

Hades ensures it happens. He presses hard on her piercing and her pussy clenches so tightly around my cock that I curse. I forget myself, forget my orders. I grab her hips and drive into her again and again, chasing my own pleasure as she milks my cock with wave after wave of orgasm. I slump back onto the couch, a boneless mess, and Meg does the same against Hades. He presses a kiss to her neck and strokes her stomach, her breasts, her arms, before shifting to give me a similar treatment. That little touch grounds me when I didn't even realize I was floating. Hades carefully eases Meg down onto my chest and presses a soft kiss to my mouth that I'm too dazed to return. "Don't move."

As if I could even if I wanted to. I wave a hand vaguely and wrap my arms around Meg, cuddling her into me. She kisses my neck and nuzzles me, obviously as blitzed as I feel. Damn. I just… damn. I didn't know sex could be like this. It was beyond good, beyond great. It was fucking life-changing.

And I can't shake the feeling that we've only scratched the surface.

Hades returns quickly with blankets and a warm damp rag that smells faintly of clean laundry. He helps us sit up and cleans us up a little. Though he doesn't linger on that aspect, there's an element of softness in his caretaking that I didn't expect. Maybe I should have. Several minutes later, he has us wrapped up in our respective blankets and leaning against him on either side. It feels so fucking right, I don't bother to question it. Meg reaches across his lap and laces her fingers through mine, another little point of contact, a connection I crave as much as Hades's warm strength.

I don't know how much time passes while Hades acts as

rock to our respective storms. Long enough that my heart is no longer trying to beat its way out of my chest and my breathing evens out. Finally, as if he's as reluctant to break this peace as I am, he sighs. "I suppose it's long since past time to talk."

CHAPTER 20

I don't have the energy for this conversation now, which must have been the point when we began this night. It doesn't seem to matter, though, because Hades is speaking in that careful way of his that seems to come out when he's negotiating. I push up a little, needing to see his face as he talks. My body resists the call to action, but I power through the languid feeling coating my muscles. Some things are more important than the afterglow. On his other side, Hercules does the same, shifting back to rest against the arm of the couch. His legs are still pressing against Hades; he doesn't seem to be able to give up that contact any more than I can.

Hades plays his fingers along my knee and sighs. "I targeted Hercules specifically."

I know that already. He does nothing without reason, and we were in that restaurant with the sole purpose of netting Hercules. "Yes, I'm aware of that, even if you didn't bother to tell me." My voice comes out sharper than I want it to, giving too much away, but I can't seem to help myself. My defenses are down, crashed to pieces by these two men.

He continues as if I haven't spoken. "I did intend him as a gift to you, love. But that's not the reason I picked him specifically."

A gift. I still haven't quite wrapped my mind around the fact that Hades knew exactly how messed up we'd gotten and instead of talking to me like a normal person, he served me Hercules on a platter. I don't know that I can throw stones at this point, though. As Hades pointed out, I didn't exactly tell him everything I was feeling.

Maybe he's right. We *aren't* normal people to fix our problems in that way. And I can't deny that Hercules's presence helps in ways I wasn't expecting. Not solely in prodding us to talk to each other, but he's a soft ooey-gooey center to all our harsh edges. He blunts us, allows us to connect in a softer way.

I clear my throat, bringing my attention back to this room, this conversation. "Why did you pick him, specifically?"

"A long time ago, before I came to Carver City, I lived in Olympus."

"I know." Just that he lived in Olympus and was exiled. Nothing more. Maybe I should know more about him, how he grew up, what his family was like. It's not something we've ever talked about. My parents were hardly saints, and they turned their backs on me when I ran off with Declan all those years ago. I couldn't bear to admit that they were right about him, so I've never gone back. And they've never once tried to reach out. It doesn't hurt quite as much as it used to, but that tenderness causes me to never push Hades about his past. What is the point? We have our now and our future.

Obviously, I should have paid more attention.

"I..." For the first time tonight, Hades hesitates. He glances at Hercules, a connection so brief, I wouldn't have caught it if I weren't watching them so closely. "I had a family. Wife. Son. A promising future as one of the most powerful people within the city."

A wife.

A son.

Each word hits me in the chest with the force of a sledge-hammer. Two things I can never, ever give Hades. Two things I desperately don't want, even now. I start to pull away, but his hand bracketing my knee tightens and he turns to me. "Listen."

I don't want to. I don't want to hear how happy he was. How *normal* he was. Some truths aren't mine to bear, and this one is too much to handle. I might laugh if I could find the breath for it. Of all the secrets lurking in his past, this will be the one to break me. Not the horrible things he's done. Not the people he's hurt along the way in his quest to secure power. Not the legion of people he's fucked. Just this. A wife. A son. An entire life I knew nothing about. I swallow hard. "I'd really rather not."

"Listen." This time it's Hercules who speaks, his deep voice steadying something in me despite every molecule in my body demanding I get the hell out of here.

Hades gives me a long look and continues. "We didn't last the year after I inherited the position of Hades. I was too young and too... innocent. I couldn't protect them."

A pit opens up in my chest. "What happened?"

"Zeus killed them."

Hercules makes a choked noise, but Hades doesn't look away from my face. "He killed them," he repeats. "And he drove me out of Olympus with nothing but sorrow to accompany me. For thirty years, he's been untouchable, well beyond my reach, and now I have the chance to balance the scales. A son for a son."

My mind is racing and my body tenses as if I'm about to

166

flee for my life, rejecting the things he's saying. "You... Hercules... *His son*."

"Zeus is my father, yes."

More pieces fall into place. The reason Hercules left Olympus, because of his father's monstrosity. It never occurred to me that it could be connected to *Hades*. I grab Hades's wrist and wait for him to look at me. "You are not killing Hercules."

He gives me a small smile. "Hardly, love. I'm not in the business of murder."

I could argue otherwise. He's more than happy to hand people over to their enemies, which may or may result in their death, even if his hands remain relatively clean. He was more than happy to hand *Jasmine* over to a man who terrified her. I can't blame him for that, though, not when my hands are equally dirty with his deals. I look from Hades to Hercules and back again. "So you seduce the son to hurt the father. I'm assuming there is some footage or photographs that will make their way to him."

He shrugs. "It's possible."

I point at Hercules. "And you're okay with this, with him using you like this?" It can't last forever, no matter what Hades negotiated as terms. He's going to drag Hercules down to our level and then cut him loose to drown. "You can't be okay with this."

"My father is a monster." He says it so calmly, as if remarking on the weather. From the little I know of Zeus at this point, I can't argue with him, but surely he sees this isn't as simple as Hades has laid it out to be.

They knew and spoke about this and didn't loop me in until I forced them to.

I feel like I'm falling. Every time I hit the bottom it collapses beneath me, revealing farther to drop. I am completely immaterial to this place. Just the lure Hades placed to draw Hercules in. He didn't tell me. And Hercules seemed more than content to keep *his* silence too. It hurts. It hurts way more than it fucking should. I can't help feeling like Hades has drawn a circle in the sand and I'm on the outside of it. Why bother to tell me the plans? My part in them has been served. He's only doing it now to placate me, to keep me content and avoid rocking the boat further, not because he genuinely wants me involved or sees me as an equal partner. Even offering Hercules as a gift feels secondary to his vengeance.

I swallow past the hard knot in my throat. "So you take the pictures, send them to Zeus and... what? How is that even close to equal to what he did to you?"

"It's not." Just that. Nothing more.

Even with all this talk of *talking*, he's still shutting me out.

I wait, but no more information seems to be forthcoming. He's given me enough that I'm supposed to be satisfied, but even now, he's holding back. I want to shake him, to scream at him, to list all the ways he's breaking us even as he appears to take actions to heal us. I don't. It won't change anything, not really. Instead, I lean over and take his chin the same way he does to me when he wants my undivided attention. "Hades." I pitch my voice low, but it shakes with the sheer intensity of the feelings I'm determined not to show. "If you hurt Hercules, that's it. I'm out."

"You have a lifetime sentence, love."

I give him a sad smile. "We both know that won't stop me if I want to disappear. You deliver harm to him, and I'm gone for good."

He searches my face with those dark, dark eyes. All amusement flees his expression. "You're serious."

"Yes."

"Megaera—"

168

I drop my hand and push to my feet. "Good night, Hades." I nod at Hercules, who's watching us with a stunned expression on his face. "Sleep well."

I don't bother to retrieve my dress before I leave the office and take the back stairs down to the residential floor. Tomorrow, I have to spend more time in the club, to see and be seen. The old saying about the mice playing while the cat's away is never truer than with a bunch of kinky criminals in a sex club. They'll push just as far as we'll let them, so likely I'll have to make an example of someone tomorrow. Once upon a time, the thought would fill me with glee. There was nothing I loved more than bringing a proud person down a few notches, to strip them to their core self and rock their world. Now? I'm just tired. So fucking tired.

Hades won't change whatever his plan is for Hercules. I know him well enough to know that. No matter how much he cares about me, no matter how much he claims to want to fix things, he's been harboring the need for revenge for thirty years. Justice for his wife and child. I stop. How goddamn selfish do I have to be that *that* is the thing that trips me up? Not his vengeful, potentially murderous, intentions. No. It's the kid who makes my chest hurt and my eyes burn.

I don't want kids. I never have. It was something I thought Hades and I had in common, a total and complete lack of desire to procreate. But I know what I heard in his voice when he mentioned his son.

Longing.

I am selfish beyond measure to be hurt by that longing, so incredibly selfish to hate that he's lied to me. Ten years we've been together, and he's wanted children this whole time? I *hate* the guilt that eats away at me. I haven't done anything wrong. If he'd communicated with me—and the very idea is laughable now—then we wouldn't be together. Some things a

169

person cannot compromise on, and having children numbers among them.

How dare he hide this from me?

I shove through my door and drop the blanket to the floor. I can't do this. I thought I had a clear understanding of my life and relationship. Nothing is perfect, but at least I know the boundaries I'm willing to compromise on. I thought I knew *him*. It hurts beyond measure to realize I didn't know anything at all.

A quick shower does nothing to clear my spiraling thoughts. I wrap myself in my robe and stare down at my bed. The thought of sleeping alone is unbearable, which might make me laugh if I had anything resembling a sense of humor left after tonight. The temptation rises to call Jasmine and make the drive over to Jafar's penthouse, but we don't have that kind of relationship. Fucking and friendship, yes, but not the depth that allows me to crawl into bed with them and take comfort from their presence.

I'm being a coward.

Before I can talk myself out of it, I walk out my door and pad down the hallway to Hercules's suite. I lift my hand to knock and it's only then that I pause to consider that he might not have come back to his room. Even now, he might be settling into Hades's giant bed. I lower my hand. This self-pitying spiral is exhausting. I'm not fit company for anyone right now, and looking for a shoulder to lean on is just as selfish as everything else I've done today. This week, this year, this decade.

The door opens before I can turn and walk away. Hercules leans against the doorjamb, his hair wet from a recent shower and a towel wrapped low around his hips. He studies me for a long moment before he pushes off the frame and steps back. "Come in."

"Actually, I—"

"Meg." He gives me a soft smile. "Come in."

It's what I want. Why am I so conflicted about taking it? I finally nod and follow him into his room. He doesn't speak again, and I have too much to say to get anything out. Hercules disappears into the bathroom for a moment and comes back naked. He eases off my robe and takes my hand, tugging me to his bed and tucking us both in with an efficiency that's truly impressive. I rest my head against his chest and listen to his strong heart beating.

The comfort he offers comes without strings, without manipulations. Maybe that's why it's so easy to speak my pain into the dark room. "Tonight hurt."

"I know." He smooths a hand over my hair. "I'm sorry."

"I love him." I don't even know why I'm saying this, why I'm treating this man as my own personal confessional, but I can't seem to stop. "I don't know if it's enough. I don't know if it ever was."

Hercules cuddles me closer, his strong arms acting as a barrier between me and the rest of the world. "He'd walk through fire for you."

Maybe once. I don't know if it's true any longer. "When we first fell for each other, yes. But the years have a way of taking their toll. We've grown apart. The stupid thing is that I don't even know when it started. It's something I should know, right? But it feels like I just woke up one day and realized that he's almost more a stranger now than he was when I first made my deal."

"It happens like that sometimes." His lips brush my forehead. "I think he's trying, though. In his own way."

I'm not so sure. What kind of man throws *another* man at a problem instead of wading in to fix it himself? Hades, that's who. I manage to keep that doubt inside, though. Hercules has enough to worry about without adding my wavering emotional health to the mix. I hold him as tightly as I can. "If you were smart, you'd run. I can get you out if that's what you decide."

Hercules presses a kiss to my temple. "I'm not going anywhere, Meg."

That's what I'm afraid of.

CHAPTER 21

HADES

I let myself into Hercules's room well before dawn. The faint light of the full moon shines through his windows, illuminating the scene on the bed. I knew Meg would need comfort tonight, but I also knew she wouldn't accept it from me. Not this time.

Is that what she wants? To walk in the sun with a man like the one holding her so close while she sleeps? The thought carves out my stomach and leaves me curiously empty. If I was a better man, I'd let them both go, let them attempt to find whatever happiness there is in the world with each other. If any two are able to do it, it's Meg and Hercules. For all her scars, she's still one of the good ones. He brings that side out of her. I'd have to be particularly dense not to recognize that.

I'm not a better man. I'm not even a good one. This woman and this man belong to me, and I'll do whatever it takes to ensure they stay.

I give a soundless sigh, and Hercules opens his eyes. We stare at each other for a long moment. I expect recrimination. Judgment. Anger. Any number of things. He simply smiles. "I figured you'd make your way here eventually."

"Am I becoming predictable?" We both speak low to avoid waking Meg, though I could have told him it's unnecessary. Once she falls asleep, she's dead to the world. A tornado could burst through the building and she'd likely sleep through it.

"You care."

Two words to encompass so many conflicting emotions. I nod at the woman sleeping in his arms. "Thank you. She wouldn't accept this from me, but she needs it."

Hercules shakes his head slowly. "You really are a good Dom, aren't you?"

"Yes." I should leave it at that, but apparently the honesty earlier tonight begets further honesty. "But not a good person."

"No, not a good person." He lifts a hand and motions me forward. "What are you waiting for?"

Will that man ever cease to surprise me? I slip my hands into my pockets and take a step back. "I'm respecting her wishes."

"You're being a fucking idiot."

I blink. "You're a mouthy little sub, aren't you?" There's a specialness to Hercules that I can't let myself enjoy. He's not for keeping, and forgetting that is unacceptable. Leaving right now is the only option. Yet my feet don't quite get the instruction.

What if he *was* for keeping?

For Meg, yes, but also…for me.

"It's not just me she needs and you know it. Stop being a fucking coward and get in here."

Now is the time to walk. Meg and I have survived plenty in our decade together, and that history suggests we'll survive this too. Hercules was only meant to be a temporary fix. Or that was the plan until he burst into our lives and the balance shifted. It's the one thing I couldn't have anticipated —his effect on both of us. For the first time in thirty years, I don't know what the future holds. Not in its entirety. I can't be sure my plan won't break us.

I strip slowly, aware of Hercules's attention on me. A small vain part of me enjoys the way he watches me so closely, but he's right. This isn't about me. Or even about us. How can this man come into such a longstanding relationship and see things so clearly? I didn't plan on *that*. Perhaps it's just who he is. He shines a light wherever he goes.

I carefully climb onto the bed on the other side of Meg. She barely shifts as I settle in next to her. She looks younger like this, less world weary with her carefully cultivated mask set down for the moment. It makes me ache. She's so formidable during her waking hours. She may stand at my side, but she doesn't need me. Not for protection, not to shore up her defenses, not for a single thing. It's such an attractive thing in a partner, to know that she can weather any storm and keep the things we value safe in the process. But somewhere along the way, we went from standing side by side to being on either end of a gulf I don't know how to cross. I'm too old, too set in my ways. I can't bend for anyone.

Even her.

"She's worth it."

For a moment, I think Hercules is pulling thoughts straight from my head, teasing them into existence through sheer force of will. That would be a neat trick, but it's ultimately impossible. No, this man is simply better at reading people than I anticipated. I shift onto my side so I can see him better, and he mirrors the movement. "Surely your anger at your father doesn't delve deep enough to sacrifice yourself for it."

Hercules doesn't blink at the change in topic. "That's really not for you to say, is it?"

He has a point, but I don't like unknown quantities, and this man has proven himself to be one. Since bargaining himself away for Meg, he hasn't quite done what I expect. I study his face, taking in the strong lines of his jaw and cheekbones, the straight Roman nose, those full lips that save his features from being too harsh. Really though, it's his eyes that hold a person captive. Contrary to popular belief, not all eyes are the windows to the soul. Too many things can counteract that. Control, fear, a skilled lie. Hercules has none of that. His eyes could drown the unwary.

I don't look away. "Explain it to me."

For a moment, I think he might argue, but he glances at Meg and sighs. "My father didn't stop doing terrible things after he… did what he did to you. I tried to make him pay through the appropriate channels, and it blew up in the face of someone who deserved it the least."

I could play with this, could tease out his willing victimhood to serve my purposes. But this blasted honesty gets the best of me yet again. "It's not going to bring him down, little Hercules. I may have had that ability once, but I don't anymore. I can kill him, but I can't dismantle his power structure."

He went pale. "You could kill him."

"Yes." No use denying it. It's what I intend, after all. If he hasn't seen what I am up to by this point, he's denser than I could have dreamed. No, that's not the truth. Hercules is too insightful by half. He just has a pair of rose-tinted glasses that color his experience with the world. Despite being slapped down again and again, they remain intact. It's the strangest thing.

He shifts a little closer and pulls the covers up when Meg shivers. "Hades." He gives me a long look. "You didn't change your name back. You know, in Olympus now, Hades is more bogeyman than real person. I always assumed he was a legend."

We're dancing too close to things best left in the past, but the past is here and shining directly in my face. "It's a legacy role, similar to Zeus. With my son…" Even after all this time, I can barely speak the words. "There is no one to assume the role. It dies with me."

Hercules reaches across Meg's sleeping body and takes my hand. "I'm sorry."

"You weren't even alive at the time. You have nothing to be sorry for."

"Fuck, Hades, I can still offer emotional support even if I wasn't directly responsible for what happened to your family." He strokes his thumb over my knuckles. "What were their names?"

"Amber. Jonah." Saying them aloud feels like summoning their ghosts to this room. I was a different man in my early twenties. They wouldn't recognize me now. Some moments, I barely recognize myself.

Hercules squeezes my hand. "You should have told her."

No point arguing. He's right. "I know." I've never lied to Meg—not really—but withholding this information is almost the same thing.

Hercules keeps stroking my hand, little movements that curl through me even as they provide the comfort I don't deserve. He finally says, "What you said before, your plan to defile me and send evidence to my father… It won't work. He won't care." He doesn't tense up as he says the next words. "For it to be true justice, you'd have to kill me."

My chest locks up and I stare at him, shocked to my very core. "What?"

"That's what this is about, right? A son for a son?" He's watching me so closely, and for the first time since we met, I have no idea what my face is showing. "He already wrote me off, Hades. You could be fucking me seven ways to Sunday, and it will barely make him blink. That's not how my father works."

Surely he didn't just suggest I murder him? I won't lie and say the thought never crossed my mind in my initial plans, but I discarded it upon meeting him for a thousand different reasons. Meg and the future of our relationship, such as it is. Even Hercules himself. "I'm not killing you, little Hercules."

"Why not?"

What is his aim with this conversation? I twist my hand and take his wrist, tightening my grip until his fingers splay out and he bites his bottom lip. There are so many things I could say, so many reasons I could give that would detour us away from this conversation. In the end, this strange addiction to honesty wins out. "Because you're mine."

He's mine.

Yes, that's my truth.

Hercules is mine the same way Meg is mine. Except it's not the same. She and I push and pull and move through an intricate dance of power in every single one of our waking moments. With Hercules, it's effortless. He slid perfectly into a slot in our lives that I hadn't even realized was lacking until his presence brought it to my attention. I acquired him as a gift to Meg, yes, but I never realized that I would feel this way about him, too.

"He knows I'm here."

He doesn't form it as a question, but I answer him nonetheless. "He knows you're here."

Hercules nods. "Maybe that's enough."

It's not. Zeus will be ripping his hair out at the thought of his son within my grasp. Not because he cares about Hercules. If he did, he wouldn't have let the man leave the city and struggle the way he has these last few months. No,

Zeus is a schoolyard bully. Hercules is a possession, a toy, and even if he's long since discarded it, he can't stand the thought of someone else picking it up and finding value in it. It will aggravate him to no end to know Hercules is in my household. Eventually, I will push him hard enough that he'll be forced to come here, to my territory, and retaliate.

That's when I'll truly gain my revenge.

I release Hercules's wrist and reach up to stroke a single finger along his jaw, tracing the hard line there. Lifetime bargain or not, I can't guarantee he'll stay, short of locking him in. I know how that story ends. I don't know how this one does, though. "You'll be tempted to break your word at some point."

He makes the conversational leap with me without hesitation. "I've never broken my word before. I won't start now."

Promises aren't worth the air it takes to voice them. I've learned that lesson time and time again. "I suppose we'll see, won't we?" I lean over Meg and kiss him.

CHAPTER 22

MEG

I wake up pressed between two bodies I know intimately. Hercules has a big hand bracketing my hip, but from the way they're moving, they're making out over my head. Both their hips shift as if seeking each other, except I'm in the middle, keeping them from closing that last bit of distance.

I'm in the way.

If I had any self-respect at this point, I'd bolt out of the bed and retreat back to my bedroom to brood in peace. I came here last night to escape the demons nipping at my heels, and yet here they are, thrusting their hard cocks against me. If I leave, will they even pause? Or will they get right to fucking without the slightest bit of hesitation? I don't know. I don't even know what I want. I'm not fool enough to think their relationship only exists when I'm in the room. It's not true for me and each of them, why should it be true for them together? Expecting that—wanting that—is ugly and horrible and selfish of me.

Hades drags his hand across my side to delve between my thighs. The shock of the touch has my eyes flying open.

Hercules breaks their kiss and looks down at me, his blue eyes already gone hazy with pleasure. "Good morning, Meg."

"I—"

Hades chooses that moment to push two fingers into me. "Did you think we wouldn't notice you waking up?"

That's exactly what I thought. I swallow hard. "You were busy."

"Never too busy for you." Hercules shifts down to kiss me, and I can taste Hades on his tongue. He barely lets me sink into him before he lifts his head. "You tensed up. Why?"

Is he seriously asking me this while Hades fingers me? I arch up to take his mouth again, but he moves back, staying just out of reach. Hades chooses that moment to withdraw his fingers and deliver a stinging slap to my clit. "Answer him, love."

When I craved being the center of their attention, I didn't anticipate *this*. I open my mouth, but hesitate. Admitting my selfish thoughts might as well pave the way for them to leave me. The fear feels a little irrational right now, with Hercules reaching down to lightly stroke my clit and Hades moving to finger-fuck me from behind. It doesn't mean it's not valid or that it won't leave me so incredibly vulnerable. "Can we please just get down to the orgasms and stop talking so much?"

Hades's lips brush the curve of my ear. "No." He pushes a third finger into me. "Answer his question."

I can't think past what they're doing to me, past the way their presence overwhelms me from both sides. The truth spills from my lips, sharp and painful. "I feel like I'm unnecessary. Replaceable."

Hercules inhales sharply. "*What?*"

Now that I've started, I can't seem to stop. "Hades shares with you what he won't share with me. He doesn't shut you out." God, it hurts to admit that, hurts more than I could imagine.

Hades stops fucking me with his fingers, but he doesn't remove them. "You're still hurting." He sounds...shocked? But surely that can't be. Hades knows all, even when I want to shove him out a window for seeing things I'm not willing to share.

"I'm always hurting." My words don't have the intended amusement in them. They come out stark. True.

I twist to face him and they allow me to do it. Hercules wraps his arms and body around my back, always giving me comfort in whatever way I'll allow. His strength buoys me to speak the truth that's been lodged in my throat for days. Longer. I look up into Hades's dark eyes and, for the first time in as long as I can remember, he's not holding himself back from me. He's right here, close enough to touch in every way that counts.

I swallow hard. I may not get another opportunity to get this out. "You didn't tell me about them. You've stopped telling me *anything*. I'm not a partner, Hades. I'm just another soldier for you to bend to your will."

"Not that, love, never that." He strokes his thumbs over my cheeks and they come away wet with my tears. Hades presses his forehead to mine. "I love you. I may not... show it abundantly at times, but never doubt that I do."

"I love you too," I whisper. "I just don't know if it's enough." The same words I said to Hercules are just as true now as they were then. That's the worst part of it. Love is supposed to conquer all, but I've known that for a lie most of my adult life. It feels different with Hades, and that used to be something I cherished. Now, it seems like every move we make cuts each other, no matter how carefully we maneuver.

"Give us time, Meg." Hercules kisses the top of my head.

Pain lances through me. "You two want—"

"No." Hades shakes his head. "Give *us* time. All three of us."

I stare up at him. Surely he isn't saying what I think he's saying. I lick my lips, striving to calm my racing heart. It's no use. "The three of us."

"Yes." He looks deadly serious for once. No amusement. No cruelty. Just Hades. "We could be a true triad." His lips quirk. "At least we could if we get out of each other's way long enough to make it happen."

What he's saying, what they're both saying... Surely it can't be that simple? I've seen poly relationships in the Underworld. Hell, I *am* poly for all intents and purposes, but we've never tried it as a *relationship*. It's always just been fucking, with Hades and I circling each other, the only constant. "What about your revenge?"

"It will take shape regardless of what happens with us here now."

The words are right, but something is off in his tone. Maybe he distrusts this perfect solution as much as I do. I run my hands over Hercules's arms where he holds me. "This can't be the life you wanted. To chain yourself to us."

"Why don't you let me worry about what I want?" Hercules gives me a squeeze. "What I want is you. Both of you."

"You *hate* us." Why can't I let this go and just accept it? It's easier to let lust and love have their way than to pick apart their solution, but I can't seem to stop. "You're furious at us for lying to you, for trapping you."

"Yeah, I was." He chuckles against my hair. "Maybe I'm still kind of pissed, but you were right before. I have no one to blame but myself."

He's too good. Too pure. We'll tarnish him. It might take a few weeks, months, years, but eventually he'll lose that shine and start compromising the values that makes Hercules the man he is. He won't be able to avoid it, not if he wants to survive this world. It hurts me to think about, but telling him to go would hurt too. "This can't possibly work," I whisper.

"We won't know unless we try it for real." Hercules runs his hands over my body like he's trying to soothe a startled animal. "We can do this. There will be some bumps along the way, a whole lot of communication, some mistakes, but we can make it work."

I reach up and tentatively touch Hades's chin. He's staring at me like he can read the doubts on my soul. I can't seem to stop shaking. "This is a trick."

"No trick." He covers my hand with his, sealing me to him. "This is… an alternate route."

An alternate route. As if it is really that simple. "But—"

"Megaera." He doesn't raise his voice, but he doesn't have to for me to know I won't like what he's about to say. "I am not Declan. After all this time, you should know that. I won't treat you as carelessly as he did. Ever."

Hercules tenses. "Who is Declan?"

How dare Hades spill forth my darkest shame like that? His eyes are still tender, but there's a challenge there now too. He's willing to compromise his vengeance, to offer a part of himself up on the altar that could be this new relationship. Am I willing to do the same? I close my eyes and let the soft sound of their breathing soothe me. I'm scared. I'm so scared. "Declan is the man who convinced me to bargain myself away to further his own goals. He wanted something only Hades could provide and so he convinced me to make a deal on his behalf. My freedom for his ambition."

Hercules's shocked inhale is too pure. "You took *that* deal?"

"I had my reasons."

I open my eyes, I can't help it. Hades is looking at me just like he did that first day, all warmth and danger and a sweet possession that calls to every part of me. I lick my lips. "Do you remember the first thing you said to me upon sealing that bargain?"

He strokes the back of my hand. "That you are destined to be a queen, not some man's pawn."

Hercules is still tense behind me. "You let her sell herself for some piece of shit. What the hell, Hades?"

He lifts his gaze to the man behind me. "I'd think you would know by now that I'm not a good man, little Hercules. I wanted Meg from the first moment I saw her, and when she offered herself to me, I took her."

Hercules huffs out a breath. "Yeah, I get that. That's not my fucking problem, Hades. You let him profit off her sacrifice."

"Ah. That." Hades presses a kiss to my knuckles and releases me. "Would you like to tell him, love, or should I?"

It's been a long, long time since I thought about Declan or the beginning of my relationship with Hades. He didn't fuck me that first year I was under contract with him. He simply trained me in everything from BDSM to the politics of Carver City. There were nights where we'd talk for hours after a scene, and I felt like I'd found another part of my soul I didn't know I was missing.

It strikes me that I have that same sensation with Hercules, too, albeit in a very different way.

My chest goes warm and tight. "Declan was running a small territory just south of Jasmine's father's." A vicious part of me rises to the fore at the memory and I smile. "About a year after we made our bargain, Hades dismantled his support system in the space of a week. And when he came crawling into the Underworld to beg for help, Hades exiled him from the city entirely."

"You can do that?"

Hades shrugs. "If I start running major players out of

town, they'll all turn on me. Neutral territory is my strength, and so I don't directly meddle with power squabbles in the various territories." His eyes go lethal. "However, it was a special circumstance, and everyone recognized it as such."

The others saw it as a courting gift, a way of balancing the scales. It helped that I was already developing a reputation in the Underworld and most of them liked me. Nine years later, and they still gravitate to me, but there's a healthy dose of fear mixed in. I'm one small step down from Hades in their eyes, and they treat me with every respect and courtesy.

Hercules is quiet for a long moment, obviously processing. "It doesn't seem like enough."

I jerk away and sit up. "What?" Did he seriously just say that?

Hades isn't looking at me now. He's got a strange expression on his face, as if Hercules has done something delightful. "He hasn't been seen in nearly a decade, little Hercules."

I freeze. "Hades, you didn't."

Now he turns that look in my direction. "The terms were clear, love. If he attempted to come back to Carver City, I would ensure it never happened again."

I remember that, of course. But no one crosses Hades. Surely Declan wasn't stupid enough to try. I open my mouth to ask, but reconsider. Does it really matter? Hades's hands aren't clean. They haven't been for the entirety of the time I've known him. They won't be in the future either. Will knowing that he killed my ex make a difference?

Yes. Yes, it would.

"Did he come back?"

He doesn't blink. "Yes."

I can't breathe. "When?"

"A week after he left. He attempted to slide back into his old role." His eyes give me nothing. "He couldn't get to me, so he blamed you for the broken bargain. I ensured he ceased to be a threat."

That sounds like Declan. Even after all these years, I remember his rage. When we were first together, I was naive enough to think it was sexy. A man with emotions. I didn't realize how toxic he was until it was far too late and I'd signed my life away. Declan never loved me. He loved that I loved him and he found me useful. Having *me* be the reason Hades turned on him must have driven him mad. Funny that I never stopped to consider it until now. I was too busy forcefully shucking off my innocence, shedding it like a skin that no longer fit. Declan was like all the other things in my past—something I wanted to leave behind and never think of again.

"You killed him." Hercules still has that strange expression on his face, as if he can't decide whether he's horrified or not.

"I'll do anything to protect those I love, little Hercules." Hades doesn't look away from my face. "Anything."

"I get it," Hercules says slowly. Now he's looking at me, too, his expression contemplative. "Some people are worth protecting, no matter the cost."

If I were a different person, I'd be running screaming from the room right now. Hades is a dangerous man and I knew that from the moment I met him. This information about Declan might be new, but it's not surprising. For the first time, I'm realizing that Hercules is just as dangerous in a different way. He won't play out a revenge scheme over the space of years, a spider in his web waiting for the unwary fly to come to him. No, Hercules will charge forth to do what he thinks is necessary with no thought to himself. He wouldn't have waited for Declan to break the rules. He would have chased the man down and ensured he never got a chance to try.

I shouldn't find that so sexy, either of these scenarios, but I've long since given up the concept of *should*.

Still, I can't quite believe this is real. I take each of their hands and look down at them. "You mean it when you say you want this with us. Truly?"

"Yes." Hercules doesn't hesitate.

Hades lets me see him, lets me see exactly what he's thinking for the first time in a long time. He planned this, yes, but he has his own reservations despite wanting this just as much as I'm afraid to. "Yes," he says. He drags his thumb over my palm. "The question remains—do you?"

I laugh. I can't help it. "It's going to blow up in our faces."

"No, it won't." Hercules sits up, and I'd have to be dead not to appreciate the way the muscles in his stomach flex when he does. "Come on, Meg. Let's give it a shot."

There's really only one answer. There's been only one answer from the moment I sat in that restaurant and Hades told me he wanted me to fuck a waiter. I look at Hercules and then Hades. Are they holding their breath the same way I am? I can't be sure. I finally nod. "Yes. Let's do this."

CHAPTER 23

HERCULES

I kiss Meg. It seems only right after her agreement. She barely lets me sink into the taste of her when she pushes me back to the bed. "Hades?"

"Mmmm?"

She lightly rakes her nails down my chest, but her attention is on him where he reclines next to us. "Thank you for my gift."

"Anything for you, love." He gives Meg's hair a tiny tug and she leans in to accept his mouth.

Every single time they're together, touching, kissing, coming, I can barely breathe past the perfection of it. This time is no different. When Hades finally leans back and glances at me, his satisfaction rolls off him in a wave. "Voyeur."

Meg twists to look at me. She takes in my body, my obvious desire, in a single sweep. "Oh, Hercules, we're going to have such *fun* with you." For once, she doesn't seem tormented or angry. She's grinning at me like I've gifted her the perfect present. Like I *am* the perfect present. Which I suppose is exactly what I am.

She kisses my jaw, neatly avoiding my mouth even as I turn to take hers, and moves down my body with an intention that has my cock going so hard I get a little light-headed. Hades takes my mouth even as Meg sucks my cock down, fighting against my length to seal her lips to the base of me. I groan and Hades swallows the sound, kissing me deeper. Claiming me. They overwhelm me, sensation bleeding into one another until there's no room for anything but the way she drags her tongue up the underside of my cock like she's licking her favorite ice cream or the way he grips my throat and urges my jaw to a different angle to allow him better access.

Theirs. I am theirs.

And they are mine.

I find Meg's hair with one hand. I don't guide her. I'm simply hanging on for dear life. I run my other hand down Hades's chest to grip his cock. He chuckles against my mouth. The sound vibrates through me. He lifts his head. "Slow." For a second, I think he's talking to me, until he reaches down and drags Meg off my cock. She makes a protesting sound, but Hades is having none of it. He pushes her down onto the bed next to me and uses a hold on my throat to guide me to her mouth.

Kissing Hades feels like being thrown into a hurricane. Wild and free and a little terrifying. With Meg, it's sinking into a pool of cool water. I want to stay here forever, to take every bit of her, to kiss her until it doesn't matter where she ends or I begin because we are one. I tangle my fingers in her hair and give myself over to this. I'm only vaguely aware of Hades moving down her body, but when she moans, I can't help but look.

Hades is always so controlled and restrained. It's sexy as fuck. I won't even lie and pretend it's not. But he doesn't look controlled *or* restrained right now. He holds Meg in place with a hand spread across her lower stomach and he's going after her pussy like he'll never get another chance to taste her again. Like he craves her coming on his face the same way he craves his next breath. He's fucking *lost* for her.

In that moment, I know the truth. I've fallen for him. I've fucking fallen for both of them. No matter how little sense it makes. It's the truth and not one I'm willing to fight.

I palm Meg's breasts and nip her bottom lip. "Come all over his face."

"Dirty boy." She starts to reach for Hades, but I grab her wrists on instinct and guide them over her head. The scene makes me dizzy with desire. Both my hands and Hades's holding her down. Keeping her in place until he's done with her. Until we both are. I glance down to find Hades watching me.

He drags the flat of his tongue over her clit. "You know what to do."

I guess I do. I climb up onto my knees, letting my weight press Meg's wrists more firmly against the mattress. She moans and shoves against me, but not like she wants to get away. More like she enjoys knowing she can't. I shift to grip both her wrists in one hand and use my other to stroke my cock. "Do you want a taste?"

She blinks hazy blue eyes at me. "Should have known you pick up some of Hades's bossiness just by proximity."

"He asked you a question, love."

She lifts her head to glare down at Hades, but he pushes two fingers into her and it bows her back. "Damn it, yes, I want a taste."

It takes me a second to find the right angle to allow me to guide my cock into her mouth. In her position, she can't do more than take what I give her, and I have to fight not to come just from that knowledge alone. Meg sucks me down eagerly, fighting my hold as if I'm not going fast enough for her.

"Harder." Hades's sharp command lashes me. "Fuck her mouth, little Hercules. She can take it." He gives her another long lick that has her moaning around my cock. "You know the drill if you get overwhelmed, love." He must sense my question, because he elaborates. "She will tap with her foot and I will tell you to stop. Don't hold back." Hades gives me a slow grin. "I'm not going to when I fuck your ass later."

My balls draw up and I curse softly.

I begin fucking Meg's mouth. I trust her to communicate if it's too much, and I trust Hades to tell me if she does. I find the right angle that will allow me deep. The way she relaxes to give me full access is so fucking hot, I can barely stand it. I experiment with long strokes and finally find a rhythm that works, fucking her just as Hades told me to. Just like I want to.

I want it to last forever. This control, this pleasure, this moment of pure understanding.

In the end, I am only human. Pleasure and pressure and a tiny bit of pain overwhelm me. I curse. "I'm going to come."

"Down her throat."

Hades's words drive me on, pumping into her mouth as my balls draw up and I orgasm. She drinks me down without hesitation and gives me another few pulls as if she can't get enough. That makes two of us. Three of us. I finally withdraw, but I don't release her. Not yet. Instead, I twist to watch Hades finish her. He must have been teasing her this whole time, bringing her to the edge without letting her cross the threshold. He stops teasing now. He goes after her with the kind of intention that would be terrifying in a different situation. With Meg's pleasure his focus, it's sexy as hell. In an enemy searching for weakness? Less so.

He's not my enemy. Not anymore.

Right?

Meg comes with a cry and a shudder that nearly dislodges my grip on her wrists. She's beautiful all the time, but when she orgasms, it's like the walls falling away. She's unguarded for a few precious seconds. I love those moments. I'm learning to crave them.

Hades moves up her body and kisses her. He cups her pussy possessively, but it seems the contact is meant more as grounding than to send her flying to new heights. I reach out a tentative hand and run my fingers down his back as he brushes soft kisses against Meg's lips. It still feels surreal that I'm allowed to touch him just because I want to. And, fuck, do I want to.

He finally lifts his head enough to say. "You're mine, love. And I'm yours." He turns those dark eyes my way and Meg follows the movement. "And little Hercules is ours."

"Not so little," she murmurs with the beginnings of a wicked smile.

Hades chuckles. "Not so little," he agrees.

My cock's already stirring. When I'm with these two, I feel like a man possessed, and yet I'm more present in my skin than I've been at any other time in my life. My world narrows down to touch and taste and scent. I only worry about what comes next, allowing them to lead me to new heights. I'm not in the mood to be led right now. I know what I want. "I want more."

Hades's smile takes on a mocking edge that promises wickedness. "You have a suggestion I assume."

"I fuck her. You fuck me."

Meg lifts a hand still limp with pleasure. "Sign me up."

Hades shakes his head. "Two mouthy subs."

"You love it." Meg suddenly laughs. "Maybe you have a bit of a masochistic streak, Hades."

"Perhaps." He props himself up on his elbows and looks down at her. "It's good to hear you laugh, love. It's been a long time."

Instantly, she shuttered. "I laugh."

"Yes, you do. But not like this." He smooths her hair back from her face. "You've dimmed your light, and I'm to blame, at least in part."

I find myself holding my breath. This is what I want. Well, I want a lot of things, but *this* is so fucking important. These two people are two broken halves to the same whole, and they're in danger of shattering because they don't talk. It seems the simplest of fixes, but ten years is a lot of time to build up baggage. It's easier for me to pinpoint the problems because I haven't been here this whole time. I have an outsider's perspective.

And this outsider knows they need to have a whole host of conversations before they can truly to heal the rift that's grown between them. We've started, and that's the important thing. Both seem willing to continue, but time will tell. I'm more than willing to push and pester and bully them into talking whenever it's necessary. The thought fills me with a strange kind of joy, a deep knowledge that they need me, that I offer them something they can't get anywhere else or they would have done it long since.

We *fit*, the three of us.

"You shut me out," she says softly. It's a variation of what she's said before.

"I did." His fingers linger against her skin. "I could tell you weren't happy. I thought you planned on leaving."

She stares. "You thought I was going to leave because I was unhappy, so you decided to shut me out and make me *more* unhappy?"

"I didn't say it was a smart decision."

I stroke my hand back up his spine. "It won't happen again."

"You can't make promises like that," she whispers.

"Yes, I can. You might both withdraw on instinct, but I don't. If we veer off the course, I'll stage an intervention. Promise."

"Fuck, Hercules, you're such a Boy Scout." Her words have no venom, just a strange kind of awe.

Hades moves off her to kneel between her thighs. "That's about enough talking for the moment. We're on the same page. We'll decide a course forward in regards to the rest of it later. Right now, our Hercules has a request."

My blood heats up. "More."

"Oh, *now* you have nothing to say. So strange and shocking."

Hades crawls off the bed and stands. He considers us for a moment, and it's like a switch being flipped. I'm holding my breath again, but it's with the kind of anticipation that comes before a violent summer storm. It's inevitable and I'll love every moment of it, but it may hurt along the way. He finally motions with those elegant hands. "Fuck her. Make it good, little Hercules, but neither of you are allowed to come."

My heartbeat picks up, thundering in my chest in anticipation. "Yes, Sir."

"Yes, Sir," Meg echoes, though she gives her words an ironic slant.

I snag her hips and drag her under me. "Always so mouthy."

"You're one to talk."

I kiss her in response. Truly, it's the only thing that makes sense. She's so fucking warm and soft beneath me, and she wraps her legs around my waist, opening herself completely. It's the easiest thing in the world to draw back enough to angle into her. I lace my fingers through hers and guide her hands to the mattress on either side of her head. Her pale skin is flushed and her lips are swollen from our kisses…and from my fucking her mouth. The memory rolls over me, and I have to stop moving and close my eyes for a moment, fighting for control.

"Problem?" Hades's casual question sounds behind me. I have a feeling that if I lose control, he'll punish me, and while that might be fun in a different situation, this moment means too much to derail.

"No," I grit out. "No problem."

"Mmm." The mattress shifts as he climbs back onto it. I don't need to look back to know that he's moving to the spot directly behind me. I can feel him there. He runs his hands down my back and carefully uncrosses Meg's legs and guides them wide, giving him plenty of space to work with. "She feels good, doesn't she? Tight and wet and made just for you."

"For us."

His chuckle rolls down my spine. "Yes, little Hercules. For us." He kisses the back of my neck, setting his teeth against my sensitive skin. "Sometime soon we'll both fill her. Would you like that?"

For Meg to be shared between us the same way they shared me last night? The same way they're sharing me right now? "Fuck yes."

"Would *you* like that, love?"

Her hands spasm in mine in response, but she manages to sound slightly put upon when she answers. "I suppose I could rise to the occasion." She arches beneath me. "Hercules, don't stop."

"Don't tease the poor man. He's hanging on by a thread."

Something wet slides down between my ass cheeks and I freeze, sheathed in Meg to the hilt. And then Hades is there, his hard cock pressing in, in, in to me. My breath leaves me in a whoosh. He barely gives me a moment to adjust to the size of him. His hips bump mine, sealing us together. Hades leans down until his breath teases the curve of my ear. "Move, Hercules. Seal the bargain."

I thrust into Meg and then back onto Hades cock. The first stroke is pure experiment, but he's given me enough room to move. To control this the tiniest bit, to chase my pleasure at their whim. I have every intention of going slow, of enjoying every second of this. I don't stand a chance. Not when Meg runs her hands down my chest and Hades mirrors the movement on my back. Not when they kiss me and then each other across my body. Something snaps inside me and my brakes give out. I push Meg back flat on the bed and drive into her and then drive myself onto Hades's cock. I become a rutting beast, my entire focus narrowing down to filling and being filled. I can't stop. I can't slow down. I can't do anything but fuck.

Hades grabs the back of my neck and shoves deep and that's when I lose it. I cry out as I come, pumping wildly into Meg. I collapse on top of her, and she gathers me to her, pressing kisses to my shoulder, my chest, my neck. I dimly realize that she didn't come again, and I fumble between us, but she catches my hand. "Relax, Hercules. Enjoy this moment."

"But—"

A cool cloth touches me and I jerk. I hadn't even realized Hades left the bed. Holy shit, I am losing it. I can't do anything but lay there while he does a little clean up, and then he's gone and I hear the water in my bathroom running.

I heave myself off Meg. "I'm sorry."

"Don't start that." She pushes me onto my back and climbs up to straddle me. She looks like a wanton goddess who somehow ended up in my bed, and I want to capture this moment forever. Her hair is as wild as her eyes and her whole body is flushed with pleasure. This isn't the ice queen she plays when it suits her.

This is Meg.

My Meg.

Our Meg.

CHAPTER 24

MEG

*J*know the moment Hades reenters the room. Just like I know exactly what happens next as if we've choreographed this to perfection. I ache for him even after everything we've done. It's been too long. He doesn't give me time to adjust. He just jerks my hips back and up and then he's inside me, so deep he takes my breath away. I cry out against Hercules's chest. I can't help it. It feels good but *fuck*.

Hercules catches my arms, holding me in place as Hades fucks me. I should have known he'd be a quick learner when it comes to the push and pull of dominance, should have figured it out after he fucked me on Hades's desk, probably should have figured it out before that. God, he really is perfect.

Hades digs his fingers into my hips. I'll have marks tomorrow, and I relish them. He always knows when my old marks are fading and finds a way to give me fresh ones. Never the same, but that's the point.

"You're thinking too hard." Hercules runs his hands down my arms and back up. "Stay with us, Meg."

Stay with us.

Does he know how much those words mean to me? Even having a place of my own in the Underworld, I still crave exactly what he's offering me. A place with *them*. Something permanent. I'm scared to even hope for it.

Hades grasps my throat and guides me up and back until I'm pressed against his chest and I can barely inhale past the careful pressure he exerts. Hercules is sprawled out beneath us, watching us with a satisfied look in those pretty blue eyes. He's exactly where he wants to be, totally confident that this won't blow up in his face. In all our faces. I wish I had his confidence.

Hades caresses my throat without letting up the pressure. Not enough to hurt me. Just enough to give the impression of cutting off my air supply. He drags his mouth over my shoulder and up my neck to speak softly in my ear. "You're holding back."

"No." The word is barely more than whisper.

"Yes." He sets his teeth against my earlobe and I shiver. "You don't trust me anymore."

"I do." It's almost the truth.

For once, Hercules doesn't have anything to say. He presses his hand to my lower stomach and slides his thumb against my clit. Just a casual teasing touch as if I'm not pinned in place against Hades's body with his cock sheathed deep inside me. Pleasure sparks hotter yet. Hades grabs Hercules's wrist with his free hand. "A moment, little Hercules."

"She thinks clearer when she's on the edge of orgasm."

I try to glare, but I can't quite dredge up the right expression. "Traitor."

He sits up. He's tall enough that he could kiss me in this position if he wants to. "Let go, Meg. Trust us."

Trust. As if it's really that easy. As if I haven't had every man I've ever trusted walk back on it. Even Hades, though he would claim otherwise. He didn't let me essentially sell myself for his gain, but when he shut me out, it damaged us. Hercules is the only one who hasn't, but surely it's only a matter of time. The odds are not in his favor.

"This only works if all parties are invested." Hades doesn't release Hercules's hand, but he guides it back to my pussy. "Do you want this?"

As much as part of me wants to hold back, I can't quite manage it. "Yes. Too much."

"No such thing as too much." Hercules strokes my clit again, his eyes on my face. "Not with us."

"How can you be so sure?"

He shrugs those big shoulders. "I'm falling for you."

The words shock the breath from my lungs more effectively than Hades's hand around my throat does. "What?"

Hercules drags his thumb over my clit again and gives me a startlingly sunny smile. "I'm falling for you. Is that so hard to believe?"

"Yes." The word just pops out into existence despite my attempt to keep it silent. "The only reason you're here is—"

"Because I want to be. I chose to be here when I made the deal. Now I'm choosing this, choosing you. Both of you." As if it's that simple for him. He decides this is what he wants and that's enough to go for it. His optimism humbles and terrifies me. He leans up and kisses me softly on the lips. "Choose us, Meg. Please."

In the end, maybe it is that simple.

I want the picture Hercules paints. I want it so bad, I can barely stand it. If I let fear hold me back, maybe it won't end right this second, but things will fall apart sooner, rather than later. The only way this works is full commitment on all parts. That includes me. Tears prick my eyes, though I can't begin to say why. I finally nod as much as I can with Hades's hand still at my throat. "Okay."

"I'm proud of you," Hades murmurs. "I know that wasn't easy." He pulls out of me and I sob out a breath at the sudden lack.

But then Hercules is there through some unspoken agreement. He pulls me down onto his cock and I might laugh if I had the breath for it. God save me from a twenty-five-year-old's record recovery time. I already know what Hades is about before I feel the cool slide of his lubed fingers against my ass. I lean forward and exhale, relaxing into the intrusion as he tests me. I don't want the tease right now. I want all of him, all of them, a physical representation of what we've already said with our words. Hades always had a cruel streak, though, and he takes his time with me. Making us wait.

Hercules cups my face with his big hands. "Trust us," he repeats.

"I'll try."

He kisses me. His tongue slides into my mouth the moment that Hades guides his cock into my ass, as if they planned this moment perfectly through some unspoken command. Even though I've done this before more than a few times, I can't help panting against Hercules's lips as Hades works his way into me until he's sheathed completely. I am so fucking *full* of them that it almost hurts, a growing pressure that will morph into pleasure at the barest hint of movement. I try to shift, but Hades grips my hips too tightly. "Not yet, love."

Desperation rises in time with the heartbeat throbbing beneath my skin. Too much. It's too much and not enough and I can't stand it. "Please." I manage to slide the barest bit against them and the friction nearly causes my eyes to roll back in my head. Words rise up, a torrent I fight to keep inside. I should know better by now. "Please, please, please fuck me." I try to stop, try to slow down, but they overwhelm me simply by existing. "Please love me."

Just like that, Hades's grip relaxes. "I'll always give you what you need."

"We'll always give you what you need." Hercules takes my arms and guides them to the small of my back where Hades takes over. He clasps my wrists with one hand and keeps his grip on my hip with the other, and then he begins to move. A slow slide out and an equally agonizingly slow slide back in. On the third one, Hercules picks up the rhythm, thrusting when Hades withdraws, withdrawing when Hades thrusts. I am never empty, never able to move, never able to do more than take the pleasure they alternate giving me.

I'm sobbing and I can't stop. They have made me their center in this moment and it's a balm to my battered soul. Through some unspoken communication, they both shove deep and it throws me over the edge. I shudder as I come, my body so over-sensitized that I can barely handle the pleasure. Hades and Hercules are there to catch me. They hold me between their bodies as they keep fucking me, but the tone of it changes. Even as they buoy me up, they seek their own pleasure. I twist a little to see Hades take Hercules's mouth and it's almost enough to send me over the edge again. Hercules comes first, driving into me from below, his moans muffled by Hades's mouth. Hades breaks away and releases my hands. He braces himself on the small of my back and drives deep again and again, pulling out the barest moment before he orgasms. He comes across my back in hot spurts and I shiver.

Hades slumps down next to us and I turn my face so I can see him. He looks... happy. Relaxed in a way I've never witnessed. As happy and relaxed as I feel. He takes my hand and presses a kiss to the tattoo on wrist and gives me a wry smile. We don't need words, though. Not right now, not when everything is exactly as it should be.

Maybe… maybe this can actually work.

It takes time to recover enough to regain the use of my legs, but the moment I do, they haul me into the shower and we take turns cleaning one another up. It could be a foreplay all its own, but I'm so exhausted, I'm weaving on my feet. The last twelve hours have been a lot. More than a lot.

Back in Hercules's bedroom, I stare at the messy sheets and shake my head. We've ruined them. There are a spare set in the closet, but the thought of putting even that much effort is too much. "Well, hell."

A silk robe touches my shoulders and I slip my arms into it and belt it around my waist. I glance at Hades. "Since when are my clothes in here?"

He gives me a look but ignores the question. He's wearing his slacks and pulls on his shirt. I don't know why my stomach drops with each button he closes, but I can't shake the feeling that this was only a magical moment in time. That it can't last. I push the fear away. I told them I'd trust them, and I will. No matter what.

Hercules has on a pair of lounge pants and nothing else. He stares at the bed. "That won't work."

"Come along." Hades opens the door and walks out.

I sigh. "I hate it when he does this."

"Do you, though?" Hercules chuckles and heads for the door.

I glare at his back. "Fine. No, I don't."

I half expect Hades to walk to my room, but he bypasses my door and heads for the elevator. We take it up to the top floor, and I can't help watching Hercules's face as we step out. His eyes go a little wide as he steps out into Hades's penthouse, and he turns a slow circle. "Wow."

Wow is right. The rest of the building, Hades's personal

office excepted, is all clean lines and minimalist decorations. Not so with his living space. It's... not cluttered, exactly, but filled with evidence of a life well-lived. There's a shelf filled with knickknacks he's collected on his various travels, and bookshelves filled with more books than one man could possibly read in a single lifetime.

Hades doesn't stop to let Hercules take it all in. He strides down the short hall to the bedroom. Here, it's a little darker, a little broodier, a little more expected of someone who runs the Underworld. The windows all have blackout blinds and the giant custom-made bed has deep red sheets that are an obscenely high thread count. The walk-in closet is larger than most people's apartments, and the bathroom larger yet. Hades likes his luxuries.

Hercules huffs out a laugh. "You do nothing halfway, do you?"

"Why bother?" Hades flips back the comforter. "In bed, both of you. Before you fall asleep where you stand."

I don't have to look outside to know that the sun is creeping up from the horizon. We have a few hours before I need to be in my office, and I'm tired enough to need them. I drop my robe and climb into the bed. After the briefest hesitation, Hercules follows me. Hades stands at the foot of the bed and stares at us for a long moment, possession and something like longing lingering in those dark eyes. "Mine."

I shiver and try to keep the vulnerability out of my voice. "I take it you're not joining us?"

"Not yet." His gaze softens. "Sleep, love. You two deserve it. You've pleased me greatly."

There's no point in arguing. It will waste both my breath and my time. I finally tuck myself against Hercules's chest and relax into him as he wraps his arms around me. The man is an inferno, chasing away the chill that worked its way beneath my skin on the walk up here. I always sleep well in

Hades's bed, surrounded by his presence even when he's not in the bed with me. This time, with Hercules holding me, it's doubly true. I close my eyes and let myself relax against him.

Maybe they're right and this is the start of something new. Something special.

Maybe this really won't blow up in our faces.

Maybe.

CHAPTER 25

HADES

Something akin to guilt pricks me as I sit in my private office and turn on my computer. Leaving Hercules and Meg in my bed was harder than I anticipated. They fit there, just like I suspected they would. *We* fit. The knowledge still sits strangely with me. Hercules may give himself freely and without reservation, but that's not the man I am. I know my Meg cares deeply for him. Despite herself, perhaps, but it's there all the same.

My feelings are a bit more complicated.

I click to bring up the video that was recorded earlier tonight. The three of us in my public office, Hercules trussed up with the nipple clamps and cock ring, the metal chain glinting with every movement. My cock in his mouth. Meg behind him, fucking his ass. The video is high quality and there's absolutely no doubt of our identities, just like there's no doubt that Hercules is a happy, willing participant in his fall from grace.

It takes the space of a few moments to cut the video down to size, a thirty second clip that sends the message I require. I attach it to the email and hesitate. Hercules all but gave permission for this. He wants to cause his father pain, and he's willing to play whipping boy to ensure it happens. Meg and I have our own reputations and this video will do nothing to damage them, even if it's shared widely. And I highly doubt it will be shared. That's not what this is about. It's simply to reinforce my message to Zeus.

Your son belongs to me.

He does, albeit in a way I never could have anticipated. Becoming entangled in Hercules, allowing him to attach himself to the one relationship I value above all others... I only meant for it to be temporary. A fix to bind Meg and I together until we could find our footing again. I never expected for him to fit in a way that could work in the long term. I can't say I'm sorry it's happened. Because he *does* fit. He softens our sharp edges and makes us stronger as a unit.

And I care about him.

Perhaps *that* is what's causing this strange hesitation. I protect what's mine, regardless of the reason it came under my influence. I should have anticipated my instincts fighting against my actions. Hercules knows what he signed on for. Even if he doesn't, there is no turning back now. I've gone too far, come too close. It's not a true balancing of the scales, but it's close enough. Fifteen years ago, I would have killed Hercules at the beginning and been done with it. I'm not sure I've changed for the better, regardless of how much I enjoy the ultimate outcome.

My body moves before my mind can alter course. I click to send the email. My careful exhale doesn't make me feel better about what I've done. I have no use for guilt. I don't torment myself with it the same way my two lovers do. What's done is done and that's the end of it.

At least for now.

My phone rings. I know who it is even before I answer. "Yes?"

He doesn't make me wait long. "Release him."

Satisfaction curls through me, the perfect counterpoint to the tension in his tone. I smile and lean back in my chair. "I don't think I will. He so enjoys being trapped by me."

"That is my son's throat you have your cock shoved down in this video." He pauses and, when he speaks again, a false calm bleeds into his words. "He's a good boy, Hades."

"Yes, he's a very good boy."

He growls at the innuendo. "You have a problem with me, you come at me."

I could laugh. I wrap up the urge and tuck it away. "You know better. An eye for an eye. You should be grateful I'm not going to kill him the same way you murdered *my* son."

"Better he be fucking murdered than in your bed." His volume increases with every word. "I won't stand for this, Hades. You have twelve fucking hours to return him to me or you'll pay the price."

"I've already paid the price in spades, old friend." I hang up.

The expected jubilation never arrives. Instead, Zeus's words play back to me. *You'll pay the price.* A threat, and I'm not fool enough to ignore it. Neither am I inclined to return Hercules to him. The man made his choice, for better or worse, and now we're all going to live with it. He chose us, not his family, not Olympus.

This is exactly what I wanted when I set out on this path. Zeus enraged enough to come for me.

Still… It may be prudent to make security aware of a possible threat to our people. I send a quick text to Allecto. She'll ensure all precautions are covered. There have been a few missteps in recent months, but none of those involved allowing people into the building who aren't supposed to be there. Several guests have abused my hospitality, but that is an altogether different problem. We're a fortress in the form of a skyscraper. Zeus cannot touch us here.

I push back from my desk, a nervous energy zinging through my old bones. Even knowing better, I can't shake the feeling that I've made a mistake somewhere along the way. That perhaps I should have turned my back on this final vengeance, no matter how tempered. I walk to the closest bookshelf and pull out an old copy of *Aesop's Fables*. It's weathered and aged and holding it in my hands brings a dull ache to my chest even after all this time. It's a reminder of another life. I flip open the cover and there they are. My lost ones.

I hear her behind me, her footsteps as familiar as my own. "I used to read this book to my son every night. He was too young to understand, but it calmed him."

Meg stops. "You never told me about them." She can't quite keep the accusation out of her voice.

"It still hurts to talk about them. It's easier to force forget-fulness."

She takes another step, moving around the desk to stand at my shoulder. "But you didn't really forget them, Hades. Not if you've been spinning out this plan for revenge."

She's not wrong. "Would you believe that I wanted to spare us both pain?"

"Yes, but that doesn't make it right." She wraps her arms around herself. "Don't you think the time for that has long since passed?"

I shift to include her in this painful walk down memory lane. Meg moves until her arm presses against mine. I tilt the book. "This is one of the few pictures I have of them. The others were lost." I mourned that loss for a long time, but perhaps it's for the best. Better to let their ghosts rest, to let the memory fade. It doesn't cease to cause pain, but it's not a constant low hum in the back of my mind.

"May I?"

I hand her the picture. As she studies the photo, I study her face. What does she see? A pretty young blond woman with a baby boy in her arms. They're wearing white, which only adds to the surreal nature of the entire thing. Meg finally looks at me, her blue eyes shining. "They're beautiful."

"They were, yes."

She carefully passes back the picture, and I replace it inside the book. Meg is obviously working up to something, so I slide the book back into the shelf and give her a moment to find her voice. This is a conversation we should have had long ago, and it's only my reluctance to open old wounds that delayed it. A mistake. I see that now.

Finally, she sighs. "You told me you didn't want kids."

"I don't."

"Hades, look at me."

I turn to face her. Meg's dressed in the same robe she wore for the trip from Hercules's bedroom to mine. Another time, I would take that as a clear invitation. Not this morning.

She's right. This subject deserves my full attention. *She* deserves my full attention. Instinct demands I turn this topic, avoid this old pain. I ignore it. "When I was young, I thought I was invincible. I married Amber in a whirlwind romance because it seemed the most natural thing in the world, and she was pregnant within a few months." I lift my hands, but let them fall without touching her. "I was a different man before Zeus killed them. I wanted different things. When I crawled out of the pit their deaths put me in, I promised myself I wouldn't repeat the same mistake. No innocents to depend on me. Especially no children." I finally meet her gaze and she's looking at me with her battered heart in her eyes. "I didn't lie, Meg. I withheld the reasons I felt the way I did, but I didn't lie."

"You should have told me," she whispers.

"I see that now." I'm not used to making missteps. Not on this scale. "I'm sorry, love. It still hurts at times, and in my attempt to avoid that pain, I didn't think about the harm it would cause you."

She leans against my desk and crosses her arms over her chest. "Hades... your plan sucks. It will piss Zeus off knowing that you have his son, but from all you and Hercules have said, you're out of your mind if you think he won't retaliate."

"I have it covered."

"No." She shakes her head. "No, we're not doing that again. If you meant what you said last night, then you're going to loop me and Hercules in on the plan, and we're going to discuss it. We can play submissive at your feet when we actually play, but this is too serious for you to try to shield us. We made our choice. We're in this with you, for better or worse."

There's no point in arguing. I cannot effectively protect them if they actively fight against the precautions I put into place. The only way to ensure they work with me is to include them in the conversation. No matter how much I'd like to shield them. I finally nod. "I'll arrange a meeting with Allecto to go over things this afternoon before the club opens."

"Thank you."

We stare at each other for a long moment before I sigh. "I've made a mess of this."

"We both have." She pushes off the desk and steps into my arms. "We just need a little course correcting." Meg gives a faint laugh. "A *lot* of course correcting."

I think of the man we left in my bed and can't help the wry smile that pulls at my lips. "Somehow, I think Hercules will single-handedly bully us back onto the path."

"I think you're right." She smiles up at me. It's far more tentative than it would have been even a year ago, and I mourn the lost time. I know better than anyone not to take things for granted, but I've done exactly that with this woman.

I brush her hair back from her face. "I don't deserve you."

"I think we can both agree that if any two people deserve each other, it's us." She turns her head and kisses my wrist. "Don't shut me out again. I can't bear it."

"I won't." A promise I likely have no business making, but one wrong word could send this fragile balance between us shattering into a million pieces. I won't willingly break it. The thought of losing her... "You are everything I never knew I needed, love. A partner in every way. An *equal* in every way. You don't shy from my less savory traits. One could argue that you relish them."

"I do. Sometimes it's despite myself, but I do." She leans into my touch. "What happens now?"

That was the question, wasn't it? "We wait to see how Zeus reacts. Then we adjust from there."

Meg smiles, though sadness still lingers in her eyes. "Hades, that's a horrible plan."

"He can't penetrate the Underworld's defenses. I've spent all my time here ensuring that this place is a fortress."

"Yes. But even a fortress can't provide for every need. We have to leave eventually. To stay trapped here is to let him win."

She's right. "I simply need the appropriate leverage."

"You figure that out." She takes my hand. "In the meantime, come back to bed."

CHAPTER 26

*W*hen I wake, it's tangled up between Meg and Hades's naked bodies. I lie there for a long time, soaking up their closeness. My body aches faintly from all the fucking, but not in an unpleasant way. It takes longer for the rest of what I'm feeling to sink in. I'm... happy. Content. The stress of the future still lingers, but it's nowhere near as overwhelming as it has been for most of my life. I finally feel like I'm right where I'm supposed to be.

Meg stretches, her ass rubbing against the aching cock I've been trying to ignore. "Is that cockstand just for me?"

"Mmm." I pull her closer and cup her breasts. I was planning on letting them sleep longer, on maybe slipping out and hitting the gym for a little bit before the day gets started. This is a way better way to spend my time. "Good morning."

"Good morning indeed."

I skate a hand down her stomach to palm her pussy. Every time I touch this woman, it feels so fucking right. Like coming home, if home was something to be craved, rather than something to be avoided. I touch her idly, teasing her until she's pressing back against me, trying to get closer. I lift her leg up and over my hip, opening her completely, and notch my cock at her entrance. There's no rush as I slide into her. It's the kind of fucking that feels like we've shifted from one dream to another. Slow. Unhurried. Decadent. When she comes, it's with a ragged breath and my whispered name on her tongue. I bury my face in her hair as I follow her over the edge, emptying myself into her in a way that feels downright fucking spiritual.

Hades's hands on my hips guide me out of her and onto my back. He moves between my thighs and then his lubed up cock is pressing into my ass, just as slowly and steadily as I pushed into Meg. He looks relaxed and sleepy in a way I could get used to. He sinks the last few inches into me and looks at Meg. Through some unspoken agreement, she shifts closer to press against us and kisses him. I can't stop myself from touching her again. I don't even bother to try. She draws back with a little gasp and Hades gives me a look of approval. "Ride his hand, love. We both know you're too greedy to be satisfied with a single orgasm."

She's wet and slippery against my fingers. The evidence of our dual orgasms makes it easy to push three fingers into her and press my palm against her clit. "You heard him."

She kisses me as she starts to rock, fucking my hand just like Hades told her to. That's when Hades begins to move. It takes me several breathless moments to realize he's mimicking Meg's strokes almost perfectly. Long slow glides. And then Meg moves back and Hades is there, his mouth on mine. He's nowhere near as soft as she is and I relish the difference between them.

Before, they overwhelmed me. It doesn't feel like that this time. I feel utterly cherished between these two people I care about. Like the new corner we turned last night really means something and we could be waking up like this many, many times in the future. I want that more than anything.

Meg reaches between Hades and me for my cock and gives me a rough stroke that has my back bowing. Hades leans back for half a second and then cool wetness covers her hand and my cock and she picks up her pace. She jacks me as he fucks me and, god, has there ever been a more perfect pair than these two? I don't know. I can't think, can't breathe, can't do more than lie there and take what they give me even as Meg comes apart all over my hand. I try to hold on. I do. But it's too fucking good. I come with a shout, coating my stomach and chest. Hades jerks and curses softly, and he pulls out of me in time to come across my stomach and chest too. I stare down at the mess and, holy shit, this is real. Maybe I shouldn't be so turned on by the way we mix, but I am and I'm not sorry.

Meg rolls away and stretches her entire body. She doesn't come close to reaching the end of the bed. "Shower time."

Hades catches my mouth in a devastating kiss that ends all too soon. "Time to clean up, little Hercules. We have a long day ahead of us."

Showering in Hades's huge-ass bathroom feels so strangely domestic. There are enough showerheads for six people, but we linger together under the water. Hades washes Meg's hair with the ease of someone who's done it many, many times before, and I'm captivated watching his graceful hands work her dark locks. And then he gives me the same treatment, easing away the tightness in my temples and neck while Meg soaps up my body. I feel utterly cared for. This is what I wanted, but I had no idea their edges would come with this unexpected softness beneath. A true tenderness that makes the warmth in my chest bloom.

By the time we make it out of the shower and dry off, I'm grinning like a fool.

Meg drags a comb through her hair and smiles at me in

the mirror. "Look, Hades. We've made our little Hercules a happy man."

"Didn't take much," he murmurs, disappearing into the closet on the other end of the bathroom. It's tempting to follow him, but I get the feeling that Hades isn't even remotely comfortable with adding someone into his care the way he's added me. He didn't intend for this to happen, and I'm willing to wait him out until he comes to terms with exactly what he feels for me. I have all the time in the world, after all. When I made my bargain with Hades, I never anticipated this outcome. It feels so right, I don't question it. Before, I gave him forever in that moment of pain and anger. Now, I'm choosing it. Choosing *them*.

I hop up to sit on the counter and watch Meg get ready. She moves about the space easily, but then that makes sense. Even if she has her own suite on the employee level, she must spend a lot of time up here with Hades.

She dries her hair and then twists it back and begins her makeup. I watch, fascinated, as she uses a variety of products to sharpen her already natural beauty, finishing with the bold red lipstick I've come to associate with her. She glances at me in the mirror. "Are you about to tell me I look prettier without the makeup?"

"I like you every way, Meg." I shrug. "Whether you're wearing makeup or not makes no difference to me."

"Smart boy." Hades walks back through the door. He's once again dressed in a suit that's black-on-black. He gives me a significant look. "I'll have some of your clothes brought up here so you aren't wandering the halls in a towel in the future."

Another indication of the permanence of our arrangement. No, not arrangement. This is a fucking relationship. I grin. "And here I thought you'd want to show me off."

"Trust me, little Hercules, I'll do that and more tonight on the floor of the public play room."

All my amusement disappears, replaced by pure heat. "Tonight?" I may not have worked at the Underworld long, but I've already heard about how rarely Hades plays in public —and what an event it is when he does. Even though I know what this must be—him continuing to prove a point to my father—I can't quite catch my breath as anticipation lances me. He's also claiming me as his for everyone else. The only one he publicly scenes with is Meg.

"Yes." He stops and presses a kiss to Meg's temple and then walks to me and does the same. "Behave, you two. We have a meeting with Allecto in an hour. You don't have time to get distracted." And then he's gone, silently walking out of the bathroom and through the bedroom. I don't exhale until I hear the door click shut.

"Why are we meeting with Allecto?"

Meg heads for the closet, and I hop off the counter to follow her. The closet is filled to the brim with black clothing, but there's a section that's obviously Meg's for all that it appears to be menswear. She dresses quickly in a pair of gray slacks and a white halter vest thing that gives glimpses of her pale stomach and the curves of her breasts. Heels finalize the outfit, bringing her well past my shoulder. She finally looks at me. "Hades taunted your father last night. It's possible Zeus will retaliate."

He taunted my father last night. I pick apart the words and delve beneath to what she's not staying. "He left our bed to go play power games with Zeus."

"Yes." She doesn't bother to pretty it up, but then Meg isn't one to mince words. "He's brushing up the security in order to ensure his people remain safe. Allecto is already the best, but she can't anticipate an enemy she doesn't know exists."

I should have known that reality wouldn't wait long to intrude on this little paradise we created. Just like I should have known that Hades would be the one to invite it in. I scrub a hand over my face. "How Zeus responds will depend on what Hades did to provoke him—and how public it was." My father has a mostly sterling reputation despite everything he's done in the shadows and behind closed doors. It's one of the things that tipped the scales against Leda, in addition to her being a virtual unknown and Zeus holding significant power. Zeus will fight to maintain his public persona.

"I can't speak to that." She stops in front of me and runs her hands up my chest. "I hope you were serious with everything you said last night, because there's no turning back now." She hesitates. "But if you do change your mind—"

"I won't."

Meg catches my chin, her nails digging into my skin. "If you change your mind, I'll get you out."

Shock floors me. "What?"

"It won't be Olympus and it won't be Carver City, but I have enough money set aside that you could effectively disappear as long as you aren't an idiot about it. Say the word and it's yours."

What she's offering... I hold perfectly still. I won't brush this off, no matter how unlikely I am to take her up on this. If I know Meg, and at this point I feel I have an innate understanding of her, then this nest egg she's gift wrapping for me is one she's saved for herself. Her exit hatch to ensure history never repeats itself, that she always has a way out. "I meant what I said last night." I take her hands. "I'm totally gone for you."

"You barely know me." Even as she says the words, her heart is in her eyes. She cares about me too. She wouldn't do so many of the things she's done since we met, culminating in offering me everything to leave if I need it.

"I know enough." I lean down slowly, and though she maintains her hold on my chin, she allows it. I kiss her carefully, cautious of the red lipstick. "Thank you for offering me this. I don't need it, but I know what it represents to you and what losing it would cost."

Her fingers tremble, just a little. "You can't possibly be real."

"I am." I cover her hand with mine. "I'm real. I'm right here." A pause. "I'm yours."

Her lips finally curve into a reluctant smile. "Yes, you really, really are." She drops her hand and shakes her head. "I don't know if this is the beginning of something new and wonderful—or the beginning of the end. But apparently we're taking this ride to its conclusion."

"It will be okay, Meg." A reassurance I have no business offering her, but one I can't help making despite that. I don't want her sad and stressed. I sure as fuck don't want to be the cause of it. "We'll figure this out together."

"I suppose we will." She casts a critical eye over me, lingering on the lounge pants I wore up to this room last night. "We better get moving or we're going to miss the meeting with Allecto, and then Hades will think up some ridiculously uncomfortable punishment." She leans into me. "But if we had time, I'd be sucking your dick right now and let you fuck me in front of Hades's giant mirror."

I glance over her shoulder at the mirror in question. It stretches from floor to ceiling and is wider than it has right to be. A heavy frame that must be custom-made borders it. With all that space to work with, I would be able to watch my cock slide into Meg with each stroke, would be able to see every wave of pleasure roll through her expression. I swallow hard and try to get my physical reaction under control, but my cock isn't listening.

Meg gives a low laugh and strokes me once through my pants. "Mmmm. Makes my mouth water."

I narrow my eyes in a mock glare. "You're trying to get me in trouble."

"Maybe." She's totally unrepentant, her wicked grin lighting up her face. "What can I say? I have a bit of a sadistic streak when I'm inspired, and you, my dear Hercules, inspire the fuck out of me."

CHAPTER 27

MEG

*T*he security meeting goes about as well as I expect it to. Allecto details the extra protocols we'll need to go through in order to leave the building and the new cameras she's having installed around the exterior. We already have more cameras in the Underworld than we probably need, and I appreciate her thoroughness, but I can't help feeling that it won't be enough. We can't live in this glass castle forever. The building may be strong enough to withstand a subtle siege, but there are more factors in play. Our clientele, for one. If we have to close down operations for some reason...

No use thinking about that.

Even with the sky threatening to fall down around our heads, I can't help the bubbly feeling in my chest as I sit between Hercules and Hades. My men. *Mine* in a way I barely dare comprehend. I meant every word when I offered Hercules a way out. I'd slip him out the door and stand in Hades's way while he escaped us. It might break my heart to do it, but I don't want him trapped here through circumstance. Unlike Hades, I want him to choose it with eyes wide open.

Once Allecto is done giving us a run-down, we disperse. Hades to his office and Hercules to occupy himself. I suspect he'll end up in the gym or maybe sneak in a few more hours of sleep. It's tempting to follow him, but I have a job to do. Which is why I don't even sigh when Allecto walks into my office a few minutes later and shuts the door.

She's in her daywear: ripped jeans, a black silk shirt, and boots that are probably steel-toed. Her long braids are in a top-knot and her lipstick is just as red as mine. She leans against the door and crosses her arms over her chest. "Give it to me straight. how bad is it?"

"Bad." No use mincing words. Hades may or may not downplay the danger, but I'm not willing to. "He's in a pissing match with the guy who effectively runs Olympus."

Allecto curses softly. "This guy will have personal security."

"Probably. With the kind of influence he brings to the fore, it's entirely likely he has the equivalent of his own militia. Large staff, large number of people working security." In the regular world, security details aren't utilized like soldiers, but ours is not the real world. We can't take anything for granted. Allecto, for example, might run security, but she also has a plethora of unsavory talents that lend to working in the shadows if the situation calls for it.

She nods. "Okay. I'm going to set up a secondary circle a little farther out. If they come for us, we'll at least have a little notice before they're on our doorstep."

I lean forward. "Can you do that? Won't people notice you putting up cameras?"

She grins. "You're pretty, but you're not that smart."

"Yes, yes, you're superior in every way." I wave that away. "Now tell me how it works."

"I'll have Tis hack into the businesses' camera system. Most of them are connected to an off-site network to store the video, so they won't even realize that we're piggybacking on their signal. Enough of them exist that we should have most of the circle covered."

I lean back and give her a smile of my own. "You're pretty *and* smart. Very impressive."

"Yeah, yeah." She laughs, but instantly sobers. "I'm going to get her working on that now. I don't like this."

I wish I could give her some inspiring words, but Allecto and I don't lie to each other no matter how barbed our conversations can become. "I don't like it either."

She gives me a long look. "I'll keep you assholes safe as long as you don't do anything stupid."

"Do anything stupid?" I press my hand to my chest. "Me?"

"Yes, you." She shakes her head. "Don't leave the building without letting me know, Meg. I mean it."

"Yes, ma'am."

"Bitch." She says it fondly. "I'll show you the secondary camera circle once we have it set up." She walks out my door, not bothering to close it behind her.

I huff out a sigh. The damn woman always has to get a last word, and while I can admire it most of the time, I still want to snarl as I climb to my feet to shut the door. I'm still a step away when Tink steps into my office. I stop short. She looks like shit. She's wearing the same clothes from yesterday and her hair has... dirt in it? Most telling of all is the bruise darkening the space around her left eye.

I stare at that bruise. Fury rises, swift and nearly overwhelming. Someone *hurt* her. "Who?"

She doesn't pretend to misunderstand me. "It doesn't matter."

I reach past her and close the door, forcing her into the office. "Sit."

"Meg—"

"Sit your ass down, Tink. That's not a suggestion." I follow her to the chair and carefully tilt her head back. The bruise is new enough that it's still going to swell like a motherfucker. "Do not move. I'll be right back."

"Meg—"

"Now is *not* the time to argue with me." I stalk out of the office and to the little kitchen we keep stocked for employees. Among other things, we ensure there are a lot of ice packs. One never knows when they'll come in handy, though I can't remember the last time someone had a black eye. That shit is not sanctioned, and I know Tink's preferences. No way did she consent to this. If she *did*, then that's one thing. If she didn't…

I'll get the truth out of her. And then I'll deal with it.

I close the door to my office and press the ice pack into her hand. Once she has it against her face, I perch on the edge of my desk and study her. "Tell me."

"I came in here to request some time off. Not because I wanted the third degree."

I give a mirthless smile. "You know how we operate, Tink. You can try to brazen your way through, but it won't work. Tell me what happened now or we go to Hades and you tell him later. Either way, the truth comes out." When she goes to speak, her expression stubborn, I hold up a hand. It's time to try a different tactic. "Your contract still has two months on it. An injury to you is an injury to Hades. You know he can't allow that."

Tink sinks down in her chair and leans her head back. "You're such a bitch."

"You're not the first person to say so today." I prop my arms on the desk and wait. She's holding out for pride's sake at this point, and pushing her will result in her digging in her heels. Better to let the silence spin out until she works herself up to speaking.

Tink, being Tink, doesn't make me wait long. She sighs. "I'm an idiot." I want to jump in and tell her that she's probably the least idiotic person I know, but interrupting at this point will just make her clam up again. Tink closes her eyes. "You know why I have this deal with Hades?"

"I know enough." Safety in exchange for service. I don't know what drove her to that level of desperation, but in the end it matters little.

"I don't know what I thought would happen if I left him. I guess I didn't really think about it beyond getting out." She opens her eyes, and they look greener than I've ever seen them, filled to the brim with guilt. "He's got a new girl, but apparently he learned from his mistakes with me because he's got her brothers too. It's… It's never going to stop. If not her, then someone else, forever and ever until the end of time."

In all the time I've known Tink, I've never seen her look so despondent. I know better than to offer sympathy, though. She's like me. She'll see it as pity and shut down completely. I hold perfectly still. "So you went to get her out."

"Stupid, I know. I thought if I talked to her, she'd see that it didn't have to be that way. She punched me in the fucking face." She laughs and winces. "I might like her under other circumstances."

Damn it. This isn't something I can fix. I sigh. "What can I do?"

"Nothing." She straightens and takes the ice pack off her face. Her eye is already swelling and it will be completely shut soon. Tink pushes to her feet. "I have to handle this myself, one way or another. But I needed to let you know I can't work tonight for obvious reasons." She motions to her face.

"Don't worry about it. I'll see if Aurora is up for another shift, but even if she's not, the club will be fine if it's short a submissive." I lean forward and tuck a strand of her hair behind her ear. "Go pop some meds, take a shower, and get some rest. We'll survive without you until you're healed." I wait for her to start for the door before I continue. "And Tink?"

"Yeah?"

"If you change your mind about wanting to take care of this yourself…" I allow a sharp smile to creep over my face. "I'm more than happy to lend a helping hand."

She goes a little pale but manages a smile of her own. "I appreciate that."

I spend the rest of the afternoon finishing up small tasks that don't require too much thinking involved. Tonight feels monumental for a number of reasons, not solely because it's an open declaration of war. I don't know what exactly Hades did to piss off Zeus last night, but dominating Hercules in front of all the important players in Carver City is the kind of public message that Hercules is sure his father will respond to. I know Hades thinks he has it locked down, and he may even be right, but I can't shake the feeling of dread the suffuses my entire being. Something bad is coming and it's too late to avoid it. We're on this path, for better or worse.

An hour before the Underworld opens, I head down to my suite to change and get my head on straight. I can't afford to hesitate or doubt, no matter what the night brings. Any reaction on my part will feed into the conclusions people will draw. It's important they come to the correct ones.

I haven't been this nervous in a very long time. I find I don't like it much.

I manage to nibble on half a protein bar before I give it up for a lost cause. To distract myself, I change into one of my favorite dresses. It's a sleek black sheath that hugs my body like a second skin. I pair it with tall boots that hit mid-thigh, drawing attention to exactly how indecently short the dress is. I touch up my makeup, and there's nothing left to stall with.

My phone rings before I decide that I need a drink. The sight of Hades's name gives me a little flutter in my stomach, but I manage to keep it out of my voice when I answer. "Yes?"

"Come up to my office. I want to speak with you before we begin."

That could mean anything and nothing. I frown. "Is everything okay?"

"Now, Meg." He hangs up.

I mutter under my breath a bit, but it breaks the tension a little. I don't have to think too hard when I'm obeying, though it doesn't always work out like that. A few minutes later, I shut the door to his office and pause. Hades and Hercules sit next to each other on the couch, their heads close as they speak. They look... My heart skips a beat. They look so good. All youthful glow and well-aged whiskey. And they're all mine. The thought barely feels real as I take a few slow steps toward them. "Am I interrupting?"

Hades crooks his fingers, motioning me forward. "We're going to make tonight easier for you, love."

I blink. "What?"

"Did you think we wouldn't notice?" He waits, the ever-patient wolf, as I cross to him and tentatively lay my hand in his. Only then does he take in my body with a single sweep. "This dress is a gift. Don't you agree, little Hercules?"

For his part, Hercules is looking at me like he wants to eat me up with a spoon. "Definitely a gift."

I don't understand this. There isn't some silly rule about not spending time together before they scene, but they aren't acting like I expect. It strikes me then that I was bracing for rejection, even after everything. I might laugh if I weren't so damn ashamed of myself. I wet my lips. "So glad you like it."

"Mmm." Hades leans back, taking me a step closer to them until my legs bump their knees. "I would hate for you to feel left out tonight, so we're going to give you a little something to remember us by until we can take care of you later."

My mind whirls, but I don't get a chance to do more than tense as Hercules runs his hand up the inside of my thigh. He urges me to take a wider stance, and I do so in a daze. Hercules slides easily to the floor between my spread legs. He gives me a happy smile. "I've been thinking about your pussy all day."

I've been the recipient and giver of dirty talk for years. Nothing has made my legs shake the way his simple sentence does. Because of the words, yes, but also because of what they represent. I look up at Hades to find him watching with a hungry expression. No masks this time. Just sheer need. He combs his free hand through Hercules's hair. "Get her ready."

He doesn't hesitate. He pushes up my dress until it bunches around my hips and then his mouth is on my pussy, licking me like he may never get another chance to. I can't stop myself from moaning. My knees buckle as he sucks on my clit, and he catches me under my thighs. He lifts me and spins us, and for one dizzying moment, I think we're going to end up on the floor, but then Hades is there, guiding me down onto his lap, my back to his chest.

Onto his cock.

I whimper as he stretches me, fills me. I try to shift to accommodate, but Hercules isn't giving me an inch, he uses his hold on my thighs to keep me pinned in place, spread and open and impaled on Hades's cock. He watches me with those big blue eyes as he drags the flat of his tongue over my clit. Hades presses his hand flat between my breasts and pins me to his chest. I'm trapped, unable to do more than take what they give me, and I've never felt safer than I do in that moment.

Pleasure rises in wave after wave, each driving me closer to oblivion. I lace my fingers in Hercules's hair and writhe against them. "Let me move. *Please.*"

Hades sets his teeth against my neck and then soothes the spot with his tongue. "No."

I try to hold on, but they're too overwhelming. I come with a cry, shuddering into one of the better orgasms I've ever had. I slump back against Hades's chest and for a moment, I think this is what they meant when they called me in here. I really should know better by now. Hercules leans back and holds my gaze as he licks me from his lips. "That's a start."

He lifts me and slams me back down on Hades's cock. I try to help, but they're not interested in my assistance. Hades's hands at my waist. Hercules's under my thighs. They use my body to fuck Hades, as if I'm a toy in human form, a pussy solely for his use. It's so hot, I can barely stand it. Hercules pushes partially to his feet and shoves his tiny shorts off. Even damn near out of my mind with the lingering effect of my orgasm, I can't help clenching around Hades at the sight of him naked. "Glorious, isn't he?" Hades murmurs.

Nothing but the truth between us. "Yes."

Hercules pushes me back against Hades chest and lifts me again, but this time it's *his* cock that pushes into me. He gives me a quick kiss, and that's all the warning I get before he braces one hand on Hades's shoulder and starts fucking me in long, brutal thrusts. Like he's trying to fuck me right into Hades. All the while, Hades holds me down, ensuring I can't do anything but play the willing victim.

As if he can sense my thoughts, he begins speaking in that

sinful voice of his. "Have to take care of our Meg, little Hercules. Fill her up so while she watches me beat you, the reminder of who she belongs to is dripping down her thighs."

I come again, and I must black out for a moment because when I blink, Hercules has followed me over the edge and is pulling out of me. Hades topples him back onto the couch and shoves me onto his chest. Hercules bands his arms around me, keeping me pinned. "Fuck her like she needs, Sir."

Hades rams into me hard enough to have a helpless noise emerging from my lips. Hard and rough and utterly perfect. He mirrors the rhythm Hercules took, fucking me just shy of brutally. And then Hercules's mouth is on mine, swallowing my cries as Hades drives me toward another orgasm. I can't handle it, don't want it to stop, need them to keep fucking me until I'm marked as theirs forever. Hades presses down on the small of my back, grinding me against Hercules's stomach. The friction against my clit is all I need. I scream as I orgasm. I'm distantly aware of Hades following me over the edge, pumping me full of come. And then he's there, covering me with his body, he and Hercules holding me close between them.

I have never felt so loved as I do in this moment.

CHAPTER 28

HADES

I can feel the buzz of anticipation in the Underworld even before I leave my office. Earlier today, I instructed Tis to quietly put out word that I'd preside over a scene tonight. That always brings in the wolves from the outer boundaries of Carver City. Even the people who only darken my doorstep occasionally manage to make an appearance on the nights I take up a whip. Or flogger. Or any number of my toys.

Hercules shifts from foot to foot. It's the first time he's shown nerves since he agreed to this, and I find myself moved by it. "Come here, little Hercules."

He pivots and immediately crosses to kneel by my feet. It seems beyond belief that he's been mine for such a short time, and yet here we are. Being with him feels as natural as breathing. I trace the hard line of his jaw, allowing myself to linger. "Your safe word remains the same. Say Olympus and it all stops. Our having an audience changes nothing when it comes to that."

"Okay." He stares at me with blue eyes that have somehow retained an element of innocence. It's intoxicating. Hercules wets his lips. "Are you going to fuck me in front of everyone?"

"No." I don't know why I'm surprised to witness disappointment on his face, but it amuses me. "Greedy thing, aren't you? Just as greedy as our Meg, wanting to claim me the same way I'll claim you."

He lifts his chin. "Can you blame me?"

"Not in the least." He's still holding back, though. Something isn't quite right. "What is it?"

"Meg should be here with us." He starts to drop his chin, but I tighten my hold on his jaw, forcing him to continue meeting my gaze. Hercules's brows lower. "It's not just you and me. It's the three of us. It seems wrong to basically declare your intentions and not have her involved."

He's not wrong, but I have a plan and it requires the two of us, not the three of us. "She'll be feeling evidence of us for hours yet."

"That's not the same and you know it."

Yes, I suppose I do. I sigh. "I've already compromised the better part of my plans. *This* isn't something I'm willing to add to that list."

He hesitates, but in the end finally nods against my hand. "Promise me that someday it will be the three of us out there."

"I promise." Easy enough to do since that is my intention already. Not tonight, not when I need Zeus squirming and full of rage, but soon. Everyone knows Meg is mine, but it won't do to have them speculating that she's being replaced. Rumor may fly for a short time, but it's something I'm willing to risk.

I nudge Hercules back. "How do you feel knowing I'm going to strip you down to your base level in front of a crowd?"

He blushes, a tinge of pink stealing over his golden cheeks and down his chest. "I want it."

"Good." I urge him up. "I got something for you." I walk to my desk and pick up the wooden box that was delivered earlier. I turn to him and flip it open. Hercules's response is everything I could have dreamed of.

His jaw drops and his eyes go wide. "That's mine?"

"Yes." A more masculine twin to the collar Meg wears when we play. Thicker leather, fewer diamonds. I set the box down and lift it out. "Kneel."

Hercules instantly obeys. I don't know that I'll ever get tired of seeing this man on his knees. He's truly beautiful in a way that goes beyond his physical perfection. I fasten the collar around his neck and then take his hand and press it to the buckle at the back of his neck. "This removes it."

"I won't take it off until you take it off me."

Power and desire curl through me. If I were a simpler man, this would be all there is to us. Lust and love, and the only power games would be confined to the bedroom. I'm not that man. I don't know that I ever was, but any chance at that kind of life was buried alongside my family. There is only the person I've become, and the vengeance that has been a slow burn in my chest for too many decades. I don't know how to be different than I am.

I press a soft kiss to his mouth. "It's time." I move to the door, and he falls into step behind me. We stride down the hallway and around to the back door into the lounge. I stop just inside the door, a king surveying my kingdom, at least in part. The more interesting things will be going on behind the door Allecto lounges in front of. She won't let anyone through who isn't meant to be there, but it won't matter. Rumor spirals, and I have every intention that news of this night will reach Zeus's ears before dawn.

As I suspected, there is so much power in this room, it's

only my dominion that's kept it from being a bloodbath. Jafar and Jasmine lean against the bar, as wrapped up in each other as they always seem to be. Jafar pauses to glare at me, but he knows better than to push the subject, righteous revenge as motivation or no. Being banned from my club would cut his woman off from a significant resource and piss her off in the mix. I had expected to see Meg with them; she adores Jasmine and tends to gravitate to them when they visit.

I survey the rest of the room. Hook with his second-in-command on the other side of the bar. The warring generals Gaeton and Beast who are never far apart, but who I've had to threaten with expulsion if they ruin yet another piece of my furniture with their brawling. The golden queen, Malone, who's as untouchable as she is beautiful. Even the Sea Witch is here, dripping in jewels and watching the room with a predatory glint I recognize.

But no Meg.

Unease slithers through me. It's possible she's in the playroom already, but she doesn't spend time back there unless she's actually playing. I'd fully expected her to be here waiting. I can feel Hercules's tension at my back, but there's no telling if he's noticed her absence and found it as unnerving as I have.

Something is wrong.

I turn on my heel and jerk my chin at Hercules. "A small detour." It's easier—and faster—to check the cameras than to search this place for Meg. I don't care that it may be seen as a weakness to retreat as soon as I enter the room. I've spent too long honing instincts to ignore them now. Meg intended to be in that room when we walked in. It's possible she changed her mind, but even if she's having doubts about us, she knows the value of a united front. We show a sliver of weakness to the people in that room, and they'll crack us

235

open without hesitation. Our strength protects us, yes, but it protects the people within our small domain as well. No matter how angry Meg gets with me, she takes her responsibility too seriously to endanger anyone.

So why isn't she here as planned?

"What's going on?" Hercules doesn't lift his voice, but he doesn't have to since we're alone in the hallway.

I don't slow down. "Meg should have been there."

Just like that, he picks up his pace until he's shoulder to shoulder with me. "You're going to check the cameras."

"Yes." For all that Hercules is a shining near-innocent when it comes to our brand of fucking, he's smart enough to connect the dots without my spelling it out for him. I veer around the corner and have to draw myself up before I open the door to the security room. Charging in there isn't likely to panic them—they work directly under Allecto, after all—but I'll get answers quicker if they aren't scrambling to cover their asses. I take a slow breath and push through the door on the exhale.

The thin man behind the row of monitors jumps to his feet. Minh, a Vietnamese man who's worked for me just shy of five years. "Sir?"

The urge to yell rocks me back on my heels. I have no reason to panic. No reason to fear. I'm overreacting, surely. I manage to keep my tone mild. "Find Meg."

"Yes, sir." He drops back into his chair and his fingers fly over the keyboard. The screens in front of him flicker as he cycles through them, almost too fast for me to follow. He frowns. "Uh, give me a second."

Cold sinks into me. "Is there a problem?"

"I can't seem to find her." He doesn't look from the monitors. "Give me a second to backtrack and figure out where she went."

"Do that."

A warm hand presses to the center of my back and Hercules leans against me. Offering silent strength, though his expression is as worried as the feeling curling through my bones. Something is wrong, terribly wrong, and standing here while we wait for bad news sends me hurtling through time and space to a room very different from this one. To my man, Andreas, shaking and pale, spilling forth words that no man wants to hear. My wife. My son. Both lost in a fire.

Meg was sheltered between my and Hercules's bodies an hour ago. Safe. It never occurred to me that she wouldn't remain so.

The two minutes it takes Minh to pull Meg's image up on the screen take on the semblance of a small eternity. Finally, he sits back. "Here she is an hour ago." The camera shows Meg walking out my office door. She's a little flushed and has a small smile on her face. Happy. She looks happy. She rolls her shoulders and sets off down the hall.

"Follow her."

Minh clicks a few buttons and the screen changes, showing the lounge. It's not as full as it is now, and Meg strides to the bar and says something that makes Tis laugh. They share a smile. Everything is *fine*.

I find myself holding my breath, and Hercules keeps rubbing small circles against my back as if that will change the feeling of the sword about to slice through my neck. As if I summoned trouble with my thoughts, Tink appears on the screen and hurries up to Meg's side. Meg dips her head and listens intently to what the other woman is saying. She flinches.

My woman *flinches*.

Just like that, the joy is gone from her face, from her posture. She turns with a wooden expression I haven't seen since that first few months when she lived under my roof.

The memory steals my breath. The implication of what it means seeing it now? "No."

The cameras follow her as she walks out of the lounge and takes the elevators all the way down to the ground floor. There's a black car idling at the curb.

"Do you have sound for this?"

"Yeah." A push of a button and we can hear soft traffic noises.

The door opens and a man's voice says, "You came."

"Let her go." Meg doesn't sound terrified, but I know my woman. It's there in the line of her shoulders and the hardness of her voice. She's holding onto anger to shield herself from fear.

"Of course. A deal's a deal. You know all about that, don't you?"

Movement within the car and Aurora spills onto the street. She rushes to Meg and wraps her arms around her. Meg smooths back her hair, checking her expression. "Are you okay?"

"I'm sorry, Meg. So sorry. I didn't know—"

She presses her fingers to Aurora's lips. "Go."

The man speaks again. "Remember, princess. You say a single damn thing to *him* and your mother pays the price."

"I remember." She doesn't have Meg's poise. She's obviously been crying, and though she moves as if she's not injured, she's plainly terrified. Instead of coming into the building, Aurora bolts. I don't need to follow her path to know her destination. The hospital where her mother is on life support.

I speak without looking away from the cameras. "Send two of our people to watch over her mother—and her. When she's ready to come back, escort her."

"Yes, sir."

A hand emerges from the backseat. "Come along."

"I don't think I will." She takes a step back. A red light appears on her chest. A tiny little dot, its significance sending ice cascading through my veins. Meg looks down and freezes. "Impossible to claim you came in good faith when you have a sniper in a nearby building."

"I had a feeling you'd be difficult." A deep laugh. "Get in the car or the next person who's on the wrong end of my sniper is that old bastard."

Meg hesitates, but only for a moment. She steels herself and takes the man's hand, letting him draw her into the car. The door shuts and it veers away from the curb and into traffic.

No.

"How long ago was this?" I barely sound like myself. Even without seeing inside that car, I know exactly who it contained. Zeus. I took his son, and even if that doesn't begin to balance the scales of what he did, he still sees the injustice of it and is determined to punish me just like he did all those years ago. I thought he'd come for me when he was furious enough. It never occurred to me that he'd get to Meg first.

"Thirty minutes."

"He's going to take her to Olympus. Beyond our reach."

"No. Fuck that." Hercules glances at Minh. "Could you excuse us for a minute?"

Again Minh hesitates, but he finally nods and slips past us out of the room. Hercules barely waits for the door to click shut before he grasps my shoulders. "Get your fucking head in the game, Hades."

I blink. My thoughts move slowly, the past, the present, and the future melding together into one unforgivable emotional blow. "We can't save her. It's too late."

Hercules gives me a hard shake. His blue eyes are twin flames of fury. "If he wanted her dead, he'd have shot her right there in the street. He wants to punish us, and that means we have time."

"She trusted me to keep her safe and I failed."

He shakes me again, harder this time. "If you're going to go maudlin and defeatist, you don't deserve her. Choose now, because I'm going after her."

I could lose them both.

The thought staggers me. I close my eyes and try to focus, to think past the memories trying to claw me down to hell. "He'll take her to Olympus," I repeat. It's several hours' drive. He has barely a half hour head start on us. I nod and push Hercules back. "We go after her." I give him a long look. "You will follow orders, no matter how unsavory you find them."

His jaw sets like he wants to argue, but he nods. "As long as we leave now."

I call Minh back into the room. "Tell Allecto to meet us in the garage. She gets three people—her best."

He nods, but I'm already moving. I stride back into my office and collect the gun I keep in a locked drawer in the desk. Hercules doesn't blink as I withdraw a hostler and shrug into it. I take a moment to check that the gun is loaded and the safety is on. I prefer not to use firearms. They're so incredibly clumsy and blunt when it's just as easy to accomplish my will with words and careful manipulations. I don't have the luxury of that now. I don't have the *time*.

I hold Hercules's gaze. "It may come down to your father or Meg."

"I know." The pain written on his face isn't only for our Meg. Zeus is a monster, but he's still the father of the man I care deeply for. Killing him will hurt Hercules. It may even take our potential future together and damage it beyond repair.

Even knowing that, if it comes down to a choice between them, I know what I'll choose. "I'm sorry."

"Don't be. She's the important one."

We detour to his suite long enough for him to throw on a pair of jeans and a T-shirt and then we're off, rushing down to meet Allecto in the parking garage. She takes one look at me and her mouth tightens. "That bad."

"Zeus has Meg. If he makes it to Olympus with her, I can't guarantee we'll be able to get to her. He has roughly forty-five minutes on us." I scrub a hand over my face. "I expect he'll pick the most direct route, but I'm not sure."

Allecto takes it in stride. It's one of her strengths—seeing the battlefield as a whole before she ever takes the first step. She turns to the three women at her back. "You three take one car. We'll take the other. Keep your damn phones on because we'll need to coordinate carefully to drive them off the road and we have to catch them first." She glances at us. "You two, with me." Allecto stops short. "But if you're going to be wringing your hands and distracting me, you can damn well stay here."

Hercules bristles, but I touch his shoulder. "We have it under control."

"You had better. We don't have room for error on this." She turns on her heel and marches to the nearest car. "Get your ass in the backseat. We're doing this."

CHAPTER 29

MEG

Fear is a strange thing. I thought I've known it in the past. Walking into the Underworld at twenty-six and bargaining away my future for the man I thought I loved was scary. But even then, I must have seen something in Hades and known that he wouldn't hurt me in any irreparable way. Like recognizes like, after all. A broken heart is one thing. But my body has always been safe with him.

I don't have that assurance with the man lounging in the seat across from me.

No, Zeus will hurt me and hurt me badly. Nothing personal, of course. He simply intends to send a message to the men I love, the kind designed to bring Hades to his knees.

It may be easier to stomach if he looked like a villain, but he's got the same golden boy perfection that Hercules possesses. The carved jawline that translates to strength for those who don't know better. The big, broad shoulders and wide hands. The blond hair and beard that have the faintest sprinkling of gray in them. He's Hades's age, but where time has honed Hades to a fine blade, it's done something different to Zeus. The laugh lines around his eyes probably inspire trust. Just a good old boy, someone people want to sit down and have drinks with.

I haven't moved since I took this seat, and though the silence wears on me, I haven't spoken either. Zeus scares the shit out of me, but I've played longer games than this with Hades. I don't always win with him, but I'm determined not to break first now. I occupy myself by counting down the seconds.

"I've heard about you, Megaera."

I slowly turn my face from the window to look at him. I may have won the standoff, but it feels petty now. What difference does it really make? I'm in over my head and there's no rescue in sight. I give him a blank look. "Funny. I haven't heard a single thing about you."

Oh, he doesn't like that. His blue eyes that seemed so similar to Hercules's a few moments ago light up with a rage that leaves me breathless. He leans forward and props his elbows on his knees. "Loyalty that's purchased with a deal is hardly loyalty at all. Your first man threw you away as soon as he was done with you and didn't look back. Hades has done the same now that he has my son to occupy him."

It's my worst fear given voice.

I don't believe for a second that Hades would bargain me away, not like my ex did. But I can't stop myself from reacting to his words. I swallow hard and my head spins a little. "I'm here. You've got what you wanted." A calculated risk on my part. Even if he didn't shoot me, the sniper would have had a clear shot of Aurora fleeing down the block.

Then there was the threat to shoot Hades. I can't let that happen. I don't know how I'm going to stop it, but getting in this car was the first step. I should have stopped, should have talked to someone, should have done anything but react emotionally, but the threat to Aurora put me on autopilot and panic drove me. Stupid. So fucking stupid.

Allecto would have found and removed the shooter before they became a danger to Hades. She just needed time to work and a knowledge of the danger. But time was the problem. We didn't have any. We still don't.

"I'm only getting started." He grins suddenly. "Hurting you is as good as hurting him, but don't worry, I have no plans to kill you." He pulls out his phone and begins typing something on it.

That doesn't reassure me nearly as much as I'd like it to. I'm a connoisseur of pain. I know exactly how a person can draw out the pain until it's a symphony. The difference is that I only play with the willing and Zeus isn't talking about kink. He's talking about torture.

I am so sorry, Hades. I really fucked this up.

Headlights over Zeus's shoulder draw my attention. My heart leaps even as I tell myself that it's a lost cause. I *know* those headlights, the ridiculous blue tinged lights bright enough to blind the unwary. Allecto has a thing for lights, and she's pickier about them than I am about my floggers. I've had to sit through countless conversations where she gushes about the new technology and her plans to install them in the Underworld's vehicles. Still...

The car behind us closes the distance and switches lanes, revealing a second nearly identical one behind it. What are the odds of having two cars with the same headlights? I blindly reach for the seat belt and secure it. "You're going to regret crossing Hades a second time."

"Am I?" Zeus shrugs without looking up. "He's weak, Megaera. You'd recognize that if you knew true strength. He takes every hit lying down and when he tries for revenge, it's laughably pathetic. Seducing my son?" He snorts. "As if

Hercules won't come crawling back to me the second he realizes I have *you*."

"I won't let that happen."

"You don't have a choice."

The cars are closing the distance fast. I don't know what their plan is, but I grip the seat belt tight against me as the closest one edges near. I swallow hard. "I think you'll find that I do." I have a moment to tense and then the car nudges the passenger side of our car, right near the back tire. For one second, I think it won't do anything, but then our car begins to spin.

We hit the edge of the highway and barrel down the embankment. A rumble of impact and then I'm weightless, the car rolling with a violence that leaves me breathless. Or maybe that's the seat belt slammed against my chest, holding me immobile. We land right side up, and I let loose a sob and scramble for my buckle. It gives with a pop, but the pressure in my chest doesn't abate.

Through the shattered window, I see the other car screech to a halt. The doors fly open and there's Hercules and Hades.

They came for me.

Hercules sprints to our car and damn near yanks the door nearest me off its hinges. He starts to reach for me and hesitates. "Are you hurt?"

I try to find words, but a sob rips free and I throw myself into his arms. My chest hurts. *Ribs*, I think distantly. "I'm… I'll be okay."

He holds out a hand. "Can you get to me, Meg?"

My fingers brush his when a hand closes around my throat and I'm jerked back against a big body. Something wet coats my back, soaking through my dress. Zeus's voice sounds more animal than human. "You always were a fucking traitor."

Hercules goes pale. "Let her go."

"Move back or I wring her neck."

Hercules takes a step back and then another, his hands held up in front of him. Each increase in the distance between us spikes my panic. I struggle, but Zeus wraps his other arm around my waist and squeezes. The pain nearly makes me black out and I can't stop a shriek.

Zeus shoves us from the crumpled vehicle, dragging me over broken glass. I barely feel the cuts over the symphony of agony that is my ribs. He stops just outside the car and my vision clears to see Hades bearing down on us. Zeus, the bastard, laughs. "I thought taking her was good enough, but you're right. This is better. You can watch her bleed out and know that it's your fault."

Hades draws a gun and points it at us. "Release her."

"Is your aim good enough to hit me and not her?" Zeus laughs again. "I don't think so." He hefts my body up until my knees don't touch the ground, using me as a human shield. "Move back."

"I don't think I will."

"Come now, Hades. Release Hercules and I hand you back your woman. She's even mostly whole." He laughs, the bastard. "You've had your fun."

"No."

Zeus goes tense behind me. "You can't get out of this without losing one of them. Her or him. Choose."

"There is no choosing, Zeus. I love them both." Hades hesitates and then his eyes go hard as they meet mine. "Head wound, Meg."

I don't think. I can't afford to. I reach back and punch blindly over my shoulder, ignoring the screaming of my ribs. My fist makes contact with Zeus's head. It wouldn't be enough if he was healthy and whole, but the blood soaking me must be his because he shouts and drops me. I hit the ground and press myself down as a gunshot sounds. Too loud. Too close.

Then Hercules is there, gathering me carefully up and rushing back several steps to put distance between us and his father. I lift my head enough to see Hades standing over Zeus, who's bleeding from a gunshot wound to his shoulder. Not fatal. Not by a long shot.

Hades trains the gun on Zeus, and I've never seen him look so cold. "If you or your people set foot in Carver City, your life is forfeit." He gives a slow smile that doesn't reach his eyes. "You're lucky I care for your son or I'd empty this clip into you." He glances at me—at Hercules at my back. "A gift to you, little Hercules. Your father's life."

Hercules starts to move forward, aggression in every line of his body, but I clutch his shirt. "It's the right choice."

"He *took* you. He was going to hurt you." His eyes go hard, and he's never looked more like his father than he does in this moment. "There's only one way to guarantee that he doesn't do it again."

"No." I look between my men and put more force into my voice. "*No.*" I want nothing more than to take that gun from Hades's hand and pull the trigger several times. I hate that Zeus made me afraid, I hate that the fear will cling to me like a spiderweb for days and maybe weeks to come. It doesn't matter. I put a little wobble into my voice, and it takes far less effort than I want to admit. "Take me home. Please."

For a moment, I think it won't work. Hercules hesitates and then finally takes another step back. "If that's what you want."

It isn't. I want this man dead at my feet. I want to rip him to pieces with my bare hands and then scatter his ashes to the wind. But Hades has always seen things clearly enough for both of us. He's right. If Zeus dies today from our hand, Hercules will eventually grow to hate us. He won't be able to stop himself, no matter what he's feeling in this moment.

If there's a choice between love and revenge, I choose love.

Today, for the first time since I've known him, Hades does, too.

Hercules doesn't stop until we're on the other side of the car from Zeus. He sets me carefully on my feet and then Hades is there, running his hands gently over my body. His fingers graze my side, and I wince. "Ribs," he says, echoing my thought. "Get her into the car before someone calls the police."

Hercules opens the door and carefully guides me inside. Allecto turns around as I settle in the middle seat. "You're alive. Good."

"No thanks to you." I've never heard Hercules sound so dangerous. "You could have killed her with that stunt."

"I had things perfectly under control."

"No, you fucking didn't."

I clear my throat. "Children."

Hades opens the other door and takes a place on the other side of me. I'm safe. My brain may register that, but my body hasn't quite got the memo. I can't stop shaking. "You shot him."

"Yes." Hades leans forward. "Go, Allecto. We've lingered too long."

"Yes, sir." She veers into traffic heading back toward Carver City, as reckless as ever behind the wheel.

Hercules shifts me until I'm leaning back against Hades's chest with my legs over Hercules's lap. They hold me carefully. Gently. Words bubble up inside me, but I know better than to speak them. Not yet. Allecto is trusted above all others, but she's not part of our relationship, and I'm not willing to spill those secret parts of myself while she witnesses. Still, I can't help saying, "You came for me."

"Yes."

Hades's hands tremble a little as he smooths them down my arms. "We'll always come for you, love. You're ours."

"You're fucking irreplaceable."

I can't stop shaking. The impact of the last few hours hit me in waves. There was no time to process before, just to act. "Are you sure it will work? Banning him?" He made it to the Underworld before. Just drove right up to it without the slightest hint of difficulty. I shiver.

"Yes."

Hercules looks over my head at Hades. "How can you be sure?"

"Every single territory leader in Carver City graces my doorstep at one point or another, and most of them regularly." The cold satisfaction in his voice warms me in a strange way. "If they want to continue to have access, they will bend to my will in this one small thing."

If every territory in Carver City ceased to be a welcome place for Zeus and his people, it would create that many more hurdles he'd have to get through in order to reach us. No one wants to fuck with Hades, not when he offers such a particular service. Neutral ground. The sex and kink and everything else, yes, but the true value of the Underworld is the sheer number of deals made beneath its roof, facilitated by Hades's enforcement of neutral territory. It might actually work.

We sit in silence as Allecto drives us back to Carver City. My men don't stop touching me, as if they're afraid I may disappear at any given moment. As if they're afraid this isn't real. My adrenaline fades right around the time we hit the city limits, and then all I know is pain. I've definitely broken at least one rib. My knees and shins is full of pinpricks of agony from the broken glass and I'm getting blood all over the seat.

Hades is the one who carries me out of the car and up to his penthouse. I'm so tired, I don't even bother to protest that I can walk myself. I feel safe in his arms with Hercules shadowing his steps.

Someone must have called Dr. Miranda because he arrives less than a minute after we do. He's a small white man with giant glasses and a no-nonsense attitude that never ceases to make me feel like I'm five years old and have disappointed him greatly. He casts a look at me. "The dress needs to come off."

Hades cuts off my dress as the doctor peppers me with questions that I try to answer as honestly as possible. Once I'm naked, he does a quick examination and stands back. "Broken ribs, most likely, but I'd need an X-ray to be sure. They aren't hampering her ability to breathe, and she hasn't started coughing up blood or any of that nonsense, so I doubt it's serious. Miscellaneous cuts and bruises that need to be cleaned, but nothing deep enough for stitches." He crosses his arms over his chest and glares down at me. "You'll live."

"Glad to hear it."

"Six weeks of no hard activities." He turns that glare on Hades and Hercules. "No wild sex. No swinging crops and the like. Nothing that puts stress on those ribs. If the pain gets worse or you start having trouble breathing, call me immediately."

"I will."

"Then I'm going back to bed. You two." He points at my men. "Clean her up. I'm sure you have bandages around here. Rinse the wounds first to make sure there's no glass remaining. That's it. Keep things PG."

Hades levels a severe look at him. "Thank you for your help, Doctor. Please leave."

"Good night." Dr. Miranda turns and strides to the elevator, and then he's gone.

I let out a dry laugh. "I always liked him."

"It's the only reason I put up with his attitude." Hades moves to stand in front of me. "Come on, love. Let's get you cleaned up."

It feels surreal to step into the shower with him and have him wash me. We've done this before. Hell, we did this earlier today. It feels different now. He sits me down on the tile bench and carefully cleans my legs, probing gently for glass.

Hades has never touched me like I'm breakable before. I don't think I like it, but I'm too tired and too *breakable* to complain. When we turn the water off, Hercules is waiting with the bandages. Hades combs my hair while Hercules patches me up. As I suspected, most of the cuts are small enough that they don't need much. There are two slightly larger ones on my arm, and he carefully bandages them.

"I love you," I blurt out. "Both of you. So fucking much. It scares the shit out of me."

Hercules flicks his gaze to my face, more serious than I've ever seen him. "You both know I'm head over heels for you two. I have been since that first night." He glances at Hades. "So, no shit, I love you."

I find myself holding my breath and relax as Hades strokes my drying hair. "You know I love you, Megaera. I may not say it often enough, but I have ever since you walked through my doors, full of fury and a determination to save someone who didn't deserve it." He leans over until I can see his face. "I haven't taken care of you the way you deserve, and I'm sorry for that." He glances at Hercules. "And you. You were never part of my long-term plan, and yet here we are."

He hesitates. "I don't give my love easily, little Hercules. You've slipped in when I wasn't paying attention." He gives a slow smile that makes my stomach flip over despite how exhausted I am. "Now you're mine forever."

"I'd like to propose a new bargain." He squeezes my hand. "The three of us—for good. Three lifetime bargains in one."

Hades goes still. "Three."

"Yes. Not just a bargain with you; a bargain with one another." Hercules smiles and it's so sweet, it washes over me like golden sunlight. "The three of us on equal ground, such as it is."

I find myself holding my breath. Hades doesn't make us wait long. "A bargain it is, then. A mutual claiming."

"Sounds kinky," I murmur.

He chuckles. "When you're healed, it will be. Until then, we seal it with a kiss." He brushes his lips softly against mine, and then repeats the move with Hercules. Hercules presses a quick kiss to my lips and stands.

My heart is so fucking full, I can barely stand it. "I think this is the best bargain I've ever made."

"The feeling is entirely mutual." Hades lifts me into his arms. "Come on, love. Let's get you in bed."

It's not as graceful as we've been in the past. The pain meds haven't quite kicked in yet, and I'm moving like a person three times my age. They bracket me in, warming me, comforting me with their bodies better than they ever could with their words. Surrounded by the two men I love, the two men who love me, something inside me relaxes, and despite my pain, I draw my first full breath in what feels like years.

This is right. This is exactly where we're meant to be.

This is fucking perfect.

* * *

THANK you so much for reading Learn My Lesson! I hope you enjoyed reading it as much as I enjoyed writing it! If you did, please consider leaving a review.

Need more Hades, Hercules, and Meg in your life? Be sure to sign up for my newsletter to get an exclusive bonus epilogue showing what happens when they finally take their relationship public!

The Wicked Villains series continues in A Worthy Opponent with Tink and Hook's story. With Tink's contract coming to a close, she's got vengeance on her mind. The only person who can help her? The man determined to bring her to her knees...and put a ring on her finger! But can Tink and Hook get over their animosity to bring down their mutual enemy? Only one way to find out!

Looking for your next sexy read? You can pick up my MMF ménage THEIRS FOR THE NIGHT, my FREE novella that features an exiled prince, his bodyguard, and the bartender they can't quite manage to leave alone.

ACKNOWLEDGMENTS

Whew, this book! This story was most definitely a labor of love, and it wouldn't have been possible without a most excellent group of people.

HUGE thanks to Christa Desir for editing and really helping me make the story shine. It's a thousand times better than it was when I finished that early draft and your insight was invaluable in making that happen.

Big thanks, as always, to Lynda M. Ryba for an excellent eye in copyediting. I'd be lost without you.

Thank you, thank you, thank you to the early readers of this book: Jenny Nordbak, Joanna Shupe, and Andie J. Christopher. Your comments give me life!

I have the best support team in the world. It's science. Big thanks to Piper J. Drake and Asa Maria Bradley for always being in my corner.

Thanks and a whole lot of sorry-not-sorry to my FB group, The Rabble. I promise that tormenting you with sexy teasers is only a positive thing, because it inspires me to up my game. Your enthusiasm is priceless.

All my love to Tim and my family. You may never understand my obsession with villains, but I appreciate you indulging me. Kisses!

ABOUT THE AUTHOR

Katee Robert is a *New York Times* and USA Today bestselling author of contemporary romance and romantic suspense. Her titles The Marriage Contract and The Bastard's Bargain were both RITA finalists. Her books have sold over a million copies. She lives in the Pacific Northwest with her husband, children, a cat who thinks he's a dog, and a Great Dane who thinks she's a lap dog.

www.kateerobert.com

Keep up to date on all new release and sale info by joining Katee's NEWSLETTER!

facebook.com/AuthorKateeRobert
twitter.com/katee_robert
instagram.com/katee_robert

Made in the USA
Las Vegas, NV
15 June 2021

24775352R00156